THE MOON IS DISTANT
BOOK THREE OF THE SERPENT'S THRONE

Dan Ackerman

Supposed Crimes LLC • Matthews, North Carolina

All Rights Reserved
Copyright © 2021 Dan Ackerman

Published in the United States.

ISBN: 978-1-952150-20-3

Cover Art by Vincent Pesce

www.supposedcrimes.com

This book is typeset in Goudy Old Style.

For David

There were some things that would never feel familiar, no matter how many times they happened. Sitting down to eat with the Schreibers was one of them. Their family dated back to when the walls had been built and maintained the record office in Hell; their guests were equally distinguished. Tonight, they dined with Ulster, captain of the First, and some of his family members, including their son's betrothed.

Ira was there because he had attached himself to Ulster's niece, Astrid, and because he had made friends with the only son the Schreibers had left. He didn't know for sure which of those things had garnered him a spot at the table. Everyone's true intentions had become harder to read following the coup.

Astrid kept her hand on his thigh for most of dinner, her fingers always coming to rest high on his leg, in danger of brushing against his cock. Several times, she made contact and he had to struggle to keep a straight face as he passed bowls and platters around the table.

"You mentioned you saw Eodus the other day," Georg Schreiber said to Ira around a mouthful of bread.

"Georg," his mother scolded.

He swallowed and rolled his eyes, waiting for Ira's response.

"I did. Yesterday morning."

"How's he?"

"Good. Busy. They've got all the soul workers pulling extra shifts, no matter what Precinct they're in," Ira informed him. "He says they found a mutilator holed up in one of the empty cells in the Second a few days ago. Had a bunch of skin tacked up all over the walls and they're not sure who it belonged to."

"To whom it belonged," suggested Georg's father.

Ira and Georg widened their eyes at each other in mutual exacerbation.

"That's not a pretty picture. Wonder how long it will take to get them all off the streets; it's been months already," Georg said.

Astrid's delicate heart-shaped face contorted slightly.

"It is taking a while," Ira agreed. "Eodus shook worse than usual telling me about it."

"He ought to get something for his nerves," Georg suggested.

"Oh, I don't want to hear any business talk over dinner," Mrs. Schreiber requested.

Ira didn't point out that it wasn't business, exactly, since neither he nor Georg worked in the Precincts punishing souls. As Master of Records, it might have been her business in a roundabout way, but Ira didn't think it counted. He wished she'd said what she'd meant, which was no politics.

Ulster chimed, "I've certainly heard enough of it! Up to my ears with reports. I have to say, I'm jealous of Rema. She's got that fellow writing up all her reports. Henry?"

"Inri," Ira corrected.

Ulster nodded. "Right, right. Inri. We should all be so lucky."

The table ate in silence for an uncomfortable stretch.

"I was reading Birsam's latest article on metallurgy," Georg told his fiancée.

Astrid sniggered.

Georg made a visible effort to ignore her.

Amaranth turned to look at him. "Since when have you been interested in metallurgy?"

With a shrug, Georg told her, "You mentioned it the other day."

Leaning close to whisper, Astrid confided to Ira, "She *hates* Birsam." She knew her cousin well; they'd been thick as thieves since Astrid had helped to overthrow the Devil.

To Georg, Amaranth responded, "Oh." She didn't seem to know what to make of his attempt at conversation; she never did, whether it was about books or metallurgy or magic or gossip. "What did you think of the article?"

"That alloy he talked about, what was it? Electrum. I thought what he had to say about it being a better conductor than silver for some magics was interesting."

"He stole all that from Greshan," Amaranth informed him.

Georg faltered. "What?"

"They used to be partners but after Greshan ended up in prison, Birsam published everything under just his name," Amaranth said.

"Oh. I. I guess I didn't know that," Georg admitted sheepishly.

"With what Greshan did, prison was too kind for him," Astrid declared.

"He's a brilliant man," her cousin countered, "Maybe unorthodox, but killing him would be a waste."

Astrid glowered.

Ira tried to soothe them both, saying, "The queen was merciful, he was lucky. Maybe he'll come to know her better. It was an abrupt change, really, a lot of people needed time to come around."

Ulster agreed, "Yes, some people always need a little more time to settle than others."

A maid came out to clear the dishes and Ira stood to help her. The others had long since stopped trying to tell him he didn't need to do it because he persisted each time. "It doesn't feel right not picking up after myself," he'd insisted over and over again until they'd stopped saying anything about it.

Georg followed suit; he gathered his parents' plates and brought them into the kitchen. He plunked them into the sink and stepped aside when Ira did the same.

They lingered in the kitchen.

Yenni, the maid, fidgeted.

"Go on for a smoke, Yen," Georg told her. "You'll need it with all this washing to do."

Yenni nodded, produced a pipe and pouch from her apron, then headed out the servants' entrance.

When she had gone, Georg gave Ira's back a rub.

Ira folded into his arms immediately, hugging him tightly. "I can't keep this up," Ira confessed into the younger man's shoulder.

"You can."

Ira shook his head.

"You can, darling," Georg insisted. He pulled back and settled his hands on Ira's shoulders. "And you must. We're close."

Ira swallowed and nodded.

"Besides, I like dinner much better now that you're here."

Ira managed to smile.

Georg leaned in, touched his forehead against Ira's, and pressed a quick kiss to his lips. "We'll survive tonight to dine again, I promise."

Ira nodded.

Georg led him back into the dining room, an arm slung around his shoulder.

They had to release each other to return to their seats beside their partners. Astrid took Ira's hand again once he'd sat down, which made him wonder if it relieved Georg that Amaranth didn't try to touch him. Amaranth, Ira firmly suspected, was keener on women than she was on men by a long shot, or maybe she was keen on no one at all. Either way, she'd agreed to marry the future Master of Records for his money, not his cock.

They sipped after-dinner drinks. Mr. Schreiber gave a lengthy, detailed report about the welfare of his great-nephews, twins who had started to walk a few days ago. They sounded precious as anything and Ira wanted to poke his own eyes out.

"And did I mention Lecia is expecting again?" Mr. Schreiber told them all.

"Goodness, that family keeps growing! Same father as last time?" Mrs. Schreiber inquired.

"Oh, I'm not sure," her husband said, "I don't think she mentioned a name..."

Ulster inquired, "That's a tricky business, though, isn't it? Having a father who isn't part of the family. You never know what they'll be after."

"No, no," Mr. Schreiber assured him, "They do it with all kinds of paperwork to make sure things like that don't happen."

"Lecia's smart about it," Mrs. Schreiber agreed.

"Maybe you two should give it a try," Georg suggested and, when he received scalding looks from both parents, he clarified, "Adopting! Plenty of orphans to go around. Or I bet you could even go down to the Eighth and pick up a few who aren't strictly orphans."

"That's about enough," warned his father.

Georg didn't argue, looking cowed as he sipped from his glass.

Ira took pity but also wanted to be gone from an awkward situation. "I ought to be heading home. Work tomorrow and all that. Thank you, again, for having me. Everything was lovely."

"Of course."

"Any time."

To the table, he broadly said, "Nice seeing all of you."

Astrid took his hand.

He leaned in to peck her cheek before she could say anything. "You don't have to get up, I'll see you soon." He retreated to the foyer.

Georg followed him, telling his parents, "I'll see him home," and exiting the dining room before they could consent or protest.

Outside, he put his arm around Ira again, this time around his waist, pulling him so they walked hip-to-hip.

"Someone's got to make sure you get home unmolested," Georg told him.

"And who's getting you home?"

Georg laughed and teased, "I'm not the one that looks like a little boy!"

"I don't."

"You do. You're a little lost lamb," Georg insisted.

"Shut up."

Georg kissed his cheek to soften his teasing. "But it's fetching. On you. On your wide-eyed ingénue lover, not so much. I swear, if she throws one more simpering look your way, I'll pluck those pretty blue eyes right out of her face."

"If I didn't know better, I'd say that's jealousy talking."

"Who says you know anything at all?" Georg asked, his voice a little lower and rougher than Ira had ever heard, enough so that he glanced at him and hesitated.

Ira sucked in a nervous breath and thought, for a second, that Georg might do something. That thought disappeared into a thousand pieces when a pair of guards on patrol stopped beside them as their paths crossed.

"There's been a sighting, you ought to get indoors as soon as you can," one of them advised.

Georg nodded at the guard. "Almost home!" he promised her.

"You two shouldn't be out so late."

They both bobbed their heads and took off, their pace quickened. "Late," Georg scoffed, "It's barely gotten dark."

"I don't know, there's marauding souls about!" Ira warned. He grabbed Georg about the ribs, giving him a little squeeze. "You don't know if they might get you!"

Georg rolled his eyes. "Color me terrified."

"Still...I liked it better when there weren't things like that loose," Ira admitted.

"I liked it better when we had a proper Devil instead of some up-jumped angel on the throne," the young man declared.

"Quiet with that," Ira warned.

Instead of arguing, Georg let out a long sigh.

Their walk progressed silently from there.

Ira fretted somewhat about the state of Hell and the odd timbre of Georg's voice just then, until he became aware of a sound. It took him a moment to realize that the wet, sort of slapping noise came from neither him nor Georg. He looked over at his friend to see that he had a similar look of unease on his face.

Together they glanced back to find a shambling, stumbling many-limbed thing flopping its way down the street behind them. It had several faces and not quite enough skin to cover all of its flesh.

At ten yards, it's uncoordinated movements were disconcerting and it took them both a length of time to process what they saw. At five yards, they realized together that they should flee.

Several of its mouths stretched open, their jaws oozing low into their necks or chests and at least half a dozen arms stretched out in front of it.

Ira gave Georg a push away from it as Georg grabbed onto Ira's arms and pulled him into a run.

They bolted down the road until they reached the Inverness. Ira shoved his key into the lock and pulled Georg into the lobby, where they remained, panting and quivering.

Mrs. Spiros opened her door and demanded to know what they were doing making so much noise.

At least, Ira figured that was what she asked. He'd picked up a little Ancient Greek but was nowhere near fluent. Gasping, his mouth sticky, he told her, "There was a thing out there, a big...uh. Like a bunch of them stuck together or something!"

She shook her head, checked the locks on the door, then retreated back to her apartment, grumbling.

Georg tugged on Ira's sleeve. "We should tell the guards."

"I'm not going back out there!"

"No, stupid, I'll send a note."

"And what runner would take it!" Ira cried.

"You know, you should bother to learn a little bit of magic someday," Georg scolded. "I need a piece of paper."

Ira bit back the smart answer that came to mind and brought Georg up to the fourth floor, letting them into his apartment. He found him a piece of paper and watched as the younger man scribbled out two notes, one to the guards and one to his parents.

To the guards, he wrote what they'd seen and where they'd seen it. He folded it into the shape of a little bird, then with a bit of chanting and handwaving, sent it zooming out the window.

Before he sent the note to his parents, he hesitated, glancing at Ira, the note grasped between his fingers.

"Of course, you're staying, don't even pretend," Ira told him.

Georg nodded and sent that note, too. It fluttered out of his hand, moving along with less urgency than his first one.

"Like I'd send you back out there with that roaming around." Ira pulled the window closed and latched the shutters for good measure.

Mrs. Spiros had put shutters on all the windows since the souls in the Seventh had gotten out; at first, Ira had thought her paranoid, but as the weeks had worn on and the souls had gotten into more trouble, he'd been glad she'd had them installed.

Georg hung back nervously as Ira got ready for bed, cleaning his teeth and his face and finally stripping off the ring Astrid had given him, leaving it with his keys. It had the shape of a raven, the wings forming the band. He found the book he'd started last week and didn't notice Georg's hesitance much, too busy recalling every sickly detail of that many-faced thing, malformed and claylike. When he started to undress and saw that Georg still lingered in the bedroom doorway, he stopped and threw his book onto his pillow.

"What?"

Georg shook his head. He'd washed his face and looked younger and more vulnerable without any makeup. He didn't look any less handsome, but being fresh-faced lent a different quality to his looks. Less coquettish and wild.

"Are you staying up?" Ira asked.

"No."

"Do you want something to read?"

At that, Georg nodded, though Ira knew it couldn't have been what had bothered him initially. Georg had stayed over plenty of times and had always made himself right at home.

Ira nodded towards the bookshelf in the corner of his bedroom. "Help yourself, love."

Georg selected a book and came over to the bed.

Ira hung his clothes that could be worn again and put the rest into the hamper; he told Georg, "Hangers in the closet, anything you want to be washed you can leave, I'll bring it by to work when it's done."

"Thanks."

After that Ira settled into bed, determined to focus on his book and not worry about what had Georg acting oddly. He'd open up eventually, Ira figured.

He was wrong, of course, Georg never did say what was on his mind and left in the morning in the same mood from the night before.

Satan was dead.

No. That wasn't right.

The Devil had died, that much was true. But he wasn't dead.

He reached up and poked at the open wound in his chest, feeling the slick flesh beneath his skin, a bit of bone. Something rattled as he moved. He dug his fingers in deeper, his long, skinny fingers crawling inside the gash, pushing in deeper until his nails scraped against his heart.

It moved, steady, calm and it comforted him. He was not dead. Not anymore.

He took his fingers from his chest; they pulled out with a wet, sucking sound and he wiped his hand on his trousers.

Worn out silk. Unwashed, greasy. It had been a while, then.

He wished he could see more but the room was dark, darker than if his eyes had been closed.

He stood. Weights pulled at his wrists and when he stepped forward he felt them on his ankles, too.

He ignored them and tried to move forward, rattling as he went until something tugged at his limbs.

He prodded at the rough cuffs around his wrists and found them attached to chains. The links were as thick as a man's fingers, which felt like overkill considering that Lucifer would have struggled to fend off a particularly vicious kitten.

He could make it no more than five paces from where his chains were tethered. He explored what he could of the room. Stone walls, stone floor. Not a window he could find or a door he could reach.

The process took about fifteen minutes and left him exhausted.

He tucked himself into the corner, his stomach growling.

He reached up to prod at the wound on his chest again, trying to recall how he had gotten it.

Things would come back to him. Eventually. Things always came back eventually. The older things came back first.

He knew he was the Devil and how he had garnered the position, that he had a wife and a daughter. He knew that he had souls to punish. He recalled some of the Fallen in his service and some of the creatures he had made.

The rest would come.

He waited in the darkness, rattling his chains every so often, just so there was something to break the silence.

Someone would have to come eventually. No one kept a prisoner without wanting something from them.

He had no doubt that he was a prisoner.

He closed his eyes and the world looked no different. He slept and dreamt of bees, fat and lazy, buzzing from flower to flower in a meadow.

He woke hungry and he went to sleep hungry. He did this again and again, each time his hunger growing and his strength fading and his mind drowning in endless thoughts of meat, of hot, wet flesh and the iron taste of blood.

He started to dream of doing monstrous things and it did nothing to soothe the hunger churning his guts to shreds. His own fingers and calves began to seem appetizing and he wondered if they would grow back if he gnawed them off. He wondered if he even could starve to death or if he would simply waste away forever and ever.

Maybe no one would come. Maybe whoever had taken him prisoner had forgotten about him or had perished themselves.

In that case, he would have to wait for the chains to rust away and the stone around him to crumble. He thought it more likely that a rogue explorer would find him before that.

He conjured up a world in his mind full of intrepid adventurers grown from the ruins of the burgeoning civilization he left behind. A world where he was nothing but a myth, where there had not been a Prince of Darkness on the serpent's throne for a millennium.

The only thing that hampered his imagining was not knowing the state of Hell when he'd last ruled it.

He pictured a city but didn't know if it had been built or just the thing he had always thought about building.

With a sheet of paper in one and a pencil clenched between his teeth, Ira tried to inventory the bar while Marius continued to bartend.

Most of the newly formed guard, as well as those who worked in the Precincts, had been pulling double duty lately, which meant that Hell had seen a boom in leisure spending. Brothels were no exception to that.

"Do you think you could wait?" Marius snapped as he danced around Ira with a drink in each hand. He came dangerously close to spilling the drinks.

Ira yanked the pencil out of his mouth. "*No.* They're not going to clear out for hours yet and I need to know what I need to order and the orders go out tomorrow—"

"Tomorrow morning, I know, I know, lovey, I'm sorry."

Ira held no grudge. Marius had always been good to him, whether he was working as a whore or bookkeeper. He returned the pencil to his teeth and resumed counting the bottles of spirits and mixers, then moved on to see what they had for garnishes.

Before he could retreat to the back office, Marius snagged his sleeve. "Glasses."

Ira stared, trying to remember what that meant.

"Cause that tray—"

"Right!" Things came back in a flash.

"The short ones," Marius reminded.

Ira scribbled down that they needed to order two dozen highball glasses, then went to the back office to fill out the order forms.

When that was done, he headed back out to help Marius run the bar. Ira had been trying to get him to hire another bartender for a while now and the pander insisted that he would as soon as he had the time to find someone he liked.

Several patrons tried to buy Ira drinks, which he refused, or tried to proposition him, which he also refused.

"I'm just the bookkeeper," he told them.

"A bookkeeper shouldn't have such a pretty mouth," was the answer he got most of the time, or something similar concerning any of his other body parts.

Once or twice, he was informed, "I've had you before," to which he always replied, "That was then. Only thing I serve now is drinks."

They usually took it well enough, considering that there were plenty of others to choose from. If they became obstinate, Marius would shoo them away or Elle, a guard who seemed to be made only of sinew and wrath, would scare them off.

During a lull, when most of the customers were occupied, Ira leaned against the counter and asked, "How's Hasbani?"

Marius glanced over, an eyebrow raised.

"He hasn't come by lately."

Marius answered slowly, "They've been busy up at the palace, I think. He came over for dinner the other night. He didn't have any news if that's what you're asking."

"No, I like him! He always seems so..." Ira debated the right word. "Skittish when he comes by, though."

"Brothels are different on Earth," Marius replied. "I think it was a shock for him to find out what...well, you know, what it is I do for a living. And what I used to do."

"I've heard they get funny about all kinds of things on Earth. Still, you think he'd have adjusted by now," Ira said.

"Twenty-something years up there is a lot to unlearn. I don't know how much he wants to unlearn either." The pander stared into the bin of dirty glasses for a while.

Ira felt he had the right to pry a little so he asked, "You two...I mean, you weren't close when he was growing up, were you?"

"His mother and I had a falling out. I think he must have been...thirteen or fourteen at the time."

Ira instantly wanted to know more but sensed this wasn't the time for that line of questioning. "I understand." He glanced around the brothel. "Well, he'll have to get used to it eventually."

Georg traipsed downstairs, perhaps the handsomest thing the brothel had to offer and definitely the most aware of his looks.

Marius elbowed Ira when he caught him staring.

"Done for the night," Georg announced as he sidled behind the bar, his fingers trailing on Ira's waist as he made himself a drink, if it could be called that. Two fingers of amber liquid, though Ira hadn't seen which one he'd chosen.

"You have to pay for that, you know," Marius informed him.

Georg dropped a fat silver coin on the counter in front of him. It was one of the new coins, not a serpent but a raven with the profile of their new queen on one side and a bird in flight on the other.

In value, there was no difference between a silver serpent and a silver raven, but to Ira, any coin felt counterfeit without the snake and the beast stamped on the faces. Of course, the old coins were still in circulation. Rivka had tried to make it mandatory for people to exchange their currencies but that had only led to panics; instead, she'd introduced the new coins by paying wages in them.

People had balked until they'd found that the new coins were exactly the same weight as the old ones; then they'd accepted them, for the most part.

Ira wondered if his old mistress had maintained a trade-only policy. He hadn't been anywhere near the Trade House in over a year and he pushed the thought out of his mind as soon as he could.

He focused on the speed with which Georg had downed his drink and reached for a second one. When he finished that one in two swallows, Ira stopped him from pouring a third.

"That more than covers it," Georg told him, nodding towards the coin.

"I'm not about to let you drink a serpent's worth of straight liquor." Ira took the bottle away from Georg and took him by the hand. To Marius, he said, "I'll be back."

Georg went with him to the back room, his lovely mouth twisted into a fierce scowl. "If I've paid then I don't see why not."

When he'd closed the door to the office, Ira inquired, trying to keep his tone soft, "Did something happen, darling?"

Georg raised an eyebrow. After a moment, he said, "Oh. You mean with one of the clients? No."

"Then what?"

"Nothing. I can't have a couple of drinks?" Georg asked.

"Sure, but you haven't got to down them like that!" Ira said. "Come on, love. What's bothering you?"

Georg shrugged.

Ira leaned back to perch on his desk, crossing his arms and not knowing what to do. He and Georg had gotten off to a poor start when they'd first met but after that, things had been good between them. They were not each other's only friends, but Ira considered their friendship closer than any other he had.

Georg collapsed into the chair across from the desk with a dramatic sigh. He surveyed the office, his honey-colored eyes sweeping over everything with bored irritation.

Checking the urge to rake his fingers through Georg's tousled, coppery hair, Ira reminded, "You know you can tell me anything."

Georg ignored him so Ira nudged his foot with his own.

"I've been thinking about that thing," Georg admitted.

"So have I."

"I." George licked his lips and looked around, less bored now, more agitated. "I don't like these things roaming our streets. This is *Hell*. It's supposed to be the other way around."

"We should be roaming their streets?" Ira asked, not able to keep the smile off his face.

Georg scoffed and smacked his leg. "You know what I meant!"

"I do. You should come with me—" Ira began.

"Where are you going?" Georg demanded, his voice hitting an unusually high note.

Ira finished, "To Earth. I've got some business up there."

Georg shook his head. "I don't know."

It would be a risk, really, to bring Georg and it was a secret that wasn't Ira's to reveal, but he wanted company. He'd only ever made the trip once before and he'd had a guide then. Now he had to go alone. He was the only one who knew where to go other than Imogen and he hadn't seen her since the coup.

He'd gotten a single note, unsigned, that he suspected was from her. It had informed him that there was a property outside the city in need of some repairs and that she would be in touch when everything had been taken care of.

He didn't know what it meant but felt that she wouldn't have told him if it hadn't been important somehow.

"What business do you have on Earth anyway?" Georg asked.

Ira glanced towards the door. "It's a secret."

Georg shook his head again. "I really...I don't know. I've seen their souls, I don't want to see them in person."

"Only the bad souls come here," Ira reminded.

"And the ones that think they should. All those miserable fuckers in the Fourth? I don't want to see where that comes from."

Ira couldn't blame him, not really. "I understand."

"I'm sorry."

"You don't have to be sorry," Ira assured.

"I am. I'm sorry that I'm not brave."

"You—"

Georg insisted, "Don't tell me I am! I'm not. If I were brave I wouldn't be keeping secrets from my parents."

"You could tell them, then," Ira suggested. "Tell them you're a pleasure worker, what's the worst they'll do? They hardly seemed to care that I was."

"That's because *you're* not their son. You serve and that's fine. For *you*. Those who serve have their place. But as part of the family? Never. We don't serve anyone but the Devil."

Ira couldn't take offense. He knew that high society people felt that their station kept them far above those who served, just as the working classes sneered as those who needed to hire someone to handle their affairs. "I don't think it would be that bad. And Astrid wouldn't be able to keep holding it over your head and I know you've been *dying* to tell her off for all kinds of things."

"They'd never let me out of their sight. Amaranth would probably call off the engagement and then no one would have me," Georg explained. "Listen to me! Whining about having to marry a captain's daughter. You must think I'm such a brat."

"You are a brat, dear, but it's what I like about you." Ira clasped his hand. "I can't think of anyone who complains in quite the way you do."

Georg's grip on his hand tightened, not enough to be painful. He pulled Ira closer so that Ira stood before him, looking down at him. Georg straightened up and placed his other hand on Ira's hip. "Before all this went to shit we had sort of..." Georg swallowed. "We'd discussed the possibility that maybe the three of us...But now there's only two of us and I know you miss him and I feel like a monster even bringing it up."

"Oh." It took Ira a few moments to piece together what Georg had said. Or had tried to say.

"You think I'm horrible, don't you?"

"No."

Georg said, "I know you love him, I do. I don't want you to think that I'm trying to weasel my way in or take his place or anything."

Ira brushed his thumb against Georg's cheek and reassured, "I don't think that."

The younger man embraced Ira, his cheek against his belly. "I don't know how things are supposed to be anymore."

"We're supposed to be friends. I know that much." Ira rubbed his back. "Anything else is sort of peripheral."

"Sort of?"

"Sort of," Ira confirmed, then elaborated, "So if we fucked, it'd be as friends and if we didn't, it'd be as friends and if I happened to decide that you were allowed to fuck our Prince, that would be an agreement between friends."

Georg chuckled at that and confessed into Ira's shirt, "I really do think he's handsome."

"Then we'd better get him back and we can decide if you're allowed to sleep with him or not."

His mood lighter, Georg tugged Ira onto his lap. "How'd you end up being the one making those decisions, anyway? You'd think the Devil would do as he pleases."

Ira shrugged. "He does do as he pleases, it just happens to be that listening to me is what pleases him."

"He really is a queer sort, isn't he?" Georg asked.

Ira agreed, "Absolutely."

Outside the back room, the clamor of voices picked up again as the hour ended and clients came downstairs. They'd be wanting drinks, Ira figured, so he pulled himself out of Georg's arms and stood.

He kissed the younger man. "We'll have to pick this up some other time, I am technically working right now."

Georg pulled him back, though, and twined his fingers in Ira's curls, drawing him in to kiss him deeply. His slipped his tongue inside Ira's mouth and Ira found himself capitulating to the kiss, responding hungrily. He went to climb back onto Georg's lap, but the other man broke the kiss and put a hand on Ira's chest, giving him a gentle push back.

Georg flashed an impish smile and informed Ira, "Just seeing how much you'd changed your mind about not wanting to sleep with me."

That boat had likely sailed, Ira realized, when he'd first grasped that the Devil wanted Georg. Ira had imagined the two of them laying together and that had stirred interest that hadn't really been there before. "You could have asked, I would have told you."

"But I had more fun doing it my way. Go on, back to work."

Ira headed towards the door with Georg on his heels. The younger man headed out into the night as Ira returned to his place behind the bar. Marius hadn't gotten swamped yet, but he showed visible relief when Ira came back and started taking orders again.

In the small hours of the morning, when all the workers had left with coins buried deep in their pockets and all the customers had sauntered out, lighter in mood and bank than they had been before, Marius and Ira cleaned.

"So."

Ira looked over and paused his application of club soda to a couch cushion. It had a splash of either blood or red wine on it; whatever it was, it didn't seem to be responding well to the club soda. "What?"

"You and Georg."

Ira abandoned his efforts to scrub out the stain. One of the cleaning staff who'd be in later would have to deal with it. He approached the counter, setting down the rag and glass. "What about me and Georg?"

"I thought you and Lucifer were exclusive."

Frowning, Ira asked, "What's it matter to you?"

"You haven't given up on getting him back, have you?"

"Oh!" Ira forgave the pander's questioning; he was one of the Fallen and remained loyal to his Prince. "No. And I won't, either."

Marius nodded, gathering up the last bin of dirty dishes. He brought them to the kitchen and when he returned, he had a more amused look on his face. "But you and Georg, though."

Ira shrugged. "We're friends. We've been friends for ages."

"Aye, and I've seen you kiss him and not look so flushed as you did coming out of your office tonight."

"Lu wouldn't care," Ira replied, feeling the need to defend himself.

"Probably not," Marius agreed. "I can think of a few things he would care about. That girl—"

"Don't you dare ask me if I want him back and then give me a hard time about doing what I need to do to bring him back!"

"Peace, lovey," Marius soothed. "He'd want you to take care of yourself, that's all I'm saying. Making yourself spend time with that girl...I know it keeps you close to the Ravens and I know that's important. I do. But if you can't get rid of her, find something that will help you deal with it."

Ira nodded, mute. He didn't know how to respond to that. Before Lucifer had taken him from the Trade House, the idea that he should take care of himself had not even been a niggling concern in the back of his mind. He had to be clean and presentable, he had to be pleasant and willing and obedient, but he hadn't needed to be satisfied or happy in any sense.

He had read in his spare time and that had been enough to keep him from growing melancholy or losing his mind. It would be enough to hold him together now, he was sure of it.

Except that at the Trade House he hadn't known anything else and now he did.

Marius gave him a pat on the shoulder when he left and repeated his advice to take care of himself.

At home, Ira tucked himself into the armchair he'd bought a few months ago. It was really too late for anything but bed but from the chair, he could see the single star in Hell's sky. He liked to read here, sometimes with a glass of wine or a cup of tea, and glance up at the star between chapters.

He stayed up until the sky grew red, illuminating the world and rendering his star invisible again.

Dinner tasted worse when Astrid was around, Ira realized. He loved this dish, this restaurant. It was a little place tucked away on a small street between the Trade House and the library. He hadn't been able to go there often but sometimes a customer had slipped him a tip, a few secret coins that Mistress had never known about.

He'd learned not to spend them on anything he could keep; once he'd been daring enough to buy himself a book. She had wanted to know everything about where he'd gotten it, who had given it to him, how many other things had he been given.

He'd lied, of course, he'd told her he'd found it on the street. She hadn't believed him and she'd given him forty lashes for stealing, first twenty and then twenty more when his scabs had healed.

She'd been careful not to do too much damage, never enough to put him out of work, never enough to leave scars, never anything that would dissuade customers from trading for him.

He pushed the chunks of potatoes and carrots around in his stew, searching for another piece of lamb.

At first, he'd thought the restaurant had started using poorer cuts of meat or that there might have been a new chef. When he'd sipped the wine and found that lacking, too, he started to wonder if it was the company that had him enjoying things less.

She'd sketched him on a napkin. She was always sketching him, that was nothing new.

He ate, knowing the meal had flavors his tongue couldn't taste, knowing the texture should have been pleasant instead of just something irritating he had to chew.

"You should take more classes," he suggested.

She looked up. "Why?"

He shrugged. "I don't know. Always something worth learning, I guess."

"I've taken all the art classes the university offers."

He nodded then took a large swallow of wine. He just wanted her to have something other than him with which to fill her time.

"Besides, I've been busy with work," she reminded.

Not busy enough, he thought, surprising even himself with the idea's vehemence.

She reached over to put her hand over his. "I know I haven't been seeing you as much as I should."

He shook his head and immediately assured her, "No, no, what you're doing is *important.* A new reign means new history."

Right now, he knew, Astrid and the Master of Records had been tasked with creating an illustrated text of how the Ravens had taken the throne. When he'd read the draft, he'd considered it more narrative than informational but hadn't thought that needed pointing out.

His skin had crawled when he'd read the parts he was in. If Rivka's reign lasted, he'd go down forever in Hell's history as Satan's betrayer and scorned lover.

"They've finished making the new crown," Astrid told him, pulling him out of his thoughts.

Ira nodded. The Devil's crown had gone missing when Imogen had. "That's good. Coronation will be soon, then, won't it?"

She beamed. "I can't wait. Not everyone's had the chance to really meet our queen yet. I mean, they've *seen* her, of course, but once they meet her, they'll understand."

"They will." Ira feared that. Rivka was an angel and she *felt* like an angel. She was serene and radiant, with silver eyes and skin and hair. She was tall and slender, like a blade, and when she'd fought the Devil, she'd moved with grace. She was what a queen should be and Ira worried that the citizens of Hell would like her too much.

He hoped that prejudice would win out. Demons didn't trust angels or anything to do with Heaven. Most of them didn't even like humans.

Some people had rumbled about her being an angel but so far, the more pressing matter had been the souls roaming the streets. She had handled that to the best of her ability, relying on Precinct workers and the newly swelled ranks of city guards instead of the monstrous shape Satan had taken.

Astrid squeezed his hand and gave him a smile. He did his best to return it.

After they'd eaten, they walked through the streets, arms linked. He made the occasional comment as she told him all about the meeting she'd had with the queen, all the comments Rivka had made about the sketches for the text. He nodded and made small comments when appropriate, but mostly he worried that she had steered him in the direction of the apartment building in which she had taken up residence after her time at the university.

He'd managed to avoid going there by saying that he needed to get to work the next morning, but she knew that he wasn't working tomorrow.

It was a nice apartment, tastefully furnished with quality items that might have been costly but would last. She came from that kind of money, the kind that considered well-crafted goods an investment, not just a luxury.

It had a large window that must have let in an impressive amount of light. Beside the window, she had set up her work station. Without asking permission, he went over and riffled through her sketches and illustrations.

He found one that showed the night of the coup, the Devil bleeding out on the ground as they all watched. He couldn't help touching the image, wishing he could see his ash-gray fingers against the whiteness of the Devil's skin instead of against that of the paper.

He put that one aside before it made him delve too deep into his memories only to find another, this one depicting a white-clad angel with golden eyes, sun-kissed skin, and lush, strawberry blond hair tumbling about his shoulders. His teeth were white and his nails were clear, instead of the black they were now.

"Rivka thinks that reminding people that the Devil was an angel, too, will help win people to her side," Astrid told him, coming up behind him to put an arm around his waist. "I can't imagine him ever looking like that."

She'd made him look more sweet-faced than Ira had ever pictured him before the Fall. Ira had never been able to imagine him without a hint of mischief, even at his most angelic.

He'd had freckles, Ira knew, but found himself glad that neither Astrid nor Rivka had known that detail.

Astrid kissed his cheek. "But don't look at those. You haven't got to worry about him anymore."

He left the illustration and followed as she brought him over to the couch. She kissed him, her hands roaming and he wished that he had a dozen more layers of clothing between his skin and the warmth of her hands.

His body didn't seem to know that. His body knew that she was pretty and warm, that her touch was the right mix of tender but passionate. His body knew that they'd been together before, that she'd been one of his most frequent clients.

His mind, however, conjured memories of being too drunk, of her climbing on top of him and shushing him so that others wouldn't hear. Of her hands on his skin and her mouth on his and being inside of her while he had wanted to be anywhere else.

That seemed to get the message across to the rest of him. The slow heat that had started to grow in him abruptly faded and his throat tightened.

He moved away from her, coming close to pushing her away.

She frowned at him. "What?"

He shook his head. "I can't."

"What do you mean you can't?" she asked, a confused smile playing on her lips. She reached for him again.

He stood up without thinking about it, taking several steps away from her. He needed a lie and he needed it to be good, otherwise, she would try it again. She wouldn't understand how he felt, she didn't even understand how terrible that night on the couch had been for him. She thought they were in love.

"I can't." He had to force the words past the lump in his throat. "He would make me do things," he told her and then immediately lost his composure, feeling disgusting that he'd done so much to paint the Devil as a terrible person. He let people think that Lucifer had abused him and now he'd named him a rapist as well.

"Oh, Ira," she breathed, her hands covering her mouth.

"Please don't make me," he sobbed.

"Of course not," she vowed, coming over to him and wrapping her arms around him. "I won't ever do anything to hurt you."

He curled tighter in on himself and she tightened her embrace. He buried his face in his hands and sobbed for a little while.

When he regained his composure, he couldn't look at her. She continued to hold him, saying soothing inane things and making him promises that he would be safe.

Stepping out of her grip, he said, "I'm sorry. I am. It...I need time."

"Of course." She clasped his hand. "I'm here for you."

He nodded, hating how she looked at him with adoration. An uncomfortable mixture of repulsion and pity stirred in him whenever she looked at him like that. He didn't know what he'd ever done to inspire her infatuation and he didn't know how to break it.

Right now, he needed her but even when he hadn't, she'd pursued him.

"I understand, you know," she assured him.

He didn't think she did.

She brought him back to the couch and told him about how the little boy next door had terrorized her throughout her childhood, pulling her hair and cornering her to steal kisses. One day, he'd cornered her as always and shoved her hand up her shirt.

"My father came and scared him off when he heard us. I don't know what he would have done otherwise," she admitted with a tremble in her voice. Anger or fear, he didn't know, but he hadn't ever seen her grow truly angry about something.

He wished she hadn't told him. All of this would have been easier if he could have hated her as much as he felt he deserved to, but every now and then she would come out with a little story like that or do something kind for him. He wanted her to be a monster.

"Tea?" he asked, starting to stand.

"Oh, I'll make it, sit down."

He sat back down, picking at his nails as she bustled about in the kitchen.

When she returned, she handed him a mug and a plate with a little cake on it. It had the shape of the carrot and had been frosted to be the most adorable approximation of a root vegetable he'd ever seen.

"I hope the tea's alright. Just a little milk and sugar, right?"

He nodded.

"I feel awful," she told him, "Really. I didn't mean to upset you."

"I know." He continued to stare at the cake. "Did you make this?"

"Yes. Well. Me and Adrienna."

Adrienna, he recalled, was her younger sister. "Does everyone's name start with 'a' in your family?"

"Just the girls. It started with my grandmother and her sisters, I think. It's sort of a nice tradition. I know Amaranth has a list of names picked out."

Ira wondered if Georg knew.

"If Georg ever stops puttering around and finally marries her," she added.

"He's taking classes still."

She made a face. "Sure. And then a whole other course sequence after he's done with this one."

"Being Master of Records is an important job, he just wants to be prepared."

"Ira, I know he's your friend, but even you have to admit he's immature," she chided.

"He's young."

"Only a few years younger than me. And the same age as Amaranth," she reminded. "I do have half a mind to tell Amaranth that he's been whoring around behind her back."

"Don't!" he insisted. "He'll get in trouble, you know he will."

"He *should* get in trouble."

"Astrid, don't," he pleaded. "He's going to spend the whole rest of his life working a job he didn't choose and married to a woman he didn't choose either. If he wants to spend a few years screwing around in a brothel, what's the harm? He's got a contraceptive tattoo, I know that's what Amaranth and Ulster are so worried about."

She surveyed him for a while and he worried that he'd said too much. Astrid's family took more issue with out-of-wedlock relations than most people in Hell did, but that was because more than half their family fortune had been doled out to bastards over the past few years. Her grandfather had not bothered with any contraceptives, not tattoos or charms or even spells, and he had left something to each of his bastards, always as much as he'd left his legitimate children, but sometimes more.

Ulster had been one of the legitimate children to receive less than a bastard. Amaranth's family had respectability and Georg's had money; their match made sense, especially after Georg's brother had been bludgeoned to death under suspicion of molesting a little girl.

Georg, of course, insisted his brother hadn't done anything of the sort and Ira believed him, but it had tarnished the Schreibers' reputation nonetheless.

"Better him than that brother, I suppose," Astrid finally pronounced.

Ira knew better than to defend the brother. There weren't many rules in Hell, but the Edicts explicitly forbid coupling with children. "He's sweet, really, once they get to know each other, Amaranth will see."

Astrid chuckled. "I don't know about that."

Ira didn't either. He surveyed the room and found a clock. It was late enough that he could pretend to be tired. He ate the little cake and finished his tea, then tried to say his goodbyes.

Her face fell. "Oh. You don't have to go, do you? I thought you didn't have work tomorrow."

"I'm sort of tired," he attempted lamely.

She smiled. "You can sleep here."

He bit his lip.

"I promise I won't do anything, we can just sleep," she vowed. "We can take things slow until you're ready."

He felt he had to consent to that much at least.

He crawled into beside her, keeping on his underclothes, glad for the barrier they provided, meager as it was. To her credit, she wore a nightdress and didn't do anything more than kiss him good night and wind her arms around his waist as they slept.

It had been dark for a long time.

He couldn't be sure how long that was, exactly, but he knew it hadn't been forever. He knew this because he could remember things that had come before the darkness.

At least, he thought he remembered them. He could have imagined them, but if he was imagining things he didn't think he would have imagined himself a son that had been born too early and whose mother had been slaughtered by her own family for birthing him.

And he really didn't think he would have named his imaginary son Felix.

But having a son, small and faraway and possibly not real, was a lot to consider and he didn't feel that he should be thinking too much about frail little babies with scrawny arms and serious, pink faces.

Recalling the sensation of having a small hand wrapped around one of his skinny fingers stirred a feeling of tenderness in him. Considering that he didn't know where or when he was or who had him chained like this, he didn't think he should be having tender feelings.

He took his thoughts of Felix and tucked them away into a deep part of his mind, the place where he kept all his most dangerous secrets. When he went there to hide away Felix, he found the face of God and the way past the heavenly gates. He recalled his memory, visceral and in perfect detail, of the first time he had died and knew why he had put that from his more conscious mind altogether.

He nestled his thoughts of Felix beside an achingly sweet recollection of the first time he had ever walked among humanity. That he knew he had hidden because it would have been difficult to be the Devil when he had once loved them so dearly.

He closed up those thoughts and put them away again before the nostalgia grew too strong and he lost a year or two sifting through them. He would be able to take them out and look at them whenever he wanted, or even return them to his regular working memory, so long as his mind was quiet and calm. It wasn't somewhere that could be accessed under duress, something that had always proved to be a boon. Beings under duress should not have access to secrets and he thought, given the stressful nature of his assignment, God must have made him that way on purpose.

Far off, the sound of indistinct voices reached his ears. He didn't recognize any of them, but then again, he could barely hear them.

Sometimes sounds made their way to him, but never light.

And never food. Hunger had gnawed his stomach so badly that he thought it must have eaten itself because he didn't feel anything anymore.

He thought that until he caught a whiff of something, some food thing that he couldn't name because it sent such pain ripping through his guts that he couldn't think for a few seconds.

First came the sound of a lock clicking and then a door scraping.

And then there was light.

Hardly any, just a small orange glow, but he threw up his hands to shield his eyes.

Bread.

He smelled bread and that was enough to make him take his hands from his eyes.

A thick strand of drool worked its way down his chin as he gazed, slack-jawed at the perfect loaf of bread that had been set down just out of his reach.

He hadn't bothered to look up to see who'd brought it, just knew that it was a person with a candle.

He scuttled out from his corner, hunched and weak, and tried to snatch the bread. No matter how he stretched he couldn't make contact, his fingers close enough to feel the heat coming from the crust.

He strained so hard that he thought his shoulder and wrist would pull right out of their sockets.

A whine of pain and desperation escaped him.

When it did, the toe of a black leather slipper nudged the loaf closer towards him.

He snatched it and scurried back, away from the light and the slipper-wearer.

He scarfed down the bread, swallowing it in inadvisably large chunks. When it was gone, he found his stomach tight and aching.

The slipper-wearer set down the candle on the floor and sat beside it. A sweet, musical voice informed him, "I thought you'd make yourself sick."

He pressed his hands over his ears. His eyes still had not adjusted to the light of the candle but he thought he glimpsed a bit of silver skin out of the corner of his eyes.

She said nothing else but he could feel her gaze. It made him knot his fingers in his hair, matted and greasy, and tug at it.

Something scraped against the stone floor and he glanced over to see her pushing a pitcher towards him.

She must have brought it in with her but he hadn't noticed it, not when the scent of bread had demanded his attention.

He pulled the pitcher over and guzzled straight from it, the water spilling down his chin. He had gulped down about half before he wondered if it was advisable to take sustenance from a stranger and his probable captor.

He set it down and wiped his chin, though that might have only served to replace the grime the water had washed away.

"It smells down here."

It was a dungeon that had held an unwashed and recently deceased body for an undetermined length of time, he wanted to tell her. Instead, he only squinted and tried to make out what he could of her from the scant light.

Her dappled silver skin shimmered faintly in the light and her fingers toyed with a long lock of silver hair.

"Heaven has a smell like water has a taste but this place...I can't put my finger on it."

Neither of them spoke for a long stretch of time.

"There should be enough to wash up a little," she advised, nodding towards the pitcher that he still clasped against his chest. "You're a mess."

He said nothing. He wondered if she had ever been a mess. Heaven was orderly and clean and pleasant. Angels didn't spend much time in their bodies and she probably hadn't lived in hers long enough to get messy, maybe not even enough time to get her blood or cut her finger.

Something itched at the back of his mind that told him that yes, she had been cut and he had been the one to do it.

Still, a little blood was different from *being a mess*. He was dirty and bloody, he had a hole in his chest and all kinds of nasty things matted into his clothes and hair, caked onto his skin.

Something about the smell told him that, when he'd been dead, things had been done to his body. Maybe they had pissed on him. They'd spit on him at the very least, he was sure of it, not because he remembered but because he knew that if his people had risen up to depose him they had disliked him enough to spit on him.

She studied him for a while longer, saying nothing, until she got up to leave. She left behind the candle and the water and the Devil.

He stared at the candle and hoarded the water, not knowing if anyone would return to him.

He wished he could have hoarded the light too, saved it for when he needed it most.

Ira caught sight of Hasbani picking his way cautiously across the brothel, taking his eyes off Georg to watch Hasbani. He ended up walking straight into Georg, bumping him with the bin of clean glasses.

"Hey!" Georg yelped.

Ira couldn't even make himself mutter an apology. He dropped the bin on the counter and ran over to Hasbani. He nearly clasped him by the hand, but managed to only bounce on his toes as he asked, "Any news?"

The brothel was empty, except for the three of them and Marius in the back room. Ira wouldn't have risked the question otherwise. The sky had started to grow light about an hour ago and most of the workers in the Precincts would be headed off to work. The whores would still be in bed, or maybe at breakfast if they were early risers.

Hasbani took a step back. "No news."

Ira's heart squeezed.

Georg hopped up on the counter and asked, "None at all?"

"No."

Ira went to stand beside him, leaning against Georg's legs. Georg twisted one of Ira's curls around his finger. "How can there be no news?" Georg pressed. "What's the point of having a man on the inside if he doesn't tell you anything?"

"I'm *not* your man on the inside!"

"Then you're a Raven?" Georg challenged.

Ira wished he wouldn't. If Hasbani had declared for the new queen, then riling him up could put them in danger, them and all the others who missed their Prince.

"I'm not anything. I just work there."

Marius came out of the backroom. "Thought I heard you." He greeted his son with a kiss on the cheek. "Any word?"

Hasbani recoiled from his father. "I'm not risking my job over this. I need the pay. And besides! I didn't come here just to feed you information."

"Don't be sore about it, Leila..." Marius' voice trailed to a whisper halfway through the name. He stared at his son with abject horror, then tried to put a hand on his shoulder. "I'm sorry—"

"Don't," Hasbani snapped, stepping out of his father's grasp. His fair brown cheeks had reddened. "Just. Whatever it is you asked me to come over for."

Marius offered meekly, "I thought we could go to breakfast."

"If it was just to talk about your king then I'll leave." He didn't wait for an answer but turned and headed out the door.

Marius watched him go.

Ira, knowing full well it was not of his business but with a sneaky idea in the back of his mind, pulled out of Georg's grasp and followed Hasbani, jogging to catch up with the other man just outside the door. "Hey!" he called but when Hasbani didn't stop, caught him by the arm. "Hey."

"I'm not—"

"No, you're not. You're not my spy. Come talk with me somewhere private."

He hesitated and Ira took it as an opportunity to pull him back into the brothel, past the other two and into the backroom. He closed the door.

Hasbani stood off to the side, away from Ira, his arms crossed over his chest and his back hunched.

"Would you like to be?" Ira asked.

"What?"

"My spy."

"I'm not risking my job. I—"

"Need the pay. Right. I can do better than pay you," Ira told him.

Hasbani frowned but took the bait. "What do you mean?"

"You know he's the Devil, right, our Prince?"

"Yes."

Ira continued, "And that thing you're saving for. It's not my business but I know how long it took Imogen and Garris and others to save for the same kind of thing."

"No. I don't know any of those people. And I'm not...I just need the money," he fumbled through a variety of answers.

The poor lad, not more than twenty-five and all his years spent up on Earth, looked about ready to tremble out of his skin. Maybe he'd even cry and Ira didn't want it to get to that. He put a gentle hand on Hasbani's upper arm. "It's different on Earth, isn't it? Everything's different up there. Who you get to be and who you get to love."

Hasbani swallowed. "I don't know what you're talking about."

"Darling, you're in Hell, no one cares. If I'm wrong and you already are exactly how you want to be, tell me to fuck off," Ira told him, "And if I'm not and there's some other way you'd like to be, then help us get Lu out and I'll make sure you get what you want."

Hasbani met Ira's eyes, his hazel eyes boring into Ira's dark ones, as he clearly pronounced, "Fuck off."

Ira grinned, unable to help himself.

The younger man pulled away from Ira, heading towards the door and turning the knob. He pulled it open a hair, then hesitated. He closed it again and turned back to Ira. "Can he really...can he really change my body?" he asked, his voice no more than a whisper.

"He's the Devil. Of course, he can." Ira hadn't ever seen it happen, but if Lucifer made demons to begin with, he didn't think it would be too much for him to rearrange a few things with Hasbani's body, even if his heritage was a mix of human and Fallen.

"And...and my soul?"

Ira shrugged and he repeated what Lucifer had told him, "Souls aren't worth bargaining for. We've got so many already and don't even use them."

"Then I'll do it."

Ira put out his hand to shake on it and when Hasbani had grasped his hand firmly, a strange bees-under-his-skin feeling came over Ira and he knew that a handshake was not enough to mark this deal. He took a letter opener from his desk and pricked Hasbani's thumb. "It's done," he pronounced.

Hasbani yanked his hand back, staring at Ira as though he'd done something much worse, then hurried away.

That had never happened before. Ira couldn't think clearly, not with his ears filled up with muffled humming and a strange feeling like his mouth had been stuffed full of cotton.

Georg came into the backroom, a frown etched on his face, and he asked, "What'd you do to him? He ran out of here looking like he'd found you fucking his mother."

"I made a deal."

Georg's mouth opened then closed. He puffed out a bit of air and looked over Ira. "A deal? Like...you know, a *deal*?"

"I think so."

"Fuck," Georg declared.

"But he's our inside man now."

"That's...That's good, then, I think. Why don't you sit down? You look...less gray than usual." Georg put a hand on Ira's shoulder and gave him the slightest nudge towards the chair.

Ira sat, his legs weak.

Georg pressed a glass of water into his hand and he sipped at it for a little while. Georg perched on his desk and watched him, his feet swinging, his heels bumping against Ira's desk.

"I mean, it's a good thing, yeah? Having a man on the inside," Georg declared after several quiet, uncomfortable minutes.

"Yes."

"Good. That's good. We need something good."

Ira agreed, "We did."

"Oh! I was supposed to tell you. Our dinner plans have been canceled for this evening. Mamma and Astrid are *very busy* with some *very important* thing together, something about that silly history book they're writing."

"Good, I hate eating dinner with your family," Ira said.

"Imagine how I feel! *I* have to do it all the time. And imagine how it was not being old enough to go anywhere else!" Georg smiled at him.

"You should come back to my place," Ira suggested.

"Oh?"

"It never used to bother me, being alone. I used to like it but now...now all I see is what's missing."

The smile slipped from Georg's face. He came over and pressed a kiss to the top of Ira's head. "But now we've got a man on the inside."

Ira nodded.

"Anyway. I've got to go."

"Not working today?"

"No, I've got class and then my father wants to talk about...I don't know, I think it's some party or another that he's planning and he wants help." Georg made a vague gesture that indicated annoyance. "But I'll come by to get you at the end of the night. I'll probably have to eat with my father, though, so don't wait around for me to go get dinner."

Georg swooped down and kissed him before he headed out.

Ira settled himself behind the desk and got to balancing the books and filling out all the other paperwork that needed to be done. Later, as it grew dark, he told Marius that his dinner plans had been canceled.

Right away, the pander said, "Oh! Good. You can stay and help me with the bar."

"I thought you had Shari coming in."

Marius sighed. "I do."

"Then you don't need me," Ira pointed out.

"Shari doesn't know what she's doing," Marius huffed.

"I like Shari! She's *learning*, too, you should be nice to her. It'll probably be slow tonight anyway. You'll get by fine."

Marius groaned.

"You should hire her fulltime."

"I don't want to."

Ira told him, "Well, I'm not going to do it. I told you I'd help out, not that I'd work two jobs. Get Shari trained up."

The pander still didn't look convinced.

"Why don't you like Shari?" Ira demanded.

"I don't trust people who haven't worked the job before."

"You mean whoring?" Ira guessed, going off of the emphasis he'd put on 'the job.' "You're not hiring her to be a whore."

"No, I mean..." Marius let out a sigh and scrubbed a hand over his close-cropped curls. "I don't trust her around you lot. I don't trust her to care about whether or not the customers are too rowdy or too drunk. I like to work with people who know the profession."

"She'll learn. We all learned."

"I suppose," Marius conceded. "What did you and Hasbani talk about? He wouldn't tell me."

"It's his business to tell you or not," Ira said, but it felt like an apology.

The pander let out another long sigh.

"It wasn't anything bad. He's not in trouble or anything."

The Fallen said, "I keep fucking up with him."

"I think that's parenting."

"I don't know. It feels wrong. I haven't got any other children."

Ira didn't know how Marius, who had worked as a temple prostitute and had been in or around brothels since before the Fall, had but one child, but he didn't ask that. Instead, he asked, "Have you sold him to anyone yet?"

Marius looked up sharply, his face drawn tight with concern and, it seemed, anger until he saw that Ira was grinning. "No, I haven't sold him to anyone."

"Then you're flying high in my book," Ira told him. "It might not be the best measure but it's the only one I've got."

A few minutes later, Shari came through the door, pulling her mass of thick, wavy hair back into a bun. Ira grinned at Marius, warned him to try not to break too many glasses, and went outside to wait for Georg.

He sat on the bench outside while he waited, his legs crossed, one foot resting on his knee. He brushed off a few advances, chatted briefly with a few people, customers and pleasure workers alike, that he knew well, and looked up at the sky, waiting for it to grow dark enough to see his star.

Sometimes he wondered if it had been his fault that Lucifer hadn't been able to best Rivka in combat. If he had been exhausted from making the star, if Ira shouldn't have warned him about trouble in the Seventh, if Ira should have jammed a knife into the angel's heart as soon as he'd gotten close enough.

It likely would have gotten him killed but the Devil had made him undying. Now he had to worry about everyone else involved in their schemes to get the Devil back on his throne.

Georg announced his arrival by knocking Ira's foot off his knee, sending his legs sprawling. He held out a glass bottle full of murky brownish liquid to Ira.

"Oh, no, darling, don't get me drunk tonight. I've barely recovered."

"It's not spirits," Georg promised. "My dad says it's, um, cider, I think. That it's not even got alcohol in it. It's like juice. From Earth."

"Oh." Ira still couldn't help regarding the bottle warily as he took it.

He cradled it carefully as they walked back to his apartment. He set the bottle on the counter and Georg puttered around in his parlor while he shucked off his jacket and took out glasses.

"What's this?"

Ira looked over to see Georg holding a jar filled with faint, shimmering light. "Oh. Open it."

When opened, dozens of little pricks of light tumbled out of the jar and floated through the room until they settled into place. This effect elicited a gasp from Georg, who stared at them in wonder before he guessed, "Stars?" his voice full of reverent admiration.

Ira nodded, his pursuit of glasses forgotten as he watched the lights. Lucifer had made it for him. He wandered out to touch the moon. It bobbed when he touched it, but then returned to where it belonged.

Georg put an arm around his shoulder.

"I miss how things were," Ira confessed.

"You'll get him back."

Ira could only sigh.

"You will. And you'll take him to the lake. Maybe you'll even still want me to go with you."

"I do."

Georg moved in a little closer and Ira leaned his head against Georg's chest. "I've never been asked to go away on a trip with anyone. I mean, not like that. With my family or a group of friends but never, you know, because someone really wanted to spend time with me."

"Me neither."

Georg tipped back his head and let out a laugh. "And how long as it been since either of us has had a first time for anything?"

"How old were you? Your first time?"

Color crawled up Georg's neck to his cheeks. "Twenty."

Ira did a bit of math in his head. Georg, he knew, hadn't yet finished his twenty-second year and he had worked at Marius' for less than a year, maybe only nine months or so. Ira had always assumed that Georg had been the sort of lad who'd started early.

"Not like I wasn't interested!" Georg added. "I just. I don't know. I was sort of an awkward-looking kid."

"I can't imagine that."

"I hit this growth spurt when I was nineteen, grew about six inches and filled out. All that, you know. And I used to have this really horrible haircut."

"Oh?"

He nodded, his fingers going up to rake through his hair.

Ira nudged him. "Go on."

"I used to wear it long and one of the boys at school thought it was funny too." Georg swallowed. "You know. Sometimes he would pull it or dip it in ink or stick bits of food or gum in it. One day he, uh, he grabbed me by the hair and wouldn't let me go until I'd licked all the chalk off his slate. I hacked it all off after that. It looked atrocious but I kept it short like that for years."

Ira put both arms around him, wondering how old he could have been. "I can't believe anyone would be so mean to you."

"Aye, well, they all thought I was going home and begging my brother to fuck me," Georg mumbled.

Ira tightened his embrace, not knowing what else to do.

Georg nestled his face into Ira's shoulder, then sucked in a deep breath. "Would you mind if I kissed you?"

"No."

Georg clarified, "I mean, really kissed you, with tongue and everything."

"No."

"Good. You know, normally I have a better feel for these kinds of situations. I still don't think you really want to sleep with me very much."

Ira's feelings for Georg existed in an exceedingly strange limbo between friendship and attraction. He found the other man handsome and he enjoyed his company and, more than either of those, he wanted to feel something nice again. He wanted to hear Georg tell him they would get the Devil back.

Ira had not known exactly what he'd wanted from Lucifer, just that he'd wanted something. It bothered him that they'd never been able to figure out exactly what they were to each other before everything had changed. He didn't know if Lucifer would even want to be with him anymore, after everything that had happened.

Dying might change a person. Being held captive almost certainly would.

Maybe Lucifer would find someone else, someone who would give him all the things he wanted, the things that Ira hadn't.

He touched his forehead to Georg's. "I thought you were going to kiss me."

"You look sad."

"So kiss me and make it better," he said like it wasn't an outlandish request, like kisses from a friend could fix anything.

Georg kissed him, his mouth soft, his hands lightly resting on Ira's waist. Ira leaned in, reminding himself that he wanted this, opening his mouth against Georg's, aching to feel a bit of warmth. He'd felt it before, he knew that he could get there, but it was like fumbling to light a match.

Then it started when Georg tightened his grip on him, sliding his hands to Ira's hips and pulling him closer. It rushed in all at once, a surge of need that came with flushed skin and a pounding heart. Georg untucked Ira's shirt and pushed his suspenders off his shoulders. He worked at the buttons and pressed his mouth to Ira's collarbone.

"We'll still be friends," Georg said, undoing the rest of Ira's buttons and kneeling before Ira to unfasten the fly of his trousers.

Ira combed his fingers through Georg's hair, enticed and distracted by the sight of him on his knees. "What?"

He glanced up. "If we fuck. It won't ruin things, will it?"

Ira didn't understand what he meant by that and imagined his lack of understanding had something to do with growing up in a brothel. Georg had lived a real life with a childhood and schoolmates and friends. Ira had missed out on all of that and sometimes it showed. He didn't understand why they wouldn't be friends, so he assured, "Of course it won't ruin things."

Georg nodded, then pressed his mouth to Ira's belly. "I can't get this button. Oh. Never mind, there it goes."

"We could go in the bedroom," Ira offered.

"Would you rather?"

"It doesn't matter to me."

They both hesitated, neither sure what to do. Finally, Georg wrapped his fingers around the waistband of Ira's trousers and underclothes, pulling them down and touching the tip of his tongue to the head of Ira's cock for half a second. "Boop."

Ira couldn't help the laugh that escaped. "What are you doing?"

"I don't know, I've always wanted to do that, but I didn't think anyone else would appreciate me fucking around like this."

He didn't give Ira a chance to respond; he placed a hand on the back of Ira's thigh and took his cock into his mouth. Ira had not done this in months; he'd barely even touched himself since the coup. It felt almost like he'd never done this before and he edged close faster than he had since he'd first started to come at all.

Georg seemed to know he was going to come before he did and did something with his tongue that was exactly perfect, sending Ira reeling and moaning. He spilled and had to brace himself on Georg's shoulder to keep from losing his balance altogether.

The other man laughed and pulled Ira down onto the floor with him, onto his lap. Ira closed his eyes and pressed his forehead to Georg's shoulder, trying to put his thoughts back together, to catch his breath.

"I liked that sound you made," Georg told him, twisting one of Ira's curls around his forefinger.

"Thanks," Ira breathed, knowing it wasn't the right thing to say, that it wasn't even what he meant. He looked up at the artificial stars that neither of them had put back into their jar.

Georg laughed again, then kissed him. "What do you think about blindfolds?"

He reached up to tap one of the lights. "Hmm?"

"I had a woman once who *loved* it, but I don't know, I don't think I'd want some stranger blindfolding me."

"No, not a stranger," Ira agreed.

"I think that's what she liked, though, that she didn't know me. Never saw her again. I wonder if she goes around finding a new stranger to blindfold her each time."

"Do you always talk this much?"

The smile dribbled off Georg's face. "I've sort of learned not to as much."

"Oh, darling, no, I didn't mean it like it's a bad thing!" Ira assured and then kissed him to drive the point home.

"No?"

"No, I *like* talking to you," Ira insisted.

"Oh."

Ira kissed him again, first his mouth then his throat. Georg let out a moaning sort of sigh and Ira slipped off his lap, nodding towards the couch. "Go on."

Georg hesitated.

"What?"

"I..."

Ira reached over and kneaded his earlobe. "Go on, kitten, tell me what you want."

At first, Georg stared, then managed to say, "I-I, uh...Do you think we could kiss for a while?"

"Yes."

They kissed for a long time, slowly, shedding the rest of their clothes and ending up twined together on the couch. Ira didn't think he'd ever kissed anyone this much, not even Lucifer.

"Would you now?" Georg breathed.

Ira nodded and lowered his head, finding a bead of come already on the tip of Georg's cock. Georg didn't spill nearly as fast as Ira did, which he should have expected, given his profession. His jaw started to ache so he switched to using mostly his fingers and tongue until Georg let out a sweet, shuddering breath.

"Oh."

Ira tongued the tip of his cock once more then took him all the way in for the last bit. Georg thrust his hips several times, sweet moans passing his lips as he spilled then melted into the couch.

Georg drew Ira into his arms and pulled him up off the floor. He buried his face in Ira's shoulder and sniffled.

"What's wrong?" Ira asked.

"Nothing."

"You're, uh. You're crying."

"It just happens sometimes." Georg wiped his face with the back of his hands, smearing the kohl around his eyes, and sucked in a big breath. "It isn't a big deal. I'm sorry."

"No, no," Ira assured, "It's fine. You're fine."

Georg shook his head and ramblingly insisted, "I'm really sorry; this has got to be ruining the mood. You probably won't want to come back to see me, I promise I'm not normally like this."

Ira pressed a kiss to his temple, cradling him.

"Would you stay for a little while?" Georg asked, his voice small and tentative.

"I live here," Ira reminded.

Georg straightened up and seemed to realize that he'd been talking to Ira like he was a client.

"So I'll definitely be sticking around."

He looked mortified, gaping wide-eyed at Ira. "You must think I'm an imbecile."

"I don't." Ira cuddled up to him.

"Promise?"

"Of course, love."

Georg's fingers ran over one of Ira's thighs, not curious or amorous but appreciative. "I always wished I was a proper demon color," he admitted. "I always wished I was something beautiful like blue or green instead of this...peachy-pinkish kind of color. There was a girl in my class, she was so pretty, turquoise with these fantastic spots..."

"There's no such thing as a demon color. Lu, he...before he fell, his hair was reddish-blond and his eyes were gold. That's what he told me, anyway. I think you must look like him a little bit. When you look worried I see the resemblance the most." Ira pulled away to stretch and yawn, then nestled into Georg's arms. "Tell me what you like."

That seemed to take Georg by surprise. "What?"

"You're always doing what other people like, tell me what you like to do."

"Where should I start?" the other man asked.

"Tell me how you like to be kissed."

"For a long time."

"I noticed."

Georg admitted, "I've never had anyone that was mine to kiss."

"Never?" Ira asked and felt bad for asking, so he explained, "I always imagined you making eyes at all the schoolgirls and sneaking off with them."

"I would have liked to!" Georg chuckled. "No. It was me and my hands and one girl I kissed when I was fifteen. I did get to know myself very well."

"You were telling me how you like to be kissed."

"I can show you," he offered, his fingers kneading Ira's skin.

Ira shook his head. "No. Tell me. Then maybe I'll let you. Go on, no blushing. How do you like to be kissed?"

"Slow...uh. I like it when...you know I can't think when you're looking at me like that!" Georg protested.

"Slow. For a long time. What else?"

"When...I liked when you bit my lip and how you pressed right up against me. One time, um, one time this fellow pushed me up against the wall and it sort of scared me but I sort of liked it."

"We'll have to tell Lu."

"You really think he'll like me?"

Lucifer had expressed interest in Georg, but more than that, between knowing the Devil and knowing Georg, Ira felt safe saying, "I know he will."

"I didn't think you'd want to share."

"I don't," Ira admitted. "When I think about him being with other people, it...it sort of makes my stomach drop. I don't want anyone else to touch him or look at him or be special to him. That's only part of it though. The other part is that I don't trust anyone with him. I don't think they'll be good to him or treat him how he should be treated. But, uh. But I like you, so I don't mind at all that he likes you, too. I like the idea of the three of us sharing."

"If it works out..." Georg trailed off.

"What?"

"It'll be nice, I think. When I have to stop working at Marius' and marry Amaranth, it's something to look forward to, that we'll be friends still and that I won't have to spend the whole rest of my life only fucking to get her pregnant," Georg explained.

Ira shook his head. "I don't understand your family."

"I don't either. I don't understand *her* the most! I do *try* to be nice, you know. I get that she's only in it for the money but shit! We could have a bit of fun together, really. I don't think she likes men, though...I'll be fucking irritated if she ends up bedding some woman and expecting me not to sleep with anyone."

"Did you tell her that?" Ira asked.

"I might have mentioned it. Nicer than that, of course."

"And?"

Georg grimaced and relayed, "And she looked at me like I'd opened my mouth and had worms come out instead of sentences."

"I'm sorry, kitten, that's rotten," Ira soothed.

"Are you going to call me that now?"

"Only if you like it."

"I like it a lot." Georg brought him closer and kissed him, the kiss somehow managing to be warm and lengthy but also relatively chaste. "Let's go to bed, I've got to go to class tomorrow morning and Professor Jenshi is a righteous bitch of a man."

While he slept, Ira dreamed about the conglomerate of souls that they'd encountered on the street. In the morning, Georg nudged him awake. "I'm heading out. I didn't want to leave without saying goodbye."

"Okay."

"I brought your mail in; it's here on the bedside table."

"Thank you."

Georg put a knee on the mattress and leaned in to kiss Ira's cheek. "I'll see you soon, love."

Ira gave his hand a squeeze and buried his face back into his pillow. He pulled over the mail, two envelopes, and barely glanced at them. He left them to rest on his pillow and went back to sleep for a little longer.

The candle burned out. He drank the water. His stomach began to growl again. He found himself wishing that the woman would come back.

Not the woman, he reminded himself each time. He wanted food, not her. She was of no consequence.

He didn't know how many days had passed since she had been here last, but this time she came with more than a candle. She brought a tray and an oil lamp, which she once again set on the floor. She sat in front of him, out of his reach but close enough that he could have snatched her if he'd been willing to dislocate a few joints.

She pushed the tray of food towards him and he dragged it back into the corner with him. He ate crouched in the corner, staring at her, wanting to know why she looked familiar. More of his memories had started to return, in bits and pieces.

She watched him eat, her face smooth. She barely blinked.

After he'd eaten and guzzled down some water, he said, "You killed me."

He couldn't stop his fingers from going to the wound in his chest. He worried about that, as much as he could. He'd even used some of his water from last time to rinse it. An infection wouldn't kill him, probably, but he didn't want one and he didn't like having an open wound in his chest. It hadn't healed much, but something told him that it should have.

He thought that it might be related to his inability to change shape or to call up any of his power. At first, he'd assumed that it was feebleness from his poor state, but the longer it lasted the longer he started to think that something wasn't right.

"I did."

"Are you the Devil now?" he asked.

"I am."

It wasn't true. He knew that right away. She was not the Devil but she could be.

"You should wash."

He glanced at the pitcher. No. He needed this for later. As much as he ached to be less grimy, he would be thirsty later.

He wondered if she had ever been dirty, truly filthy.

She left again, leaving him with the lantern.

He pulled his knees to his chest and watched the flame.

She came back sooner this time, he thought. Before the lamp had run out of oil, at any rate, and before he had grown ravenous again.

This time, though, she came without food but with a pitcher of steaming water. She set down the pitcher. She had a washcloth and something black draped over her arm. She placed them beside the pitcher. "I took some of your things."

He heard other voices floating down; they weren't in the dungeon, but they were nearby, maybe at the top of the stairs across from Imogen's office.

Imogen! Her face came back to him in a rush. He wondered if she had survived the coup. She'd advised him against going out that night but he had gone anyway. He'd felt strongly about going, too, though he couldn't remember why. He'd been looking for something, he thought.

The angel stepped outside and returned with food. She placed it within his reach and advised, "You'll feel better when you've washed."

He couldn't fathom why she'd brought him any of these things. There had to be something she wanted. Information, maybe. He didn't think it was any sense of kindness or mercy.

But he took what she gave anyway, scarfing the food then scrubbing himself as clean as he could get. He discarded the clothes he had died in and when he pressed the hot, damp washcloth to his skin, he let out an involuntary moan.

It sounded weak even to his ears, the sound of a kicked dog begging for a kind touch. With the grime and grease gone from his skin, his hair felt a thousand time dirtier in comparison. He rinsed it as best he could with the water he had left.

He wanted a bath, a real one, he wanted to sink up to his chin in hot water and close his eyes. He wanted to soak and scrub his scalp and clean the grit from under his fingernails.

He wanted to know who it was that he was remembering in the bath with him, a thin-limbed young man with dark eyes and ash-gray skin. He wondered if he had imagined him. When he pulled on the fresh clothes and found them laced with the floral, slightly fruity aroma of lavender and the sweetish and almost medicinal scent of hyssop and rosemary, he knew that he couldn't be imagining him. Those smells filled him with an overwhelming ache and more frustratingly vague recollections of that man.

By the time the woman returned again, he hadn't even started to feel hungry or dirty again.

If she had taken his throne, he didn't see why she was the one bringing him food. His instinct was to distrust her but that was, this time, outweighed by the heady scent of meat.

She set the tray down a fair distance away from him, then approached him. She lingered out of his reach and told him, "Bring me those other things. The tray and the pitchers."

He eyed the hunk of plain, brown meat and the chunks of yellow carrots, then looked at her. He wondered for a while, torn between his options.

She would have to cross into his territory to gather the requested items. In doing so, she put herself in danger and tempted him with the chance to have a meal, a real one, to gnaw all the flesh from her bones.

But if he did that then he ran the risk that no one would bring him anything else to eat and probably nothing with which to wash.

He pushed the trays towards her and set all but one of the pitchers onto them. He pushed them towards her, not wanting to go too close.

"What about that one?" she asked, her silver eyes flicking towards the one he had kept.

He carried that one over more carefully, not wanting to spill the contents on himself or his living area. He, as rule, did not like to keep close quarters with his own waste.

She carried the tray and pitchers out, then returned to place his food and drink beside him. She didn't stay to watch him eat.

A fork and knife rested on the tray and he wondered if the blade was an oversight or a test or if she thought he wouldn't use it against her.

He ate, carving the meat into little pieces and savoring the meal, trying to make it last as long as he could, not just so he wouldn't upset his stomach but so he would have something to do.

For the first time in what felt like years, his thirst was slaked and his hunger sated, his body felt relatively clean and his clothes were still passably fresh. He wouldn't want to be making any public appearances like this, but he didn't feel so worm-like as he had before.

His fingers found their way to his hair, as they always did, but couldn't manage to braid it. The long tresses, which he had always vainly kept shiny and soft, were clumped together. They pulled him down, feeling like a blanket of filth draped around his shoulders.

He took up the knife and grabbed a fistful of hair. Without hesitating, he sheared off the first fistful and dropped it to the floor.

It lay, dull and heavy, like some kind of long-dead snake. Some hideous thing.

He ran his fingers over the spot, feeling his scalp and the short fibers, unable to stop himself.

He had started and had no choice but to carry on, he knew, but still, it took more effort to hack off the second fistful. By the fourth one, it felt more like being scalped.

But he took it all off and itched for hours, covered in tiny hairs.

When the angel came back, she stopped further away than she usually did, her eyes fixed on the thick ropes of hair lying all around him.

She stepped back, panic on her face, turning her silver eyes into full moons. "How?" she breathed.

That took him off guard. He sat up straighter, taking his chin off his knees and looking her over.

Another moment passed and her face relaxed. She moved further in, no longer upset by whatever had bothered her before. She placed the tray within his reach and sat on the floor to watch him eat.

He burned his tongue on the soup and ate more slowly after that.

The day he had died had returned to him more. He had left the palace to go out looking for that gray demon; the creature had promised to come back and hadn't. In the Ninth, not too far from home, he'd encountered a beggar girl with sightless eyes and she had asked how to get to the palace.

"What's your business there?" he'd asked.

"I have a message for our Prince."

"You've found your Prince."

She had opened her palm to show glimmering coins. "A boy gave me these. Told me that if I loved my Prince I would tell him that there was trouble in the Seventh."

He had promised her a boon and run back to the palace to fetch his sword.

The last thing he'd seen had been that gray demon with his black cherry curls in the arms of a woman.

He had, he was sure, called the demon a traitor. He wished he remembered more.

She stayed after he had finished his meal. "Did you design the city yourself?"

He ceased his contemplation of his warped reflection in the back of the spoon. He didn't recognize himself, not the black hair or the red-gold eyes or the black teeth. He felt strongly that he should have had freckles, that the blank, pallid canvas of his face was wrong. "Nnnno? Yes. Maybe."

"They say you did. All the texts insist that you did so much for Hell."

He returned to looking at the spoon. He had shorn his hair unevenly, which shouldn't have come as any kind of surprise.

"Which makes me wonder."

He didn't ask what she wondered.

"You put so much effort into this realm, what is it that has you fooling around on Earth all the time? Making deals with humans. What could you need with more souls? We're almost overflowing!"

"There's a war on," he said, not sure how he knew it but deeply convinced of its truth.

She sat and continued to watch him. He gave up trying to get a real feel for what he looked like in the spoon. He stretched out his legs as far as they would go then drew them back against his chest.

If she kept feeding him, he wondered what would happen when he started getting bored instead of spending all his time thinking about food.

"How do you know?"

He looked at her.

"What to do with all of them," she clarified.

He widened his eyes at her. "You're the Devil now and the Devil *knows* what to do with souls."

She leaned over, blew out the oil lamp, and left him in the dark.

Ira sat on his bed, his legs crossed like a pretzel, with the contract sitting before him. He had his elbows resting on his knees and his face cradled in his hands. He had been staring at the contract for a long time now.

He didn't know what to do about it.

The sheet of parchment had a bloody thumbprint at the bottom of it and detailed an agreement between Hasbani Ibn-Marius and Ira, companion to Lucifer and proxy to the serpent's throne. The handwriting was a neat, practical script that reminded him of the writing on library cards. He knew it was not his or the Devil's and doubted it would be Hasbani's either.

A wax seal sat at the bottom of the page, bearing the same monstrous silhouette as Hell's coins.

Since he'd received this one, he'd gotten two more envelopes with the same handwriting and type of parchment in the mail but didn't know why. He hadn't made any other deals with anyone; he'd been too afraid to open them to find out what they said.

Someone knocked at his door. It took him a while to recognize the sound but when he did, he answered it to find Georg looking flustered.

"What?" he asked.

"We had plans."

Ira stared.

"You and I and my fiancée and your...Astrid. Whatever she is to you. At The Pennywhistle."

Ira knew a response was required of him, but the world felt far off and dim. "Oh."

"I was worried," Georg sulked.

"I'm sorry."

"You don't *sound* sorry."

Ira couldn't conjure the appropriate emotions. He shook his head, feeling uncomfortable in his own skin. "...Did everything work out?"

"We ate if that's what you mean. Astrid was beside herself."

He stared at Georg, taking in the irritated concern scrawled across his face, the way he moved his hands from his pockets to his hair to his hips. "Can I show you something?"

He retreated back into his apartment, sure that Georg would follow, which he did. He retrieved the contract from his bedroom and held it out to Georg.

"What's this?"

Ira shook his head. "I...I, uh, I'm not exactly sure. You're the Master of Records, though."

"I'm not."

"You will be."

Georg glanced at the parchment. "Where did you get this?"

"The mail. What is it?" he asked.

"It's a fucking contract, Ira. It came in the *mail?*"

"You brought it in," Ira reminded.

"You're not fucking around?"

"No."

Georg sighed and examined the parchment more closely. "It's an authentic article. It is. And it names you his proxy."

"Is that...is that a real thing?" Ira had never heard of anyone being a proxy to the serpent's throne; he'd had schooling and knew the history of Hell as well as anyone else.

"It is now," Georg said.

Ira took it back and read it over again. "How?"

"The contracts are like that. Normally they go to him but...well, you made that deal with Hasbani, didn't you? A proxy. Shit, Ira. I haven't seen *any* contract with that on it," Georg marveled, though not without a bit of concern.

Ira whined, "You can't tell me this hasn't happened before."

Georg took Ira by the arm, pushing up his sleeve to show the scars that Lucifer had left on his arm. The Devil had done something to him, carving runes into his skin and imbuing him with some part of himself. Ira didn't understand it, exactly, and Lucifer hadn't even asked permission to do it. "How many people has he done this to?"

"There's me. Maybe his wife...I don't know about that, though, I never saw any runes on her...but who knows with the two of them? They're probably carved on her ass," Ira grumbled and took his arm back. He had been exceedingly careful to keep those marks hidden from the Ravens.

"He named you companion, he made you undying. That's got to, I don't know, grant you some kind of official status in his affairs. You must have accepted it when you entered into a deal on his behalf."

Ira shook his head. He and Lucifer had been public, socially, with their relationship, but they had not entered into any type of legal contact declaring their relationship status. The laws in Hell were meticulous when it came to things like defining the parameters of a family and partnership; if it wasn't a formal affair with proper documentation than it might as well have been nothing at all as far as the courts were concerned.

Before things had been so tightly defined, the social liaisons and inheritance structures had been chaotic and just as likely to cause a blood feud spanning seven generations as they were to allow someone to amicably inherit something from a parent or partner.

"This is fucked," Ira declared.

"What's more fucked is how Astrid is taking you not showing up. The invitations for the coronation came today."

"Oh."

"She was going to invite you—"

"Has she changed her mind?" Ira asked, panic shoving the words out of his mouth. Having Astrid bring him to the coronation wasn't his only way into the palace, but it was the only event when the palace would be full enough that he might be able to slip away.

"Of course she is, but you've got to go make amends."

"How?"

Georg opened his mouth, a rascally smile starting on his lips, but it slipped from his face and his eyes lost a bit of their usual glimmer. He recovered, saying, "Tell her you weren't feeling well. She likes to think you're as fragile as you look. She'll buy it especially considering those bags under your eyes."

"I slept like shit." Ira sighed and rubbed his face. He looked around for his jacket, then decided not to bother with it.

Georg reached over to take Ira by the arm and shook his head. "It's dark, love, wait until tomorrow. Please. I don't want to have to worry about you anymore tonight."

"I thought I had to make amends."

"Send her a note. Ask her to lunch tomorrow. Special. Just the two of you," Georg advised.

Ira nodded. He'd have to give Astrid something to assure her of his affections, though what that could be he hadn't decided. He didn't know what he could give her without losing a bit of himself. It had been easy once to give things away to people without ever feeling like it mattered.

He found a pen and bit of paper and neatly wrote his apology, telling her that he was sorry he'd missed their dinner, that he'd overslept and had felt under the weather lately. He told her that he would come by her work tomorrow to take her to lunch and that he hoped she wasn't too disappointed.

He handed it to Georg for approval. "Add something sappy," the younger man advised.

Ira didn't know what to write. He added *With all my affection* then scrawled his name.

Georg folded up the note and threw it out the window. "Imagine if it just landed in the rubbish heap," he joked. When he noticed that the idea didn't amuse Ira, he came over to him and embraced him.

There weren't any words to make things better and he must have known that because he stayed quiet. They held each other for a long time and Ira took comfort in the sound of Georg's heart.

"You have to let me stay, you know, they haven't caught that thing we saw," Georg reminded him.

"I will beg you to stay."

Georg stepped out of his arms. "I mostly came over to borrow something to read," he told Ira, plainly lying. "Recommend something."

"Trash?"

"If you've got it!"

Ira went over to the bookshelf and handed him a well-worn book with a painting of a splendid, nude youth on the cover, stretched out on a soft, grassy hill beneath the red sky. The title read *Learning to Yield*. "It's about a lad who fancies his sister's girlfriend."

"What's he yielding to?"

"Oh, uh, he's got this thing like he thinks he's better than everyone and he won't do shit for anyone else and he's kind of got to learn that other people deserve things too. It's garbage."

"Sounds like it." Georg tucked the book into the inside pocket of his jacket, then shrugged off the jacket and tossed it onto Ira's couch. "You should offer me a drink because I just had to sit through dinner with both of them all by myself."

"Clearly you survived unscathed."

"How can you say that when you haven't even *bothered* to check me for injuries?" Georg pouted.

"What kind of drink do you want?"

"Whatever you've got. Neat, please."

"I've got wine, kitten," Ira clarified. "Do you want red or white?"

Georg came into the kitchen and poked around in Ira's cabinets, taking out a pot and a lot of spices that Lucifer had bought but that Ira had never used. He took what was left of the cider and poured it into the pan with a bottle of red, then added in a spoonful of honey and some of the spices, cloves and cinnamon, things like that. He turned the heat on and stared into his creation, declaring, "It feels like a cozy kind of night, what do you think?"

Ira couldn't think of the last time he'd felt cozy. "Let's go up on the roof."

"What's on the roof?"

"The sky."

"The sky is on the roof?" Georg asked.

"Shut up, you know what I meant."

Georg put an arm around his waist and rested his head on his shoulder. "I did."

They sat on the roof with their hands clasped around their mugs. Georg had brought up a blanket and wrapped it around his shoulders.

"Are you sure you don't want to come up to Earth with me?"

Georg glanced over, pausing mid-sip. "You're really worked up about that."

Ira nodded. "I've got to go, though."

"Why?"

Ira thought about telling him, but only leaned in close and nudged his shoulder. "If you come you'll find out."

"When are you going?"

"The day after tomorrow. Yatha is sending me up."

"I've got class."

Ira cried, "No, you don't! You're such a liar."

"Fine."

"Fine you'll come with me?" Ira prompted.

"Yes."

Ira beamed.

"But only because I don't think you'd make it back if I let you go alone. Who knows what kind of awful things they get up to on Earth. You know we keep records, right? Of all the souls that come through here and the things they do. They're all...murderers and rapists and liars and thieves!"

Ira giggled. "I didn't know you worried about me so much."

Georg kissed his cheek. "I have to worry, that's what we do about things that are important to us."

Ira sipped his drink and fixed his eyes on the star, wondering how he would repair things with Astrid. He bounced a few ideas off Georg, who after a while told him, "I don't know, love, I never know what to do with women anywhere but the bedroom."

Ira bit his tongue.

"Or men," he confessed. "Fuck, I am just a slut, aren't I? My mother is right about me."

"What's your mother say about you?" Ira asked. Mrs. Schreiber hardly ever had anything bad to say about anyone, but he believed Georg when he said that her opinions changed when company wasn't around.

He counted on his fingers as he listed, "That I get stupid ideas in my head about things. That Hansel should have been the next Master of Records cause he could do more than think with his cock. That I need to grow up. That I better not mess things up with Amaranth." He wiggled his fingers, one still down. "Come on, there's got to be another one. Say something mean about me."

"You cheat at cards."

"Oh, come on, you can do better than that. I'm talking about deep, personal flaws," Georg said.

"You don't let anyone know what you're really like because you're afraid they won't like you."

Instead of putting up his last finger, Georg dropped his hand to his lap. He bit his lip. He murmured, "You know what I'm really like."

"And I adore you," Ira assured. "Even when you cheat at cards."

"Even when I'm being immature?"

"Then, too."

"And when I'm thinking with my cock?" Georg asked, a bit of liveliness coming back to his voice.

"Especially when you're doing that."

Georg rolled his eyes and scoffed.

"No, I mean it! You always look...exuberant. Your cheeks get so flushed and your eyes have this sparkle. I love seeing you happy." He put an arm around Georg and pulled him close, kissing his cheek. "I *adore* seeing you happy."

"Maybe you should have been my father."

"You can call me daddy if you like," Ira purred, nipping his ear.

Georg threw back his head and laughed, a belly laugh that rang out across the rooftops. "Daddy, will you get me something pretty for my birthday?" he simpered, all pretend pouting.

Ira dissolved into giggles. "Whatever you like, kitten, as long as you're a good boy."

Georg snorted unattractively.

When they had finished with the farce, Ira caught his breath and wondered aloud, "But really, what am I supposed to do about Astrid?"

"Go down on her."

Ira shook his head, all the fun going out of the moment as a slick queasiness oozed over his skin.

Georg looked immediately reticent. He pulled Ira close and pressed his forehead to Ira's temple. "I'm sorry, dear, I didn't...I wasn't thinking. Give her something. What's she like? Does she read?"

"Not really."

"Something. Uh. She does art. Something with art," Georg fumbled.

In the end, Ira ended up buying her a small sketchbook, because he remembered that she'd mentioned not having enough time to draw what she wanted anymore.

"You can just carry it in your bag, that way if you get an idea...well, you know," he told her when he handed it over.

She didn't seem upset with him and insisted that he stay the night. She cautiously propositioned him and he gave her a few kisses, but couldn't summon the will to do anything more.

The sky was not the crystalline blue it had been last time Ira had visited Earth, but a sheet of pale gray. The drizzle had turned his curls into an untidy mess, though Georg only looked rakishly disheveled.

People stared at them as they made their way down the street and Ira chalked it up to the color of his skin. It had puzzled humans last time, a lot of them had wanted to know if he was all sorts of things.

One man had asked, "Are you some kind of colored?"

"We've all got some kind of color," Ira had responded cautiously.

"No, I mean to ask, are you...a member of the black race?"

Ira hadn't known how to respond since he was clearly gray and not black at all; he had only shrugged. One person had asked if he was from the Orient and he had changed the topic.

Georg took Ira by the hand, pulling him out of the way of a horse that had strayed close to the sidewalk.

"Love!" Ira cried, startled by being pulled.

Georg looked at the ground. "Sorry, I...I thought it would come right out of the road."

"It's fine."

Ira used the moment to evaluate his surroundings. Yatha had gotten him to the right city but that was about it. He didn't have directions, but he had carefully memorized the address of Hiram Reinhart and Phaedrus Queen. Imogen had asked him to learn it shortly before the coup. Ira hadn't wanted anything to do with the information but now he understood why Imogen had wanted him to have it.

She was always full of back-up plans; he saw that now.

"Excuse me," Ira called over to a woman.

She turned in his direction, then frowned and hurried away.

He sighed and scanned the crowd, looking for someone who might not be put off by his appearance. He saw a group of pretty young women gathered together on a street corner. He tapped Georg's arm and nodded towards them. "Go ask for directions."

"No!"

"Georg."

"No, Ira, don't make me. You go," the younger man insisted.

"But they're looking at you, darling. Please," Ira begged.

Georg pressed his lips together, then let out a hard breath through his nose. "Fine."

Ira handed him the slip of paper on which he'd scribbled the address and Georg headed off towards the girls. Ira hung back and observed as Georg made all the girls blush and giggle.

"What did you say to them?" Ira asked when he came back.

"Nothing, I just talked to them! Anyway, it's this way," he said as he took Ira's hand. "Straight until Marsh then a right, a right on to Regent and the first left. It's a big old house, they said. You said Phaedrus Queen lives there?"

Ira nodded. He felt mildly queasy at the idea of meeting the author, though what really churned his stomach was seeing Felix.

Georg tried to talk to him throughout the walk, pointing at things that Earth had and Hell didn't, like automobiles and the advertisements for all kinds of bizarre drinks and rare foods.

"Pepsi-Cola, what's that?" Georg asked.

"It's...it's like this sweetened soda water, I think. I don't know, I tried one of them but I didn't like it."

"No?"

"Well," Ira recalled, "It was the first time I'd ever had anything carbonated."

"What do you mean?"

Ira shrugged. "It's not like Mistress was serving me highballs at the Trade House or anything."

"Shit," Georg breathed appreciatively.

Ira put his hands in his pockets, scanning the street signs. He still struggled to get around the Ninth Precinct and navigating a foreign realm seemed a stupider idea with each minute that passed. "Was it Marsh?"

Georg nodded.

Ira paused and looked around. He spied the street they needed two intersections up and hurried towards it.

Finally, when they stood before a large house, Ira gingerly climbed the front steps and raised his hand to knock on the door.

He stood frozen like that until Georg gave him a nudge.

He knocked, his teeth dug into his tongue.

An eternity passed, or maybe only half a minute, and the door opened. A tall, thin man with fair peach-colored skin opened the door and stared at them. His sleeved on one arm was pinned up, revealing that he was missing a hand and some of his forearm.

Ira unstuck his tongue. "Uh. You've got, uh. You've got the baby."

Immediately the man frowned and started to call up a spell that sounded distinctly unfriendly.

Ira shied away and cried, "No, no, not...!"

Georg bounded up the steps, his own small spell bouncing around his fingertips. He stepped in front of Ira and warned, "Don't, or I'll do mine and I've heard humans aren't very sturdy."

Still holding a spell at the ready, the man said, "There's no baby."

"Lu hasn't been able to come," Ira told him.

The man pressed his lips together.

"I...Can I come in?" Ira glanced down the street.

"No."

"Please! I. I don't know who's listening and I know what I've got to tell you isn't for passers-by."

The mage hesitated and Ira thought he'd failed to convince him, but he stepped back and allowed them inside. "Sit." He nodded towards the couch.

Ira skirted around him, eying the spell warily. He whispered for Georg to get rid of his, which the other demon did, begrudgingly. They sat stiffly on the couch and the tall man stared them down.

"Hiram?" Ira guessed.

"Who are you?"

"I'm Ira."

"Ira who?" the human asked.

"Just Ira."

"Not *just* Ira," Georg corrected. "Ira, the Devil's companion and proxy to the serpent's throne."

Ira said, "I know you probably...you've probably been wondering where Lu's been all these months."

"No," Hiram answered coldly.

Ira swallowed. "I know he tries to visit as much as he can and...I don't know if you've heard what happened in Hell, but I...when I see Lu, I have to be able to tell him how Felix has been."

Hiram said, "I thought the Devil was dead."

"Well, he died," Ira conceded. "But he doesn't stay dead. He's got to be back by now."

Hiram studied him then dismissed the spell. He put his hand on his hip. "And who, exactly, are you? His proxy?"

"That's sort of tangential, really. I think he did it by accident. But mostly he and I are..." Ira didn't know how he wanted to categorize their relationship. It felt like something other than what he'd read about in romance novels. "We're companions."

"And in Hell that means, what, exactly? I don't imagine demons adhere to the same sort of relationship models as humans do."

Ira glanced at Georg. "It means we're more than casual lovers, that we care about each other. It means sometimes he threatens to eat me alive so we won't be apart."

Hiram wrinkled his nose.

"That is serious," came a voice from the kitchen. "Do you think he means it?" asked the Fallen to whom the voice belonged as they exited the kitchen.

Ira could only stare at the once-angel.

They waited, one eyebrow cocked.

"You...I. I liked your book," Ira blurted lamely.

They smiled. "Thank you."

Ira continued to stare and they grew uncomfortable beneath his gaze, their smile fading.

"Not what you expected?" they asked, their tone taking a bit of a sour note.

"No, I...I just don't know what to say, I'm sorry. I know..." Ira pressed his hands to his cheeks, knowing he was blabbering. "I know you don't like it when people gawk, I know, I just...you know, Lu talks about you whenever he's visited..."

Georg poked him hard in the ribs and Ira stopped yammering.

Phaedrus Queen frowned at the pair of them and glanced at their husband, who shrugged.

"I didn't think I'd ever meet you," Ira told them, the words slipping out before he could stop them.

"Well. Here I am."

Ira nodded, clenching his jaw to keep from saying anything else.

Phaedrus came over to him and extended a hand. "Well, let's see it then."

"See what?"

Phaedrus wiggled their fingers and Ira put his hand in theirs. They pushed up the sleeve on his left arm and eyed the runes Lucifer had carved there. "He must like you something awful. Did you say you were his proxy?" they asked.

"Yes. But I don't think he meant to..."

"There's no way to tell with him, really," Phaedrus sighed. More clearly, they said, "You came to see Felix."

Hiram protested, "I don't think—"

Phaedrus released Ira and put their hand on Hiram's shoulder. "Three-quarters of a century and you still don't trust me."

"It isn't you," answered the human.

Phaedrus didn't argue but took their hand from Hiram's shoulder and headed upstairs, gesturing for Ira to follow.

Ira wished he could have stayed downstairs but followed anyway. Phaedrus lead him into a nursery and nodded towards the crib.

Ira edged closer, not sure what he would see. The last time he'd seen Felix, he'd been a frighteningly small and frail infant. He would be about a year and a half now, maybe a little less, Ira wasn't really sure given how unlike time could be in different realms.

He peeked over the edge of the crib and peered down at the sleeping boy, pale as his father with white-blond hair. "He's been doing well?"

"Yes. Better than we hoped for. He knows seven words."

"I don't know if that's good or not," Ira confessed.

"It's more than he knew the last time our Prince came to visit. Am I correct in believing that you haven't seen him since the coup?" Phaedrus asked.

"I haven't."

"They say he's really dead."

Ira shook his head. "He can't be."

"No?"

"I need him not to be," Ira answered.

"Ah, that's a different matter altogether. I had heard that a scorned lover betrayed him. That's you, isn't it?"

Ira shifted uncomfortably. "That's what I've been letting everyone think. Things...things got out of hand and fast. But I'm going to put things right."

"I haven't heard that," Phaedrus said, then assured, "Which is good, because I hear almost everything. Lucifer's told me a lot about you. He says you like to read, he's always asking for recommendations."

Ira didn't know what to say. He turned his eyes back to the child, who had started to stretch and rub his eyes.

When Felix opened his eyes and looked around, his face contorted at the sight of Ira. He reached for Phaedrus, who scooped him up.

"Do you want to hold him?" the Fallen offered.

"No," Ira answered right away, then realized how rude that was. "I...I don't like babies, it's not him."

Phaedrus chuckled. "Then you're with the wrong man, darling, all that one does is make babies. Just like his father."

Ira looked at Felix, who had cuddled up against Phaedrus. "He says Felix is the only in a while."

"He's right, of course, I just like to tease. He's been good, he really has been. I have to say, I'm glad he slipped up with this one." They kissed the top of the child's head.

Ira looked at the two of them. He moved a little closer and touched the baby's arm with a single finger. "Your father really wanted to keep you, you know." He glanced up at Phaedrus and wondered if that had been the wrong thing to say. "Thank you for letting me see him. Lu will be glad to know he's well."

"You think you'll be seeing him soon?" the Fallen asked.

Ira nodded but didn't offer any details.

"Why don't you and your friend stay for something to eat? It's a long way to come just to look at him. It's about time for lunch."

"Uh. Alright, thanks."

Phaedrus led him back downstairs, where they found Hiram and Georg filling the room with enough hostility to shed blood. Ira wondered what had happened.

"Calm down, boys, there's already one war on," Phaedrus chided as they handed Felix over to Hiram.

"What did you do?" Ira asked Georg.

"I didn't do anything," Georg told him and graced Hiram with a dirty look.

Hiram didn't say anything, either, but gave the baby a kiss.

The four of them sat around the kitchen table together. Felix babbled and Georg babbled back at him, which seemed to only frustrate Hiram.

Phaedrus made tea and declined Georg's and Ira's offers to help make lunch. Instead, they demanded that Hiram put down the baby and be a proper host.

"I don't like having so many demons here," Hiram confessed quietly to Phaedrus, probably not aware that his whisper hadn't been quiet enough. He'd gone over to the stove to speak with Phaedrus and still had Felix on his hip.

Phaedrus answered at a normal volume, reminding, "*I'm* a demon."

"You know what I meant," the human grumbled. He cast a glance towards Ira and Georg, who were trying not to eavesdrop too obviously.

"I have no idea what you mean, Hiram. There are about a half-dozen types of demons," Phaedrus said.

"I know."

"So what are you worried about? That they're Hell-born?

Hiram shook his head. "That they're strangers."

"If you didn't make yourself scarce every time the Devil showed his face, you'd know plenty about that one," they said as they nodded towards Ira. "You'd know that my king trusts him."

Hiram didn't answer.

"Which means I trust him, too. Put Felix down and help me," Phaedrus requested.

Hiram huffed but set Felix on his feet.

The baby immediately toddled over to Georg, his arms raised up. Georg lifted him and beamed at Ira. "I *knew* it couldn't all be made up, I knew there was a baby."

"You can't tell anyone," Ira insisted.

"Why not?" Georg asked. When Ira started to frown, he immediately added, "I won't, I won't, of course, I swear but...you know, he hasn't had any children in centuries."

"That can't be right," Ira said.

"We keep records of his get," Georg told him. "Raegesh has his own room in the record hall *and* two secretaries for it."

"All of them?"

Georg bobbed his head. "Except for this one." He grinned at the baby. "Hell should be celebrating."

Hiram turned around, a breadknife in hand. "You keep *records* of that?"

"I don't personally, I just said it's Raegesh who's in charge of that," Georg said.

Hiram asked, "Why?"

Phaedrus answered for Georg, "To grant them status, to keep an eye on them. He does take some responsibility for his bastards. If they're too out of hand, he'll intervene."

"And because he was looking for an heir," Georg added. "He hasn't paid much attention to it since he found one. But he has claimed all his bastards."

Hiram didn't answer and turned around to finish slicing the bread and take down bowls, at Phaedrus' request.

"Why can't I tell anyone?" Georg asked.

"People are trying to kill him."

"You're too cute to be murdered," Georg confided to the baby.

"Or imagine what would happen if Rivka got her hands on him?" Ira asked. "His only child in centuries? He'd be...at least, I think he'd be bending to her every whim if she held Felix's fate in her hands."

Georg nodded.

Over bread and split pea soup, Ira tried not to stare at Phaedrus, knowing how much it bothered them. He knew the poems they'd written about being gawked at and treated as a spectacle, knew some of them by heart.

"Whatever you're trying not to say, you might as well," Phaedrus prompted eventually.

Ira blurted, "I just love your poems, they're absolutely my favorite, I'm sorry."

"Thank you."

"What poems?" Hiram asked.

"I had a few volumes published in Hell over the years," Phaedrus said casually. "And a few novels. Three, isn't it?"

"Four, and two novellas and a short story collection," Ira recited.

Phaedrus chuckled.

"They publish things in Hell?" Hiram demanded.

"Of course, how else would we have any books?" Ira asked.

"That's nonsense."

"A million demons and you don't think any of them figured out how to publish a book?" Phaedrus asked.

"It's *Hell*."

"Darling, you've never been," Phaedrus pointed out.

Hiram pushed his soup around and grumbled something under his breath.

Felix smeared soup all over his face and grinned. He reached out a small hand towards Phaedrus and called, "Bibibibibi."

The once-angel turned towards their son and asked, "What, love, what could you possibly want from me?"

"Bibi up."

"I absolutely will not pick you up, you're covered in soup."

"Bibi *up*."

Phaedrus reached over with a napkin and started to wipe the soup from the child's face and hands. Only once he'd been wiped down did Phaedrus pick him up, at which point Felix gurgled happily, kicking his feet.

"I love you, too," they told the child.

Lucifer probably already knew it, but Ira was glad that he'd be able to report that Felix was doing well with Hiram and Phaedrus. He hoped the news would bring the Devil a little bit of hope until they could get him out of the palace.

At the end of lunch, when Ira was helping Hiram wash the dishes, a wax-sealed envelope fluttered out of the air and landed beside Ira's elbow. He frowned and turned to look at it, spattering it with drops of water as he reached out to touch it.

He drew his hand back, frowning at the blurred ink. It was addressed in that neat, librarian handwriting to *Ira, companion to the Devil and proxy to the serpent's throne.*

He stepped away from the letter, dropping a dish in the sink and rushing out to find Georg in the living room. He grabbed him by the hand and insisted, "We should go."

Phaedrus asked, "What's Hiram said to you now?"

Ira shook his head. "No, nothing, I just...we should go, thank you for having us." He tugged on Georg, pulling him towards the door.

Hiram came into the living room, the envelope in his hand. "Is this your usual way of receiving mail?"

"*No.*"

"What is that?" Phaedrus asked, already on their feet and moving to take the envelope from their husband's hand.

"Nothing! Georg, kitten, let's *go*," Ira begged.

Georg pulled out of Ira's grip and went over to Hiram, taking the envelope before Phaedrus could. "Is this another contract?"

"I don't know, don't open it," Ira insisted.

Georg broke the wax, his honey-colored eyes darting over the page. "Who's Lewis MacAfee?"

"I don't know!" Ira cried, a whine creeping into his voice. "I want to go home."

"Lewis MacAfee lives three doors down," Phaedrus provided helpfully, sliding up beside Georg, putting one jade green hand on his shoulder, and peering down at the contract. "That's last week's date."

"Lewis MacAfee, really?" Hiram asked, gathering close to the other two. "What on Earth could he be talking to the Devil about?"

"All sorts of people make deals," Georg shared casually.

"Lewis MacAfee is a pastor," Hiram pointed out.

"A what, a pastor? Isn't that the same as a shepherd?" Georg asked. "What's that got to do with anything?"

Phaedrus sniggered, turned their face to the side, and buried it in Hiram's shoulder to stifle the sound.

The piece of paper tugged out of Georg's hand as if pulled by a stiff breeze and fluttered to the ground by Ira's feet.

That single piece of paper at his feet filled him up with more dread than if it had been a snake. No matter what that paper called him, no matter what the Devil had carved into his arm, Ira was just a whore who'd been born in the outskirts of the Eighth. He didn't know how to do anything, he was worthless except for getting on his knees or lying on his back.

He knotted his fingers in his curls and tugged. This was none of his business, these contracts.

"Love, are you alright?" asked Georg cautiously.

"I want to go home."

"Alright, we'll go home." Georg came over to him and slid his hand around Ira's waist, pulling him in for a hug. He glanced towards Phaedrus and Hiram. "Thank you."

"Of course," Phaedrus said.

Ira let Georg pull him out of the house and down the street. "You've got to tell me where I'm going, darling, how are we getting home?" Georg asked.

"Yatha...back to that pub, the one where we came up. Yatha's got that mage there, the one with the spectacles, who contacts her when it's time to bring people back down."

"Alright, good, I can get us back there."

Ira leaned against Georg, desperately glad that he'd brought the younger man with him. He kept his eyes trained on the ground and worried that he would catch another glimpse of that contract.

Once they reached the pub, Georg seated him at the bar, ordered a drink, and planted a kiss on Ira's cheek. "We'll be home quick, darling, I promise," he said and went off to find the mage who had met them in the pub's cellar when they'd first arrived.

Ira sipped at the whiskey, marveling at how different even fermented grain tasted when it had been grown in the sun.

He set down the glass directly on to the contract that had once again appeared out of nowhere. He barely contained the screech that tried to push past his lips. He pressed a fist to his mouth and dug his teeth into a knuckle.

He wanted to rip up the paper but more than that, he didn't want to touch it. Finally, he scrunched it up in his fist and threw it to the ground, hoping that it would get trod into scraps.

Georg came back over to him, put a hand on his shoulder, and asked, "Ready?"

Ira nodded and started to stand.

"You've got to pay for that," the bartender warned.

Georg threw a serpent on the counter.

"What the hell is this?" the bartender demanded, snatching up the coin and glowering at it.

Georg turned back, nose wrinkled. "It's money. And more than one drink is worth!"

The man behind the bar wrapped a heavy hand around Georg's forearm. "What kind of money looks like this?" He held up the coin to show the beast.

Georg looked down at the man's hand and then scanned the bar. He returned his gaze to the barkeep and soothed, "It's silver, no matter what's stamped on it."

The man pulled Georg in closer. He leered and told him, "If you don't have real money, we can figure something out."

"You've got sixteen Hell-born in here *at least* and you're trying to tell me no one's ever handed you a serpent before?" Georg pulled his arm out of the man's grip. "Come on, darling," he said, taking Ira by the hand and muttering to himself about people trying to take advantage.

The bespectacled mage met them in the hall and brought them downstairs to the cellar. Ira handed her the amount that Yatha had told him to bring and waited, antsy, while she counted it.

"It's all in order," she confirmed. "Should we start?"

Ira bobbed his head, overeager and sure that he must have looked touched.

The woman began her spell to inform Yatha that they were ready to return to Hell. Time flowed differently on Earth and in Hell; Ira hoped that not too much time had gone by. He had promised to help Astrid pick out a dress for the coronation after she'd nearly broken down telling him she had no idea what to wear.

He'd found himself wishing to get back to her, if only because it meant he would be safe back in Hell instead of being chased around by a piece of paper that wanted something he couldn't give. At least what Astrid wanted he could force himself to do, had forced himself to do before.

Georg took Ira's hand.

"Oh, you shouldn't do that," the mage advised. "I've seen people lose fingers that way."

Georg let go right away and gave Ira an apologetic glance.

Near to each other but not touching, they waited, fidgeting until suddenly Georg was gone.

Ira felt something tug at him and the strings of the place between worlds slithered over his skin, but that was it.

He remained in the cellar.

The mage raised her eyebrow.

A ball of paper skipped down the stairs and rolled to rest at Ira's feet. As soon as he saw it, his eyes started to sting and he pressed a hand to his mouth. He had to look at it, that much was clear. He sank to a crouch and picked it up, reading but not comprehending the details of the bargain that had been struck between Lewis MacAfee and the Devil. It had something to do with the size of his congregation.

"Are you alright?" the woman asked.

He nodded and wiped his eyes on his sleeve.

"You sure? You were supposed to go back to Hell. I can...you want me to get in touch with Yatha?" she offered.

He shook his head.

"No charge," she promised.

"No, not right now, thank you. I...I have to take care of something."

With a worried look stamped on her face, she asked, "Lad, I've never seen a transport go like this."

"I'm fine, really, I...I think I know what I need to do. I'll be back." He headed up the stairs.

"My name is Victoria," she called after him, "Ask for me when you're ready to go back."

He turned slightly and called, "Thanks!" as he headed upstairs.

He needed to find Lewis MacAfee and figure out how to complete this contract. It didn't specify what, exactly, Lucifer had wanted in return from MacAfee. Not a soul, certainly, Lucifer didn't waste time collecting souls anymore. He would get the bad ones anyway.

"Then why do all the humans think you're after theirs?" Ira had asked him once.

With a little smile, the Devil had answered, "Because once upon a time I needed souls, good souls, not the twisted ones they send down to me."

"Needed them for what?"

"For eating," Lucifer had said, but when Ira had wrinkled his nose, he'd chuckled and said, "For making things. For making demons. The ones I was making...they served their purpose but to make ones that were capable of more than straightforward thinking, I needed to either be very careful and take my time *or* to have something to start with."

"Um."

"With which to start," the Devil had amended; he had given Ira a pat on the hand and continued eating his breakfast after that.

So taking MacAfee's soul was out, not that Ira would have known how to take it in the first place.

He couldn't remember how to get back to Reinhart's house and steeled himself to ask for directions. Normally, he didn't mind asking and on Earth, he wasn't even worried that he might ask the wrong person and run the risk of harassment, but humans always looked at him like he was covered in pox.

After half a dozen people had refused to speak with him, Ira was wondering how Phaedrus managed up here; they were green, after all, and that had to be more noticeable than gray.

"Hey!" someone called over to him. "Hey, you, boy."

Ira turned around to see a woman with deep brown skin gesturing for him to come over to her.

"What are you bothering all those white folks for?" she demanded of him, "You looking to start trouble?"

Ira had not seen anyone that was white; the closest any of the people had gotten had been a sort of ivory color, but most of them had been pinkish more than anything. He glanced around and realized that his point of comparison was the milk white of the Devil's skin. He sighed, raked a hand through his curls, and admitted, "I'm trying to get directions."

"Directions to where?"

He dug around in his pocket for the slip of paper and read her the address. She pointed him in the right direction and he thanked her profusely. As he headed off, she warned him to mind himself and he had no idea what he'd been doing that needed minding.

He repeated the directions to himself under his breath so that he wouldn't have to try to ask anyone else again. It had been an unreasonable stroke of luck that that woman had taken pity on him.

Finally, he found MacAfee's house. He rapped on the door, surprised by how austere and foreboding even a door could be. Made of thick, dark wood, it might have been expensive, but was entirely unadorned. It looked like a door that took offense at being knocked on.

He rapped again when no one answered and finally, a young woman opened it. Her plain dress marked her as a servant of some kind, a cook or a maid.

"I need to see Lewis MacAfee."

"On what business?"

"Um." Ira didn't know exactly what to say. He scuffed a toe against the ground as he thought. "Tell him it's about his congregation."

She frowned.

"Please. It's...important."

She nodded. "Wait here."

She returned inside, closing the door on Ira. A few minutes later, she came back and told him Mr. MacAfee didn't want to see him, that if he wanted to know about the congregation, he could go to church.

Ira sighed and stepped away from the house. He peered up at it and saw a light shining through one window. "Alright. Thank you." Thin, white curtains fluttered in the breeze.

He waited until she had gone back inside before he sidled around to the house's small side yard and seized a drainpipe.

He hauled himself up, glad that he'd worn one of his older suits. He hadn't felt like dressing up at all lately and often found himself going about without his usual vest or jacket; not that it mattered, people wore whatever they wanted in Hell, be it layers or hardly anything at all. But Ira hadn't ever had much that was his at the Trade House and he had felt proud of how sharp and put together he looked in a nice suit.

Now he didn't care at all.

He hooked his fingers onto the ledge of the window.

He'd have to wear something nice to the coronation. It felt wrong to wear something that Lucifer had bought for him to the coronation of his usurper. Hasbani said that Rivka spent time in the dungeon with the Devil, doing what no one knew.

Ira didn't like that. He didn't want the angel anywhere near Lucifer.

With a grunt, he heaved himself through the window and swung a leg around so he wouldn't fall face first through the window. He'd chipped a tooth doing that; luckily, it had only been a baby tooth.

He stood up, brushed himself off, and straightened out his clothes. He glanced around the office. The desk had papers with wet ink.

Ira took the chance to poke around and peer at the paper. It told him nothing about MacAfee, it was just an essay about someone named Job.

The door to the office opened and a cup of tea came hurtling towards Ira; he only managed to duck out of the way because the thrower had screamed when he'd hurled it.

"Hey!" Ira shouted. "No need for that. We've got to talk, you and I."

The man, who must have been MacAfee had florid cheeks and thick, dark hair. He was somewhere between burly and athletic and Ira didn't like his chances if the man decided to assault what he must have taken to be a burglar.

"Talk?" the man roared.

"You made a deal," Ira reminded.

With that, the man seemed smaller. He drew in on himself. "You're not him."

"No." He took the contract from his pocket and handed it over to MacAfee. "This is your contract, isn't it?"

Ira already knew it was; it was a weird feeling, one that started in his gut and felt almost like the penetrating stomachache that came from seeing someone intensely attractive. This was something else, though, more aching and hungry than lustful.

MacAfee shook his head and Ira didn't think it was a denial. "Please, God, no," he whispered.

"You owe him something," Ira said, trying to think.

"Please, my boy, he's just turned eight, please, not yet," MacAfee begged.

Ira rubbed his nose and looked over the man. "A deal's a deal." He had no idea what to ask for. When Lucifer asked for favors, he almost always had a use in mind, and Ira didn't want to squander what the Devil had sought.

Blubbering, the pastor pleaded, "Not yet. It was...I was so *stupid*. I was young."

Ira smoothed out the contract on his thigh and read it over again. Not yet, the man begged, and Ira couldn't help but sympathize. This was a job for Satan, not for some pleasure worker he'd picked up by chance one day.

He read the contract a third time and glanced up at MacAfee, who'd fallen to his knees, his hands clasped in front of his chest. It reminded Ira of something, but he couldn't put his finger on it.

Not yet.

Was that even possible?

Ira thought it might be. He snagged the pen from the desk and approached MacAfee, not sure what he intended to do. He put out his hand, palm up, and MacAfee placed his hand in Ira's.

"A year longer," Ira declared, hoping desperately that in a year he would have the Devil back. "Do you agree?"

MacAfee nodded, his eyes fixed on Ira's face like Ira was some kind of idol.

He jabbed the nib of the pen into MacAfee's thumb. The big man yelped and yanked his hand back, gracing Ira with a scalding look. He stuck his thumb in his mouth.

"You mind if I go out the front door?" Ira asked, tossing the pen back onto the desk. The uncomfortable feeling in his stomach had evaporated and the contract had slipped out of his fingers; where it had gone, he didn't know and didn't care.

He didn't wait for MacAfee to answer and scurried out of the house, hoping that Yatha's mage friend would hold to her offer to contact Hell with no change.

Rivka appeared as a veritable vision in silver and white; she glimmered like a goddess, the way that the Devil should.

Ira felt nauseated just looking at her. Astrid gripped his arm and told him that she looked beautiful. He mumbled his agreement and searched the crowd to find Georg.

The younger man had a champagne saucer in both hands and a displeased fiancée at his side.

Amaranth being angry was, at least, part of the plan, and Ira thought that over drinking was to be expected, not just as part of Georg's general inclinations but as part of his preparation for what needed to happen.

Ira brought his own saucer to his mouth and wrinkled his nose. He wondered how a queen who'd disparaged the last Devil for being frivolous had gotten her hands on champagne to begin with. It wouldn't be an appropriate line of questioning, so when Rivka came over to speak with Astrid, Ira held his tongue.

He'd put on one of his new suits, the burgundy one he'd always wanted to wear but hadn't found a reason to. It felt too flashy for everyday wear and, since Lucifer's demise, he hadn't had many formal events.

"Ira," Astrid hissed.

Ira glanced up from his contemplation of the ceiling's reflection in his shoes, his concern for where Imogen had gone and when she would be back. "Hmm?"

"Her Majesty—"

"Wanted to know how you're doing," Rivka finished for Astrid, giving Ira a peaceful smile.

"I'm fine," he answered.

The queen said nothing.

"I've been well, Your Majesty, really. Thank you for asking. Bookkeeping suits me well," he told her.

"And how do you find our new reign?" she asked.

He wanted to spit on her. "Well," he answered. "The only thing I could do without is the souls wandering around."

Rivka raised an eyebrow and Astrid's face twisted.

"Not that it could be helped, of course!" he amended. "I just don't...I had a bit of a run in, it shook me a bit, I guess."

"I understand," Rivka told him and even put a companionable hand on his shoulder. "They are a fright."

Her voice sounded calm and her face remained arranged in its exquisite serenity, but Ira thought he saw something change in her eyes.

"But it can't be easy for you, either," he said, "It can't be an easy task you've shouldered."

"I did not come to the Pit because I thought it would be easy."

"But someone had to do it, right?" Ira guessed and hoped he didn't sound too glib. "I have to admit, we were...well, maybe not all of us, but we were a little worried that Hell might be different with an angel on the throne."

"Worried?" she asked.

"Ira," Astrid whispered.

"Just...well, I know for humans the Almighty has rules. I didn't know if He'd have rules for us down here, too."

Rivka shook her head. "Why would He waste time making rules to protect the souls of things that have no souls?"

"Ah." He shifted uneasily. "I never thought of it that way before."

She smiled at him again; he was starting to hate that smile.

He drained the rest of his drink and asked to be excused, promised that he would be right back.

He caught eyes with Georg, who took a deep drink from his glass and then turned to Amaranth. Ira couldn't hear what he said to her, but they'd practiced how he would say it together. Georg had agreed to take an enormous risk and cause a distraction. If he upset Amaranth, then Astrid would go to comfort her and Ira would be able to get a few free minutes in the palace.

They'd come up with the plan when they'd realized that there was no way Ira would be able to slip away from Astrid for more than a moment otherwise.

"What do you mean?" rang Amaranth's voice.

The hard part had been thinking of what to tell her. Something that would get her riled without making her break off the engagement.

"I just thought you'd...you might want to know," Georg told her, his voice perfectly audible. The whole room had quieted down to hear what they had to say. "Or, you know, that I should be honest about things."

A little bit of guilt stirred in Ira's belly.

"Why would I want to know that you've been whoring yourself out?" she demanded. Practically screeched it.

That was not what Georg had planned to tell her, or at least, it wasn't what he and Georg had practiced telling her. Maybe Georg had planned on telling her the whole time. He'd run the idea by Ira a few times, but Ira hadn't imagined he would pick now to do it.

"I, well, you know, I thought I should be honest about it."

Amaranth jabbed him in the chest. "I agreed to marry the Master of Records, not someone who takes coin for...for *whoring*."

"It's not...you know, it's just a bit of fun."

"No, sleeping around is a bit of fun, hanging around with those awful friends of yours or...or when you get drunk and stay out all night, that's a bit of fun, Georg. *Whoring* is not. Whoring is service work and I am not going to marry someone who *serves*."

He reached out to touch her arm and she pushed him away.

"Amaranth."

"Get away from me," she warbled, her voice high and thick.

Astrid rushed right over to her, which they'd known she would. Astrid was just that kind of friend, she liked to be around when people were in pain. She took pride in her ability to comfort the wounded.

It made Ira think that she liked him better as the Devil's victim than she ever would have if he wasn't.

Georg slunk away and Ira put an arm around his waist.

"You fucking him, too?" Amaranth demanded.

Ira pulled Georg away before things got too ugly. "That's not what you were supposed to say," he chided quietly.

"I know."

"Well, what happened?" Ira pulled Georg towards the front door, loudly saying, "Let's get you some air, darling."

"I could use some air..."

Instead of going out, they turned down the stairs to the dungeon, unlocking the door with the key Hasbani had slipped them when they'd first arrived and he had brought them their first round of drinks.

It wouldn't get them into the cell, but it was better than nothing.

"I'll wait up here," Georg said at the top of the stairs.

Ira nodded.

"I really would like to get some air, I think I just ruined my life."

Ira hesitated before going down the stairs and leaned in to give Georg a kiss. "You'll be alright, darling."

Georg clasped on to him for a moment.

Ira hurried down the stairs. The last time he'd been in here, it had been to leave behind the Devil's corpse.

It wasn't difficult to tell which one held the Devil; it didn't have bars like the others, but a solid wall. When he touched it, it sent an odd feeling through his fingers, making him wonder what Rivka had made the wall out of. It had to be something enough to hold the Devil, of course, and he didn't know much about magic, just knew that he didn't like the feel of the door.

"Lu?" he whispered, crouching near the lock. The keyhole was the only open spot he could find in the door. "Darling, can you hear me?"

Metal scraped against stone. Quiet and weak, Ira heard, "Yes," and it made his heart climb up into his throat.

"Oh, good. We were worried...well, Imogen said it was different every time you died and I didn't know if maybe...Anyway. How are you feeling?"

"Hungry. Afraid."

"We're going to get you out. I promise. You just need to wait a while longer."

It took a long time for the Devil to answer. "It's dark in here."

"Just a little while longer, Luci, I swear." He took a lump of clay from his pocket and pressed it into the keyhole. He'd handed over nearly fifty serpents to a sketchy fence in the Eighth for this bit of clay. Selene had pointed him in the fence's direction and the demon had sworn that it could make a mold of any lock. He stuffed the keyhole full and counted to thirty under his breath.

The Devil inquired, "She told me she's redecorated. How bad is it?"

"Tastefully simple." He carefully extracted the clay from the keyhole; it had gone stiff but would be too brittle to use for a while. It needed to set for at least a month, the fence had warned. The wait for the key to cure had seemed unnecessarily long and the fence had told him off for saying as much.

"How long would you like it to take to make a magic key?" had been the sneering response.

"There's no cat hair anywhere," Ira told him.

The Devil declared, "Disgusting."

Ira was astounded that Lucifer could manage to joke. He pressed his hand against the door and wished he could be in there with him, that he could take him out tonight. "I love you."

"I love you, too."

Ira needed to say something, he wanted to find the right thing to make things alright, to make it so he hadn't gotten the Devil killed and put a usurper on the throne. He couldn't think of anything like that.

After a moment, Lucifer asked, "Is it a good party upstairs?"

"It's a terrible party."

From the stairwell, Georg hissed, "Ira!"

"I, I've got to go." He wrapped the clay key in a handkerchief and tucked it safely in the inner pocket of his jacket.

"Hurry back."

"I will."

"I think...I've been missing you something awful."

Ira ran because if he didn't, he didn't think he could tear himself away from the cell door. He thought he might throw up. He grabbed on to Georg and pulled him out of the stairwell, his heart thudding.

"Astrid was calling for you," the younger man confided.

"Isn't she always!" Ira growled. He fumbled to lock the door behind him. He would have to slip the key back to Hasbani somehow; the man had made him promise to return it before he left. "Let's get you some air."

They slipped outside into the gardens; they weren't the only pair that had slipped off for a little more privacy. They found a bench in the garden and settled into it. Georg put his arms around Ira and turned his face into Ira's shoulder.

"I've ruined all of it. My parents are going to turn me out."

"No, they won't. You're the only son they've got."

"Then they won't let me out of the house again."

Ira kissed the top of Georg's head and rubbed his back. "Why'd you tell her?"

"Because I...I opened my mouth to lie and it just came out instead. Ira, I'm so stupid, fucking...shit. *Shit*."

"You're alright, darling." Ira kissed his hair again. "You'll be alright."

Georg let out a shuddering breath, sat up and wiped his eyes.

Ira licked his thumb and wiped away the smears of kohl from around Georg's eyes.

Georg sniffled. "You talked to him?"

Ira nodded.

"How was he?"

"I don't know. Quiet. He made a joke, I think."

"That's good, isn't it?"

"Unless he's gone mad."

Georg snorted. "Wasn't he mad to begin with?"

Without an answer to give, Ira pulled Georg back into an embrace. He rested his chin on the other man's shoulder and replayed the brief conversation over and over. It should have been longer. He should have been able to get him out now.

After they'd passed a while in the garden, Hasbani came by with a tray full of hors d'oeuvres and whispered to Ira, "Your girlfriend is looking all over for you."

"She isn't my girlfriend." Ira plucked a bit of bread smeared with something brownish from the tray Hasbani had offered him. He ate it, not displeased with the taste, though he still didn't know what exactly he'd eaten.

"Whatever she is, she's looking for you." He held out his hand palm up and for a second Ira thought he wanted to hold hands.

He took Hasbani's key from his pocket and placed it in his hand. He took another hors d'oeuvre and put it to Georg's lips.

"Ugh, Ira, I'm not hungry."

"Mmm, it's good, try it." He pressed the morsel to Georg's lips again.

With a scoff and an eyeroll, Georg sat up and took the bite of food. "You know, I hate canapés," he mumbled around the mouthful of food.

"What's a canapé?"

Georg nodded towards the plate. "Those are canapés."

"Oh. I liked it."

"Open your mouth, I'll feed it to you like a baby bird."

"Ugh, don't be disgusting!" Ira laughed, unable to help himself.

Hasbani left them, but not before Ira snagged another bit of food for himself. He didn't want to talk about Lucifer and it became clear that Georg didn't want to talk about what he'd revealed to Amaranth, so he asked, "Well if you don't like these like canopies—"

"Canapés."

"I'm pretty sure that's what I said. If you don't like them then what *do* you like? I saw you eating something before."

"I don't know, some kind of cheese thing."

"Oh, so you knew what a canapé is but not what those other things are?" Ira teased.

"Don't be mean."

"Never, kitten."

Georg burrowed into his arms.

Eventually, Astrid found the two of them like that. "Are you coming back inside?"

"Is Amaranth...?" Georg began.

"I wasn't asking *you*," Astrid sniffed. "You should go home. You don't deserve to be here anyway. And Amaranth deserves better than you."

Georg rubbed his nose.

"You haven't got to be nasty," Ira told her.

"Me? *He's* the one who's been whoring around and lying about it just so his family can crawl back up the social ladder."

Ira opened his mouth, but Georg assured, "Don't worry, darling, I'm not worried about the opinion of some sad, middle-class cousin who thinks that working with that angel on her storybook makes her important."

Astrid flushed. "The queen—"

"Is a fucking *angel!*" Georg crowed, standing up and moving closer to Astrid. "You helped overthrow the Devil to put an angel on the throne and you've got the gall to tell me that I'm not good enough for your cousin?"

"Shhh, kitten, that's enough," Ira whispered, standing and putting a hand on Georg's shoulder, worried about what kind of attention they would draw.

"Anyone who hasn't fucked their brother would be better!"

Georg barked a laugh. "You all fell into line but how long do you think your pretty silver queen can hold the throne? She hasn't even gotten all the souls *she* let out. So when she's gone and—"

"Georg!" Ira cried, tightening his grip and pulling him back. "Stop."

Astrid fixed her eyes on Ira. "You should come back inside."

"I...I wanted a bit of air, that's all."

"You should think about who your friends are, Ira, before you end up in trouble," Astrid warned him. "He's not worth it."

Ira put himself between Georg and Astrid. "He's just...he's just drunk, alright? I'm going to take him home before he says anything else stupid."

She didn't look pleased and Ira didn't want to care. He needed to keep her placated long enough to get the Devil out of the palace, he reminded himself, and then he could never see her again as long as he lived. So far she didn't suspect that he was working to get the Devil back on the throne and he needed that.

He took Georg by the arm and marched him out, pretending to scold him for drinking too much while they were within earshot of the others.

He brought Georg back to his apartment at the Inverness and found a letter waiting for him. His heart sank when he saw the seal of the beast in sky-blue wax. He almost didn't open it, not in the mood to see any contracts, but second-.guessed the handwriting. It wasn't the neat, library-card print.

He broke the seal and found a short note.

That property outside the city has been taken care of. Good to see that you've been busy, too. I'll be in touch.

It was unsigned.

He burned it, just like he'd burned the other letter he'd gotten from her.

As soon as Lucifer had heard the voice whispering through the keyhole of his cell, he'd had known exactly who that gray-skinned demon had been. A thousand and one memories had flooded back, enough to make his stomach turn.

He was not made up; it had been a relief to know that.

He was not his betrayer, either, as Rivka had assured him. He'd asked her once. He'd been sluicing warm water over his face, scrubbing it over his shorn head, and he hadn't been able to stop thinking of that face, dark-eyed and haloed by curls. "Traitor," he called him.

"Who was he?" he'd asked Rivka.

"Who was who?"

"The...the gray one. I named him betrayer."

"Oh. Ira. The memories really don't come back to you as fast as I'd hoped."

"Who's Ira?"

"He was your lover until you set him aside and he took his revenge."

"Oh."

Her answer hadn't sat right and now he knew that she had been lying, or mistaken. He had gone down to the Seventh that night to look for Ira, worried about him and worried about the message the blind girl had given him.

Hope sat in his chest, pleasant and warm, as he stared at the oil lamp that the angel had been kind enough to light for him again. Soon, Ira had promised, and Lucifer believed him.

Until.

Until he remembered how weak his will became as soon as Rivka entered the room with a bit of meat and some soap. For those things, he had started to sing like one of the little pink birds that flittered through his garden.

For a sliver of soap, he had told Rivka everything she had asked about. She'd promised to come back with more questions. She'd been slowly turning him into her counselor, albeit a chained one she paid with bits of warm food.

It wasn't wise to be hopeful and it wasn't safe for him to know that Ira had not betrayed him.

He sat with his memories for a little while, appreciating them and knowing he'd miss them when they were gone.

It took a long time for him to reach a place of calm. Lately, his thoughts had been unpleasantly crawly and full of guilt and shame and a weaseling feeling that might have been disgust.

He reached that place eventually, though, and tucked his knowledge of Ira away to a quiet place in his mind.

When he closed up those thoughts, he felt empty and uncommonly cold, though he couldn't think of why.

Something wasn't right. He scooted closer to the oil lamp, desperate for its heat and light. He slept as close to it as he could get every night. For a little while, he'd tried to pretend that he didn't crave it, but Rivka had caught on easily enough and taken it away until he'd begged to have it back.

Now all she had to do was lower the wick to get his heart thudding and his tongue loose.

"I wish you wouldn't make this so difficult," she always told him.

She was right, really. He didn't have anything to hold out for. He thought that if he cooperated more readily she might even let him live more comfortably. He thought that if he bargained for it, offered her a real secret instead of the banal bits of bureaucracy that she sought she'd even give him a bed and let him have a real bath.

He would tell her anything he needed if it meant he could get rid of this confused yearning that raked his insides.

He could hear some kind of celebration going on above him, loud enough to drift down to the dungeon, and he wanted to be up there.

He wanted to see people. He wanted someone to touch his face and hold his hand and give him something to care about.

There had been something once, but he couldn't remember what, but the idea itched at him and he picked at it, scratching open the hole in his mind until all he could think about was God and how much he had loved Him.

How sometimes he thought he might love Him still.

He thought about how stupid and prideful he had been to think that the Almighty would suffer his transgressions lightly. He thought about how he wanted to go home, not upstairs to the palace, but back to Heaven, where things had been boring but they had been easy.

He curled up, his knees to his chest; the unhealed wound sent off a bit of shooting pain when his breathing started to quicken.

It was that jab of pain that did it, that teetered him over the edge and set him weeping. It hurt to cry, but he couldn't help himself.

He didn't know how long it had been when the angel came to him next.

She came bearing her usual tray and he could smell the food she'd brought; for once, that wasn't what he wanted.

She set it down and studied him. "You look sad."

He raised his eyes to look at her and, for the first time, thought she was splendid. It was a dangerous thought, a thought that was entirely unhelpful and he dug his teeth into the meat of his hand to get rid of it.

Blood welled up through the skin.

She approached him, moving in closer than she'd ever gotten before. "You pathetic thing, it hasn't got to be like this."

He tried to push himself away from her but he was already backed up against the wall.

She crouched beside him and he felt himself wanting to lean towards her, his nose filled up not with the scent of meat but of her skin. He wasn't craving hot water or a warm bed, he wanted her to touch him.

No one had touched him in so long. Alone in the dark, he had nothing; he was disgusting and filthy, he was selling the secrets to his kingdom and he would keep doing it.

She put a hand on his shoulder, her hand cool against his skin; he might have been able to bear it cloth had separated their skin, but his shirt had slipped down over his shoulder like it always did.

He turned his head and struck, digging his teeth into the meat of her arm, hoping she would regret ever coming close to him. He needed her to stay away if he was going to maintain any of his dignity.

She didn't flinch from the bite. She shoved her arm further into his mouth, hard and fast, forcing his mouth open before he could think about it.

She put a hand on his cheek and warned, "Don't do that again or I'll have to start taking things away."

He fixed his eyes on her arm. He hadn't even managed to break the skin. He hadn't been *trying* to break the skin; there probably wouldn't be more than a bruise in the morning.

"It hasn't got to *be* like this, Lucifer," she said again. "If I didn't have to pull all these answers out of you...if I didn't need to always be holding something over your head."

She sounded as unhappy as he was. Maybe it bothered her to treat him like this. Maybe she hated the sight of a pathetic thing like him.

He shook his head but knew that she'd buy him with her touch more easily than she could with food or light or soap.

She took her hand from his cheek and stroked his head like he was a dog. He leaned into it.

"You could help me make the Pit the way it should be," she offered.

"Please."

"I want to trust you, Lucifer, and I don't want it to be a mistake."

Georg hadn't gone home since the coronation and Ira found that he liked the company. It was easy to share space with him; when he wasn't working or out with his friends, or trying to seduce someone, Georg had a quiet kind of peace to him, a stillness that acted like ballast for Ira's more harried emotions.

He had that when they went out, too; if someone gave him a hard time or got fresh, he never seemed to tremble or shy away. Ira wondered if he'd ever be able to act like that; his most common responses to unwelcome advances were fearful scrambling or numb capitulation. He'd been trying to change that but a lifetime at the Trade House hadn't prepared him to live in a world where he could say no as much as the next person.

When he came home from work, Ira poked his head into the bedroom and found Georg lying on his side in bed with a book. "Kitten, you've got to get out of bed at some point."

"I did get out of bed. Now I'm back."

"Where did you go?"

Georg set aside the book. "To see my parents."

"Oh." Ira cleared his throat. "How did that go?"

"I'm summarily cut off until I stop selling myself and repair things with Amaranth."

"Hmm," Ira hummed.

"What?"

"Well, cutting you off doesn't seem like a good way to make you stop doing pleasure work. It sort of makes it so you have to do it, doesn't it?"

"I did point out that flaw in logic. They didn't appreciate it."

Ira came over to sit beside him on the bed. "Are you still engaged, then?"

"On paper, yes, Amaranth and I are still affianced."

"And in practice?"

"In practice," Georg said, "She spat on me when I tried to talk to her."

"I don't understand your family."

"Mmm, bugger them, I don't care anymore," Georg said.

Ira knew it wasn't true, of course, but didn't think now was the right time to point these things out.

Georg stretched and turned on his side, gazing up at Ira. "How was work?"

"Someone tried to stiff Selene."

"No! What happened?"

With a chuckle, Ira told him, "She dragged him downstairs by his ear and made him send a runner to ask his family for money."

"I would have liked to see that."

"You should come back to work."

"You know I can't. Not if I want to have any hope of repairing things at home," Georg said.

"Why do you even care?"

"Because they're my family."

Ira shrugged. He didn't understand that argument. Maybe he couldn't. "You can stay as long as you need to if you're worried about having a place to go."

"No, I...they want me to come home. I just don't think I can bear it right now. My mother *cried*, you know. She *cried*, Ira, just because I wasn't sucking cocks for free."

"I'm sorry, love."

Georg stretched again. "I want to go out tonight."

"Why?"

"To find someone who will fuck me for free."

"You haven't got to go out to do that, all you'd have to do is start knocking on the neighbor's doors. I bet Yvonna on the second floor would do it in a heartbeat."

Georg snorted. "Please?"

"No, I worked all day, I'm tired. You can go out on your own if you want to go so badly."

Georg took his hand and pulled him close. "Pretty please take me out?" He drew Ira into his arms and planted a kiss on his cheek.

"No."

"Mean."

"Brat."

Georg grinned at him.

"Come on, let me up, I haven't had dinner."

Georg didn't let him up. He slipped his hands inside Ira's jacket and started to untuck his shirt. He nestled his face against Ira's throat. "If you're not going to take me out the least you could do is let me go down on you."

Since he'd spoken with Lucifer, Ira hadn't been in the mood for anything. Even now, he thought about turning Georg down.

"I'll be so good to you, I will," Georg promised, kissing Ira, drawing him closer while his hands gripped Ira's ribs. "Please."

"If you're going to insist."

He kissed Ira again, pulling him so he lay atop the younger man. Georg opened his mouth against Ira's and wound his arms around Ira's neck. After a lot of kissing and some shedding of clothes, Ira let out a sigh and buried his face in Georg's shoulder.

"What?" the younger demon asked.

"I don't know," Ira mumbled.

"Mmm, alright, come here," Georg said, adjusting his grip on Ira so that they were spooning. He molded his front against Ira's back and placed his chin on Ira's shoulder. "What's wrong?"

Ira wrapped his arms around one of Georg's, pressing a kiss to his sleeve. "I can't believe I left him there."

"Ahh, I know, love, but we'll have this taken care of soon."

"Georg, you didn't hear him, he sounded...he didn't sound right."

"He's the Devil, he's been through worse. He'll come out of this alright."

Ira didn't know if that was true; the Devil had certainly been through worse but he didn't know if there was a point where he wouldn't be able to stand it any longer.

Lying there, half-naked, somewhat aroused but mostly full of dread and guilt, felt wrong. He didn't know what he needed to do to feel right.

Things had gone so wrong so fast, not just with the coup. They'd never really gotten the chance to talk about any of the things that had happened, not the way those sorts of things needed to be talked about.

"Tell me about something nice," Ira requested.

"There was one time that Hansel and I went to work with Mamma. I was...eight, I think, so he must have been fifteen. She didn't want to bring us but Daddy and the nurse and the maids were all sick with this awful stomach bug," he began.

Somehow Ira had known that this would be a story about his brother. All his nice stories were.

"Horrible, really, just...sick and shit everywhere, the whole house stank. So she brings us into Ginara's office and mind you, Gin's got to be about two thousand years old. I don't know if she started out addled or what but...well, anyway, Mamma asks Gin to keep an eye on us, you know, all that. I swear, the poor old thing can't see more than a foot in front of her face, she's got no idea who we are, she keeps calling Mamma by my great-grandmother's name...it's a mess. Hansel and I, we're supposed to be doing our school work. Hansel has an essay to write and it was supposed to be about, uh...That captain, what's her name?"

"Which one?"

"Oh, you know, the one...she led that riot, not when she was a captain. Over wages?"

"Um." Ira tried to think. "Maliea?"

"Yes! That's the one." Georg nestled a little closer. "And Hansel hasn't brought his history book and he doesn't want to go back to get it. So he leans over to me and asks how old do I think Gin is? At first, I don't see where he's going with this. I'm trying to do my maths, you know, the kind where you have to carry and borrow? I'm ignoring him, you know, I'm terrified what Mamma's going to have to say if I don't get everything done. Hansel, he starts asking Gin about all kinds of stuff and sort of casually brings up Maliea.

"That catches my attention because I'm not sure what he's getting at. He asks if she remembers the riots or anything. And she says! She says she was *there*, not just there watching or anything, but right down in the thick of it with the workers. Which is insane, really, and he asks if she had used to work the souls. No, of course not, she tells him, but what kind of person would I be if I let my woman go to a riot without anyone to look out for her?"

"Really?" Ira asked.

"*Yes*. So he spends the whole morning pumping her for information, uses all that to write his essay. Hands it in, proud as a peacock, it's twice as long as it needs to be. Fails it, wouldn't you know!" Georg let out a chuckle. "Gets told that it was a history essay, not a creative writing assignment." He sniggered. "Poor Hansel, Mamma never let him live that one down."

Georg tightened the arm he had across Ira's chest and kissed his shoulder.

"What are you thinking about?"

"Hansel would have liked you."

"Oh."

"I know...well, with what everyone says about him, it doesn't sound like much of a compliment!"

"No, I...it is a compliment. I think I would have liked him, too." Ira rolled to face him, propped himself up on his side. "I believe you, you know. That he didn't do those things."

"I wish..." Georg flopped onto his back and sighed. "I know I can't have him back, but I wish...if I could have one thing it would be that other people knew he was a good person. That my parents would know. I think they're afraid that it's true."

"I don't..." Ira wanted to assure him that his parents didn't think that, but he didn't know Georg's parents well enough to make that assertation.

"Sometimes they look at me or they'll ask me why I'm acting the way I do and they start asking these, these roundabout questions." He sighed, rolled back towards Ira, and butted his head against his chest. "Like they think me being like *this* has something to do with him...you know, buggering me or whatever it is they think he did."

"Georg."

He sat up. "No, I...if you don't want to go out—"

"We can go out."

Georg ignored him and continued, "And you don't want to have sex, at least let me make you something to eat."

"Georg, I'm sorry."

"Why? You haven't got to do anything just because I want to do it. What do you want to eat?"

"I..."

"No, you know what? Don't answer that, I know what I'm going to make. Come sit in the kitchen with me."

Ira followed him to the kitchen and listened as Georg wondered aloud whether Yvonna on the second floor would really have sex with him. It seemed to be more idle chatter than actual intent because he made himself and Ira a plate of rice and spinach with a fried egg on top.

"Thank you."

"Don't worry about it, Ira, darling. I like to feel useful." He nudged Ira's foot with his own. "What do you think this lake house is going to be like?"

"I have no idea."

"I'll have to teach you how to swim."

Ira sniffed proudly. "What makes you think I can't swim?"

Color crawled up Georg's neck to his cheeks, turning his normally pinkish skin bright red. "I'm sorry, I..."

Ira laughed. "I was only teasing." He ran his foot along the back of Georg's calf. "I don't know if I'll have the guts to set foot in a lake. It sounds *awful*."

"No, it's fun, it really is," Georg assured. "What do you think of the rice? I told Yenni that I couldn't get it to come out right and she said I had to let it rest, showed me this thing with a towel...Anyway. What do you think?"

"It's good."

"That's what you said when it was all gummy last time."

"I thought it was good then, too," Ira admitted and meant it. His palate was not exactly refined. He glanced around the kitchen, feeling that something was missing from the meal. He got up, took down a few glasses and poured them each a glass of wine from a bottle they'd started a few days ago.

"Interesting pairing," Georg noted.

Ira stuck out his tongue.

After dinner, they lazed on the couch together, drinking the rest of the wine and taking turns reading abysmal poetry to each other. In between finishing the first bottle of wine and starting the second, they somehow shed the rest of their clothes and Georg made good on his offer to go down on Ira.

Ira wasn't exactly sure how it had happened. One moment he'd been asking for help getting the second bottle uncorked and the next Georg's tongue had been in his mouth. He hadn't minded, as he'd assured Georg several times, who'd kept asking until Ira had tilted up his chin and told him, "Kitten, I appreciate you checking in with me, I do, but would you please just suck my cock?"

It had been a brief interlude; after he'd spilled, Georg had wiped his mouth in the back of his hand, given him a kiss, and poured them both another glass of wine.

Now, Georg leaned against Ira and Ira had his fingers in Georg's hair, twisting it between his fingers as the other man read, "Your eyes like idle sapphires/glitter in the light/You laugh and I am undone."

"What is that, a haiku or something?" Ira asked, peering at the page. He wondered if he should offer Georg anything, but he felt somewhat certain that he'd already gotten himself off while he'd been taking care of Ira.

"Or something. How's a haiku go again? Five, seven, five?"

"I think so."

They both went quiet, counting the syllables on their fingers, trying to determine if it was a haiku or not.

Ira thought he should offer anyway. "Did you want me to do anything for you?"

"Hmm? Oh. No, love, thank you. I did myself at the same time. I will have to wash those trousers, though..." Georg's eyes flicked towards their heap of clothing, then flipped to another page. "Uh-oh, I think they break up in this one."

"Go on."

"You have torn me open/split me wide—"

"Maybe they were just having a particularly good time," Ira suggested.

Georg snorted. "Shut up. Split me wide enough to bleed. I am undone at your look and you cannot know the pain/of being left behind."

"Ugh, oh, I like the other one better. This is a bit much."

"I particularly liked, what was it, 'your velvet tongue haunts my dreams.' What about you?"

Before Ira had the chance to answer, someone knocked on the door.

"Late for visitors," Georg commented.

Ira grabbed his robe from the bedroom and said, "Probably Mrs. Spiros, it's not garbage day, is it?"

"I don't know, love, it's your apartment, not mine."

Ira cinched the robe and pulled open the door. At first, he didn't recognize the woman standing there, her long chestnut braid draped over one shoulder, partly because of her wan coloring and the circles beneath her eyes but also because he hadn't seen her in months. His hand flew to his mouth when he did.

"Shh, let me in," she said.

He stepped aside and threw his arms around her once she'd come in. He'd never wanted to embrace her before, but then again, he'd never met with her in quite these circumstances.

She stepped back and looked him over, then looked at Georg, who remained undressed on the couch.

Right away, Ira felt warm and stupid. "No, it's not, it's not like that, we...Lu and I..."

She held up a hand. "The three of you can hash out the details of your personal lives once we've got him somewhere safe."

He nodded, cleared his throat, rubbed his eyes. He couldn't quite think straight, but he hadn't been expecting any visitors. "Tea?"

"Coffee, if you've got it."

"Oh, I think I might..." He wandered into the kitchen to sort through the cabinets. Once he'd found what he needed, he made enough for himself and Georg, too, figuring they might need a bit of clarity to get through whatever Imogen had come to discuss.

"You know that won't sober you up, right?" Georg asked, coming up behind him and watching him measure out coffee grounds.

"I'm not drunk," he said with a scowl.

"Alright." Georg leaned in and kissed his shoulder. Quietly, he asked, "Do you mind if I borrow the other robe? I know it's his..."

"He wouldn't mind."

The sight of Georg in the Devil's robe undid Ira more than he'd thought it would. It had been so easy to settle into this shared life with Georg and Ira felt horrible that Georg had spent more consecutive nights in his bed than Lucifer had ever been able to. He thought of how badly Lucifer had wanted something like this and how hesitant Ira had been to consider the idea.

"I can take it off," Georg offered as soon as he saw Ira's face.

"No, it's fine."

The three of them settled around the kitchen table with their coffee, though Ira had only two chairs so Georg ended up leaning against the wall with his mug clutched against his chest. He had his foot propped up against the wall so that his bent leg poked out the front of the robe, and he'd cuffed the sleeves of the robe so his forearms showed; he really was gorgeous, nothing but effortless muscle, tight and smooth without being bulky or overwrought.

He caught Ira looking at him and asked, "Do you want me to come sit on your lap?"

Ira snorted.

When Imogen had taken a sip of her coffee and set it down, Ira asked, "I thought you didn't eat."

"Coffee keeps the edge off."

"What edge?"

"There are not so many vampires in Hell that I can feed as often as I like without being noticed and those that sell their blood..." She trailed off, gave both of them a guilty look and continued, "Well, those sorts of people aren't always the most trustworthy."

Ira took a sip of coffee, slurping it too loudly, trying to ignore her discomfort and the implication; most blood donors tended to be pleasure workers. "Anyway."

"Anyway," she said. "You went to the coronation and my source says you went into the dungeon."

"Who's your source?" Ira asked.

"It doesn't matter," she said, "Until we've got everything back the way it should be, it would be best if we kept other people's names out of it, don't you think?"

"Sure."

"You spoke with him?"

He nodded. "I did. I told him we'd get him out soon. Should I not have done that?"

"I don't know. I like to think the Raven hasn't got her hooks in him too deeply," Imogen told them. "But I don't know."

"We made a key."

Her eyes snapped to his face with an intensity he'd only seen when someone had shed blood in her presence.

He went to the cabinet where he'd set it to cure and extracted it carefully; the fence had warned him that too much handling would ruin the shape. "It's for his cell. Ha...my source says that Rivka has the only key to the dungeon, that she's the only one that goes in to see him. So I thought...well, you know, I thought we'd need a key to get him out, right?"

Imogen stared at the key for a while and Ira wondered if he'd done something wrong. Finally, she said, "Good work."

"It isn't cured yet."

"That's alright, I need a while longer to finish arranging things."

"What, uh, what exactly *is* your plan?" asked Georg.

Imogen glanced towards him, the first time she'd paid him any mind since they'd sat down. "You haven't got to worry about it."

"He's my Prince, you know, if I can help I will."

"We don't need too many cooks in the kitchen," Imogen warned.

"Two isn't a lot," Ira protested, not sure that he could do any of this without Georg's steady presence by his side.

"You two, plus me, and whoever we've got getting us in, that's at least four," Imogen said. "The more people involved, the more things can go wrong."

"Yes, but...Imogen, he sounded...he didn't sound right. What if it's harder to get him out than it should be?" Ira couldn't take his eyes off his coffee when he asked, afraid to see what her face might do.

Quiet, as though she didn't want to know, she said, "You think he's unwell."

"He wasn't well even before. He said he was afraid."

She sighed and leaned back. "Fine." She sighed again. "Fine, the two of you. How long until your key is done?"

"A few more weeks."

She nodded, sipped her coffee, and stared down into the mug. "You won't hear from me again until everything is set for us to go. Start telling people you've got plans to go out of town."

"Going where?" Ira asked, sure that Imogen didn't mean for them to give away the location of where they'd bring the Devil.

With a shrug, she suggested, "On holiday somewhere."

"My family has a little cabin out in the mountains," Georg offered. "My uncle used to go there for the summers to write."

"That's perfect. That's...that's exactly perfect," Imogen said.

"I'll tell them I need to go and do some thinking about everything."

Imogen stayed late into the night and informed them of what she had arranged so far. The whole time Ira thought he would be sick and when she finally left, he pushed his way into Georg's arms.

"What's wrong?" Georg asked.

"I don't know, it's, it's all too much," he whispered. "I'm not cut out for anything like this."

"Things will work out," Georg had assured and pressed a kiss to the side of Ira's head, sweet and calm.

Ira wanted to believe him.

Lucifer had finished telling Rivka everything he could remember about the Seventh Precinct. She'd brought him a list of the souls that still had not been captured and he had regurgitated answers for more than what she had asked.

At first, he'd done it to show that he was eager, that he could be trusted, but when she had leaned over and put a hand on his, he had done all the rest in the hope that she would touch him again.

"Thank you," she said, giving him a smile and sounding like she had meant it.

He nodded and hoped that she would ask him something else. When she didn't, his fingers crawled up his chest to dig into the wound there. Still gaping open, even after all this time.

He didn't know how long it had been, really, and maybe it stayed open because he kept picking at it.

She sighed.

"What?" He pulled his finger out of his chest, shivering at the feeling, wanting to do it again. Wanting to put his bloody fingers in her mouth.

That desire took him off guard and he tried to put it from his mind.

"I can't stop thinking about..." She sighed. "I saw that poor boy at my coronation."

"What boy?" he asked. The mention of her coronation did not send the roil of hate and resentment through him that it should have. He wanted to know why she sounded so sad.

"Ira." She shook her head.

"Who?"

"*Ira*," she repeated as if he'd given offense by not remembering. There were some gaps in his memories, still. "What you did to his face...I can't believe it."

He didn't know what he was being scolded for. He didn't recall doing anything to anyone named Ira, or, more specifically, doing anything they hadn't deserved to anyone by that name.

"No wonder he came to me. No wonder he wanted to see you off the throne."

"Oh." He didn't know why she was telling him any of this, about who had worked to get him off the throne. Maybe she wanted to talk. After all, she was a long way from home.

"But I can't stop thinking about *why*," she said, "Why would you do that to him?"

"I..." He wanted to give her an answer.

"Any of it, I don't understand *any* of it. Anything anyone down here does."

"Have you gone to Earth?" he asked.

She raised a barely-there silver eyebrow. "Pardon?"

"Doesn't He still send angels to Earth?"

"Not notaries."

He felt his eyes go wide. A notary. He had been deposed by a notary; more than that, he had been killed by one. He had enough of himself left to at least be embarrassed by that.

"Besides!"

He waited.

"All that meddling around on Earth, that's why I came here. I don't need to know anything about Earth, I need to know about the Pit. Why were you always up there when you should have been down here?" she scolded.

A few half-thoughts came to mind, ineffable snippets of something that he couldn't comprehend let alone vocalize. "I...I think I had things to do up there."

"Look where it got you," she pronounced, gesturing around the cell.

He looked. Dark, still, though now at least he had a bucket to shit in and a few blankets that he could wrap around himself. He didn't think he would be down here forever. Maybe someday she would let him leave the cell. Maybe if he helped enough she would let him take a real bath again, maybe he would even get to see the sun.

That thought stopped him.

There was no sun in Hell and she would never let him go to Earth.

"Have you seen the sun?" he asked.

"What need do I have of a sun when I can look upon God?" she asked.

That didn't seem fair, that she could rule in Hell and still look upon the Almighty. Had his rebellion been so bad that he was the only one banned from Heaven? "Does..."

"What?" she asked when he didn't finish his question.

"Did He ever...He never talked about me."

She didn't answer, only gave him a sour look.

He hated to see her face like that. "Is there anything else you want me to tell you?"

"No, I think that's it for today," she said. She stood and brushed off her clothes.

He stared up at her and found himself rising into a kneel as she turned towards the door, hoping that she wouldn't go. He didn't want to be alone anymore. Blankets and candles didn't help at all when the door shut and it was nothing but him again.

She gave him a curious look.

He hated her. "You'll come back, won't you?"

"If I think of anything else," she assured.

His throat tightened. "Was I good?"

She gave him a funny half-smile, her head cocked to the side.

Tell me I was good, he would have begged but knew that it would be uncouth to beg like that, that it wouldn't do anything to earn her favor. He needed to be good, he needed to get out of this place. Maybe she would let him out if he was good.

She left.

At least he had some light. At least she had brought him something to eat.

He tucked himself into the corner to wait. He looked at the blood on his fingers, once again brought back to the odd sensation of wanting to slip his fingers past her lips. He didn't understand it, not really; it wasn't really a sexual compulsion and it wasn't akin to the abandoned hunger he felt when eying a lovely piece of meat.

By the time she came back, he still hadn't puzzled it out.

He wanted to ask how long she had been away but thought the question might come across as accusatory.

She was queen, she had places to be.

But she should have been down here.

He needed her down here.

She placed a pitcher of hot water near him; she stopped bothering to keep a distance from him. When she went to get his tray, she left the door open a little and he wondered how fast he would have to be to get out.

He'd have to get out of his chains and out the door before she came back in; it took her less than a minute and it would take him longer than that to free his hands and feet.

He didn't think he would be in any condition to flee, either, if he'd resorted gnawing through his wrists and ankles.

"Don't you want to wash?" she asked when she came back in and he hadn't touched the hot water.

He immediately started to wash his face, worried that she would take it away and never bring it back if he didn't use it right away.

The water was too hot but he used it anyway, stripping down and finding the little bit of soap he had left. He soaped up and rinsed as best he could.

He wanted a bath, he wanted fresh clothes, he wanted to sleep in a bed, but all that faded away when she handed him a hand towel so he could pat himself dry. Their fingers touched and it sent a roll of warmth through him.

He wrapped his fingers around her wrist, his hand long enough to wrap all the way around and then some. She was slender as a blade, not much to her at all.

He didn't drag her closer or push himself next to her, though he could have; he didn't want to, he just wanted to touch her.

"Let go."

He didn't.

She yanked out of grip. She didn't need to move to extinguish his candles. It was light and then it wasn't; she was there and then the door was closing, he could hear the lock scrape and click into place.

He couldn't see anything, he couldn't reach the tray of food she'd left behind. He had to feel around to find his clothes and ended up knocking over what was left of the pitcher of water on to them.

Soggy and hungry, he waited.

She didn't come back.

Hasbani, Ira reflected, was a lowdown rat bastard and couldn't be trusted. No, he wasn't reflecting, he was seething.

Seething and pacing.

He paced right into a bush.

Georg caught him by the arm and pulled him close. "Shhh."

"It's been ten minutes."

"We were early," the younger man soothed. "Now stay still before someone finds us out."

They were waiting in the gardens of the palace in the pitch black; Hasbani was supposed to let them in. He had promised that he would.

Except he was late.

Ira checked his pocket for the key, the hundredth time he'd done that so far tonight. Georg tightened his arms around him.

"He's a good sort, he'll let us in," Georg promised.

Ira leaned into his embrace, forcing himself to relax, taking in slow breaths. Georg started to rock him and Ira wondered if he wouldn't fall asleep where he stood. He hadn't slept well the last week, too keyed up, his nerves always hovering somewhere between terror and desperation.

The door to the servants' quarters whooshed open and Hasbani poked his head out. He gestured for them to come in.

They all proceeded silently. Ira had one hand in his pocket and his other wrapped around Georg's fingers, squeezing hard. He must have been hurting the other man, but Georg didn't complain or pull back.

It wasn't a long walk from the servants' quarters to the dungeon, just down the hall, through the kitchen and then out into another hall. Right across from Imogen's office.

Or whoever the butler was now. Ira didn't know if Rivka had even hired herself a butler.

As they waited for Hasbani to unlock the door that led down to the dungeon, Ira started to bounce on his toes and as soon as the door was open, he flew down the stairs, doing his best to be quiet, his heart hammering and his hands shaking as he tried to pull the key from his pocket. He jammed it into the lock so hard he thought he might break it.

It twisted in the lock and he hauled the door open, digging his teeth into his tongue to keep himself quiet.

It was pitch black inside the cell and it stank, the smell of waste and bodies and something that faintly resembled the miasma of a wound that had gone sour.

He took a hesitant step inside but stopped. It was too dark, too quiet.

Georg came up and put a hand on his shoulder, making him jump and clap his hands to his chest.

With a whisper, Georg conjured up a small orb of cozy golden light, enough to illuminate the cell but not to blind them.

A horrible screech of pain and the sound of scrambling, of scraping chains, accompanied the light.

Something ragged and gangling buried itself in the corner, shaking and covering its head with his hands.

This was not the Devil, it couldn't be.

"Lu?"

The figure in the corner didn't answer, but it did look his way. Red-gold eyes fixed on Ira's face.

"Fucking shit, Lu, look at you," Ira whispered and moved further into the cell, towards the Devil, who tried to wedge himself further into the corner. "Are you...you're not alright, of course, you aren't."

He touched the chains. He didn't see a way to remove the cuffs, but they were fastened onto the chains with padlocks. He jabbed his finger into the keyhole.

"Georg, can you...maybe the key from the door?"

Georg interpreted his half-statements and brought him the key. He pushed it into the padlocks and let out a shaking sigh when it twisted and clicked.

While Georg undid the locks, Ira took the Devil by the hands, then ran one hand over his scalp, horrified to see that his hair was ragged and short. "Oh, what have they done to you, love?"

"Done," Georg whispered.

"Luci, come on," Ira said, taking his hands again, giving him a gentle pull.

"No," the Devil said.

"Yes, come on, let's get you out of here."

"No!" He pulled his hands back, pushed Ira away so that he fell on his ass.

"Lu..." Ira stood and moved in closer.

Georg hauled Ira back, away from the corner. "Careful."

"He won't—"

"He's still the Devil," Georg reminded. "*Look* at him."

Ira looked. "Lu, it's me."

"I *don't know you*," the Devil growled.

The words sliced through Ira, leaving him numb and prickling with heat.

"It's *me*, it's..."

Georg shook his head, leaned in close to whisper, "We don't have time for this, we have to go. You can get this sorted later."

"No, if I can just talk to him."

"We don't have time to talk," the younger man reminded.

"Then what are we supposed to do! I'm not going to leave him—"

"And *I* don't want to end up in one of these cells."

Ira let out a desperate whine.

"Do you trust me?" Georg asked.

"Yes, but—"

Georg, voice still low, said, "This isn't going to be pretty, alright, but go with me. Okay?"

Ira didn't answer, still staring at Lucifer, the way he huddled in the corner.

"Okay?"

"Okay," Ira agreed.

Georg grabbed one of the raggedy blankets from the floor and threw it over the Devil, then wrapped his arm around him.

Ira hesitated for just a second, then moved in with Georg, seizing the Devil's other arm.

He started to scream. "I can't leave, I can't!"

Georg clapped a hand over the Devil's face, through the blanket, and whispered a spell. His screams went quiet, though Ira could still feel his body vibrating with them and sometimes when the blanket shifted snippets slipped out.

They wrestled him up the stairs, struggling with his ungainly body.

Hasbani stared at them.

"The door," Ira hissed, almost losing his grip on the Devil, not knowing how they would get him out of the city like this.

Hasbani rushed to push open the front door.

Dragging Lucifer down the stairs made Ira's guts crawled. It was a horrendous act, unforgivable. The Devil was scared, he was more than scared, he was terrified, his whole body was trembling; Ira should have been able to talk him through this, they should have been able to do it without force.

"Lu, it's going to be alright, I promise," he whispered as they pushed him along. "You're fine, you are, I swear. We're not going to hurt you."

They reached the palace gate and Hasbani opened it for them.

They waited and the Devil almost slipped from their grasp. Hasbani rushed in when Lucifer got an arm free, holding on until Ira got a grip on him again.

They only had to wait for a minute or two until a carriage came around the corner, drawn by an unmatched team of horses, a bay and a roan.

Georg stepped back as it rolled up to them, eyes flicking over the horse.

Ira didn't blame him. Not many people used horses in the city, not unless they were heading outside the walls.

"Quit staring, get him in," Imogen hissed.

"He won't—"

"Just do it!"

Hasbani opened the door for them and, as they struggled to shove the Devil inside, helped them wrestle him in. He was the last to climb into the carriage and he pulled the door shut, one arm held up to ward off the Devil's thrashing limbs.

They all tumbled when the carriage started to move, the hooves clattering against the cobblestones.

Ira tried to keep a hold of Lucifer, tried to calm him, but it didn't work. The blanket slipped off of him and he kept screaming, kept saying that he had to go back.

"Let him go," Hasbani said.

"He'll hurt himself," Ira protested.

"Or one of us," Georg added.

"Let him go," Hasbani repeated, an odd quality of command to his voice.

Ira and Georg let go and watched as Hasbani moved forward, grabbing the Devil's face between his hands and holding tight. He pulled Lucifer in close and whispered into Lucifer's ear. Not a second later, his body went slack. He slouched against the seat, slumped against Georg.

"What was that?" Georg asked, pushing Lucifer up right.

Ira took the blanket and wrapped it around the Devil's shoulders.

Hasbani shrugged. "My father was the angel of sleep. I guess it rubbed off."

"Of sleep!" Georg exclaimed. "I always thought it had to be...well. I always thought it would be, well, you know, sex or something like that."

"No. Sleep," Hasbani repeated. He leaned back, sitting on the floor of the carriage. "I, uh...I wasn't planning on coming with you, you know."

Ira nodded towards the door. "You're half Fallen, you'll definitely survive if you jump out."

Georg gave him a smack. "Don't be mean."

Ira couldn't take his eyes off of Lucifer. He was thin and dark blue veins showed through his skin. He stank and his hair, someone had hacked off all his hair.

"I thought you said the angel was visiting him."

"I...I thought she was. She was going down into the dungeons, I didn't think she was just faffing around," Hasbani insisted.

"He looks like shit, hasn't anyone been feeding him?"

"Darling, it will be alright," Georg insisted, leaning over to give Ira's arm a pat.

"He didn't recognize me!"

"But he did last time you saw him, didn't he? It's...it's probably just some spell or maybe...maybe he was just scared. Poor thing was terrified," Georg reasoned.

Ira wanted to pull Lucifer into his arms, but it didn't feel right, not when he hadn't remembered him, not when he'd been manhandling him just a few minutes ago.

"Where are we going?" Hasbani asked.

"A house by the lake."

"What lake?"

"Oh, there's this river," Georg began.

Ira tuned out the rest of the geography lesson. He pressed a fist to his mouth and kept his eyes on Lucifer, pulling his feet onto the carriage seat and putting his back against the sidewall. "How long will he sleep for?" he interrupted.

Hasbani glanced over. "Until I wake him up."

"It's a good trick," Georg appraised. "Angel of sleep, I'm going to have fun with that next time I see him. Do you think that's what he was doing, putting people to sleep instead of bedding them?"

"No," Ira said. "Marius worked." The pander knew things about the trade that couldn't be known without really working it.

He reached out and smoothed down the blanket over Lucifer's chest.

It would take a day or so to get to the lake. Imogen had assured that they'd be going straight there, no stopping for anything.

"What'd you do to the blanket?" Ira asked, glancing towards Georg.

"Oh, that? Fun, isn't it! Good if someone's a screamer," Georg said with a smile. "Usually I use it on walls, though!" He reached over and gave Ira a pat on his hand. "What do you think she plans to feed on once we get out there?"

"What?"

"Imogen. I mean, I know she thinks all we dirty harlots will sell anything for two bits but I, uh, I'm not keen on getting chewed on."

"I wouldn't worry about it."

"I'm a little worried about it."

Ira scowled. "We haven't even made it out of the city yet, why don't you worry about that instead? That's what I'm worrying about."

Georg nodded towards Ira and asked Hasbani, "Why don't you put him to sleep, too? He hasn't in about a week."

"Shut up," Ira snapped but he took Georg's hand when he offered it anyway. He held on to it hard.

In the end, Hasbani didn't have to put him to sleep. Once they got outside the city without incident, his eyelids started to droop and no matter how badly he wanted to stay awake and watch Lucifer, he couldn't keep them open.

They brought Lucifer into the house. Ira wanted to wake him up right away; Imogen dissuaded him, saying that he'd be hungry, that they should get a fire going so he could have a bath. Ira had to admit she was right, so they settled him into an overstuffed armchair and started to get things ready.

The house was cozy without being cramped, pleasant without being opulent; it would have been perfect for a getaway, the one Lucifer had wanted to go on. Imogen had stocked the kitchen, replaced the furniture, and cleaned everything thoroughly before their arrival.

"We could have done without, but I figured, why wait in squalor?"

"What was wrong with it?"

She pointed up. "Roof leaked. He hasn't been here in a century, you know. I'd thought he'd forgotten about it."

"Who'd he bring here last?" Ira asked. He shouldn't have cared; he wasn't really sure if he did.

She shrugged. "I don't remember. Some...woman, I think."

"Oh."

She handed him a pail and told him the pump was outside.

Once things were ready, Hasbani approached the Devil, more hesitant to touch him now than he had been in the carriage. When it had been done, he stepped back and Ira checked his impulse to crowd in.

They all hung back, waiting for him to move.

When he did stir, it was to put his hand over his eyes.

Ira asked, "Lu?"

Lucifer groaned, still shielding his face from the light.

"Luci, darling." It took everything he had not to go over to him, to take him by the hand. He wanted to kiss him, wanted it so badly that it hurt not to do it.

Slowly, Lucifer brought his hands down and opened his eyes. He looked around, taking in each of them. He barely looked at Hasbani, who had moved into the kitchen, checking the soup they had on the stove.

He stared at Ira the way someone stared at a bug that had found its way into the house.

When he looked at Georg, though, his face shifted. "Master Schreiber." He didn't look any calmer. He kept looking around the room like he was looking for a way out.

"Uh...Yes."

"I have to go back."

"Um." Georg glanced at Ira. "I don't...I don't think that's a good idea. Ira, uh."

"Ira?" Lucifer asked, his voice lilting up. The name seemed to mean something to him.

Absurdly, hope bloomed in Ira's chest. He nodded.

It happened faster than anyone could follow. Lucifer was out of the chair, shoving past them, flying out the door.

Georg and Ira looked at each other.

Imogen cleared her throat. "You should go get him before he runs into the barrier."

"What barrier?" Ira asked.

"The barrier he's going to run into," Imogen pointed out. "I would hurry."

Ira ran and he could hear Georg following after him.

It worked in their favor that Lucifer had been held in such poor condition because Ira had to push as hard as he could go to even catch up to the Devil.

He didn't know where the barrier was or what it would do, but if Imogen didn't want him running into it, then it couldn't have been good.

He wanted to scream for him to stop but didn't think it would work. The Devil didn't remember him.

Georg passed him by and tackled the Devil to the ground, their bodies colliding with a thud.

Ira dropped to his knees to help corral him; the Devil was all flailing limbs.

"Hey, hey, now," Georg said. "You're alright. Come on, settle down."

Georg caught an elbow to the face and toppled off of Lucifer. When the Devil got up to run again, Georg shouted, "Don't, don't! Look, can't you see it!"

Ira looked. There was a glimmer in the air, about fifty yards away, some unnatural gleam against the night sky that Ira wanted nothing to do with.

The Devil hesitated and looked, too, but his eyes were drawn back to the blood leaking from Georg's split lip, down his chin. "I'm sorry."

Georg gaped. "What?"

"I wasn't trying...I've got to get back."

"Well, I can't let you out, I'm not the one who put that up."

"Who can?"

Georg told him, "I imagine you'll have to ask Imogen."

"Imogen!"

"Yes, she was about a foot in front of you!" Georg scolded. He gingerly touched his lip and Ira offered him a handkerchief, which felt like a stupid thing to do but it was better than sitting in the dirt watching Lucifer ogle Georg.

Ira helped Georg to his feet and the three of them stood there, staring at each other, Georg gingerly dabbing at his face.

"Come back inside," Ira tried, "We've got food and you can have a bath and...we can talk, Lu."

The Devil looked him over. "I don't know who you are."

"I can sort of tell."

"You keep talking to be like you know me."

"I *do* know you."

Lucifer shook his head and rubbed a hand over his hair. He stared hard at Ira. "You, uh, you...Rivka said you helped her."

He hated the sound of her name in Lucifer's mouth; he hated the tint of reverence. "I...it wasn't like that."

"That I did something to your face."

"No! Just, come inside, Lu, we can...you can have a bath, look at the state of you, please." He didn't know why he wanted Lucifer to be clean so badly. "And we can talk. You can tell us why you want to go back."

"I have to."

Ira wanted to scream, but instead, he nodded back towards the house. "Please."

Lucifer took a single step and Ira grabbed on to Georg's hand.

The walk back to the house was slow going and it took a lot of sweet-talking from both of them to get him back past the threshold.

Imogen waited for them, her arms crossed, leaning against the table. "You're so dramatic."

"Imogen."

"Ah, so you do remember me. I would have been wounded if you'd remembered Georg and not me."

"I didn't notice you."

"Of course, you didn't. Get in the bath."

Lucifer hesitated. "I've got to go back."

"Why?"

"Because...because Rivka—"

"The woman who murdered you and took your throne," Imogen said.

"Yes."

"Alright, just wanted to make sure we're talking about the same person. What about her?" Imogen asked.

"She...I have to see her."

"Why?"

Lucifer frowned, his whole face scrunching up in thought. "I...if I, if I can get her to trust me...Maybe...she might..." He looked around, whispered something inaudible to himself and grasped his head in his hands, his eyes shut tight. "I just need to go back."

Imogen gave him a push towards the bathtub they'd set up in front of the fireplace; the house had a toilet and some sinks, but no bath or shower. "Go on, you never wanted my help in the bath before, I'm sure you don't want it now."

He went in the direction she'd pushed him, stripping off the rags he wore.

Hasbani excused himself at that, saying something about going outside to have a look around.

Imogen went into the kitchen, turning her back on the rest of them as she started slicing a loaf of bread into thick slabs.

Ira couldn't stop watching and he couldn't help but swear, either, when he saw the wound still in Lucifer's chest. It had an unhealthy look, tight and red.

As Lucifer climbed into the bath, he let out a pathetic sound, somewhere between a sob and a whimper. He started to weep and Ira moved towards him, put his hand on the edge of the bath and said, "Lu."

It was the only word he could think of; it should have been enough.

"I don't *know you*," Lucifer said through his tears.

"You do. We spoke...it wasn't more than a month ago, we did. I came into the dungeon and I told you we'd come to take you out."

"Ira, maybe you should give him some space," Imogen suggested from the kitchen.

Ira looked around the house. There was nowhere else to go, the whole place had an open floor, the kitchen bleeding into the sitting area, the bedroom marked only by a thick carpet and the bed tucked into the corner.

Georg put a hand on his shoulder and brought him over to the bed, saying, "He's had a rough go, give him some time."

Ira nodded mutely.

In a whisper, Georg said, "The only one he's seen for *months* had been that angel, who knows what she's been saying to him."

Ira leaned against him and Georg wrapped him up in an embrace. He didn't cry. It would have been better if he could have.

Georg played with his curls and rubbed his back. "Do you think we've got any books? This is going to be horribly dull otherwise."

Ira watched from the bed as Lucifer washed himself; he listened in when Imogen came over and tutted at his state, appraised the infection in his chest and returned to the kitchen to make a poultice that filled the whole house with the sharp, pungent smell of cleansing herbs. She pressed it to the Devil's chest and bandaged him, the set of her mouth serious but not concerned.

When it was time to eat, they didn't gather at the kitchen table. Hasbani leaned against the counter, sopping up lentil soup with his bread; the Devil had migrated to a corner, scarfing down his food until Imogen warned him to slow down or he'd make himself sick. Georg sat beside the fire with his and Ira took a single bite before handing his over to Georg.

"Are you sure?"

"Go ahead, kitten."

He wandered around the house, wondering where they would all sleep.

Imogen saw him poking around and called, "There's a trundle under that one, you can go ahead and make it up if you're feeling useful."

He did so, but still only counted enough room for three, figuring that he and Georg could bunk together and that no one would try to slide into bed with Lucifer.

Imogen, who hadn't eaten either, came over and pulled a few hammocks from the closet. "Come help me shake these out, God knows when they were last used. I almost threw them away, you know."

Once they'd done that, he helped her hang them in different corners.

"We could swap out," Ira offered, "So no one would have to sleep in a hammock every night."

"We'll see," was her answer.

After he'd eaten three bowls of soup, the third stolen when Imogen wasn't looking, Lucifer took down one of the hammocks and rehung into a different corner, far from the rest of them. He crawled into it without a word to the rest of them.

Imogen brought him a blanket.

"I need to go back."

"Oh, you're definitely going back," she assured him. "Just not yet."

"Rivka's going to...she'll..." came the Devil's voice from his hammock, tremulous.

"She'll what?" the vampire asked softly.

"She takes things away."

"She isn't here," Imogen reminded, her voice so quiet that Ira almost couldn't hear her.

"She'll make it dark again."

"Get some sleep. I'll check on that poultice in the morning. And don't go trying to sneak out, that barrier will do a number on you," she warned.

"How did you know I would run?"

"I didn't. I just didn't know how you would come back. It's best to be prepared."

"Oh."

"It's what you pay me for. Speaking of which, I am expecting backpay for this," she reminded.

Hasbani took the other hammock, slinking around surreptitiously when it came time to change into his nightclothes.

Ira watched him sneak, wanting to tell him not to bother and remind him that no one in Hell cared what he had under his shirt or trousers. Instead, he tried to be polite and turned his eyes away.

Imogen went to bed last, or maybe she didn't plan to go to bed at all. She set herself up in an armchair across from the Devil's hammock.

"Come on, Ira, I want to sleep in a real bed," Georg insisted, pulling Ira towards the bed. "And you look exhausted. Tomorrow will be better, I bet. We all need time to adjust."

Ira went, not in the mood for sleep or anything else.

He lay awake for a long time, staring up at the wooden rafters, feeling that he'd been enormously deprived. It shouldn't have gone this way. He didn't know exactly what he had expected, but he'd expected something. He tried to have faith that Georg was right, that tomorrow would be better, but it wasn't.

The Devil barely left his hammock, unless there was food involved, and kept repeating his request to go back.

Imogen continued her calm questioning, asking him why he wanted to go back each time, assuring him that Rivka couldn't take anything away.

"Hey, you." Someone pushed his hammock. "I know you're in there."

Lucifer poked his head out to see that it had been the future Master of Records that had been pushing him. "What?"

"Come out of there."

"No."

"You've been locked up for months, you really want to spend all your time inside?" the young man demanded, making Lucifer feel incredibly stupid. "Come on, you've got Ira all out of sorts." He gave the hammock another push and gave Lucifer a broad smile.

"It..."

"We're safe, you know, no one can get to us out here. No one even knows where to look for us," he assured. "Imogen says so and I figure that's about as good as gold, isn't it?"

"What...Your name, Georg, isn't it?"

"Yes." Georg gave him a third push. "You've got Ira bent out of shape sitting in there all day, it's driving me insane. Please."

It was the please that did it. Lucifer crawled out of the hammock. He'd been scuttling around the house when the others had been in bed or outside. He drew himself up to his full height and stretched, his back popping wonderfully.

He felt Georg looking at him and the younger man blushed when Lucifer met his gaze. "Where are the rest of them?"

"Ira and Hasbani are trying to fish. Imogen's with the horses. I said I'd keep an eye on you, make sure you didn't try to run for it again."

"I've got to go back."

Georg threw back his head and let out a groan. "You keep saying that! Why do you want to go back?"

"I...I have to."

"Well, quit saying it. Come on outside, come for a walk with me."

Lucifer shook his head. Outside was out of the question. Even moving out of the corner felt like a stretch.

Georg looked him over critically, one corner of his mouth tipping down.

It was a lovely mouth, probably excellent for kissing.

"Ira—"

"Stop bringing him up."

The young man raised an eyebrow. "Why?"

"Because I don't know him and I hate everyone acting like I should."

Georg turned his eyes away and went over to poke around in the fireplace even though it didn't need tending. He set the poker aside and glanced back at Lucifer. "You fancy a game of cards? Or I think I saw a mancala board."

Lucifer reached up to play with his hair and his world tilted slightly when he contacted nothing. He should have been used to the short hair by now, but his hands didn't know what to do with themselves without something to braid. His cuticles had taken the brunt of the fidgeting usually borne by his hair. Imogen had bound the hole in his chest in an attempt to stop him from picking at it.

He scrubbed his hand over his head, tugged on one earlobe, then shoved his hands into his pockets. He shrugged. "If you want."

Georg nodded towards the kitchen table but Lucifer couldn't compel himself to move; the younger man took Lucifer by the arm and gave him a gentle tug. He let go right away, though, and blushed. "Sorry, uh, Your Highness..."

The title sounded strange and he couldn't help but stare. It was the first time he'd heard that since before he'd died.

"I, uh, I'm sorry, I shouldn't be bothering you," Georg apologized. "I, you know, my mother says that I get stupid ideas in my head about things. This must be one of them."

"What do you mean?"

"I thought that, uh, after so long in that cell you might want to...I know you'll need time to adjust but, I don't know..." He shrugged. "It's stupid."

"Tell me."

"Just considering that you don't remember Ira and the other two work for you, I thought you could use a friend. Figured I was the closest thing all the way out here. Not that Imogen isn't, you two seem close but in a different sort of way."

"Does the Master of Records not work for me?"

"Well, yes, but I don't *work* in the Record Office yet. I'm taking classes...I was taking classes. I told my professors I was taking the next semester off."

"Why?" Lucifer found himself asking, not sure why he wanted to know but drawn in by the cadence of conversation.

"I've got some personal things to sort out. And my parents have cut me off, which means I can't afford tuition!" he said with a little laugh. "Good thing they found all this out at the end of the semester, otherwise I'd be in debt up to my eyes."

It felt strange to have a conversation like this, with him still in the corner and Georg hovering nearby. He edged towards one of the armchairs by the fire.

Georg let out a sigh of relief and gave him a smile. "I thought you were going to stand there all day! Do you want a drink?"

"Please."

Georg brought him a glass and promised, "Just wine, watered and everything. I'm sure your stomach's a little delicate these days."

Lucifer appreciated the concern. "Why've they cut you off?"

Georg took a seat in the other armchair, drawing one leg up against his chest and looping an arm around that leg. He let the other leg rest in front of him. "Disgracing myself, polluting what's left of the family name with service work." He shrugged. "Go on, have a drink, I haven't poisoned it."

He took a sip, surprised at the taste. There was nothing out of the ordinary about the wine, just that he hadn't yet tasted it in this life.

"But enough about me!" Georg scoffed. "What about you? How are you feeling? And don't tell me you need to go back, none of us are going to bring you back there."

Lucifer had realized that. He hadn't had the chance to inspect the barrier they claimed was out there, but he would slip past it if he could. Rivka had asked to be able to trust him and this flight from the city didn't feel trustworthy at all. Maybe she would understand that it hadn't been his fault.

When he didn't answer, the demon pressed, "Why do you want to go back anyway?"

"She...she was kind to me."

A harsh snort escaped Georg. "Kind! Is that what you call being locked up in the dark?"

"I deserved it. I shouldn't have done that to her." He had only wanted to feel her skin, to feel another person; maybe if he could talk to her, she could understand. Maybe then she would come to visit him again.

"What'd you do?"

"I touched her."

Georg straightened up a little. "Touched her? That's all?"

"I shouldn't have, she told me to let her go and...I didn't." It had been a despicable thing to do.

"Angels," Georg scoffed. "What a queen we've got, treating you like that for touching her."

Her being an angel didn't have anything to do with it; plenty of angels did all kinds of touching. Rivka had some other quality about her. She was clean, still fresh from Heaven, and the world must have still felt so raw and new to her. He distantly recalled the first time he'd had a body. He had wanted to touch everything, to know exactly the feeling of flower petals and how they felt different from sand and tree bark and shells.

Others, though, hadn't taken well to corporeal forms, said they'd felt like the whole world was trying to crawl inside their skin.

A question occurred to him, one that hadn't when he'd been so fixated on when he would eat, when he would see light again. "Is she a good queen?"

"I don't care if she's a good queen or not, I want our Prince," Georg insisted. "So you work on getting well again."

Lucifer shook his head. "I can't."

"What do you mean you can't? You're the Devil, aren't you?"

He shrugged. He thought so. Eventually, he wouldn't be if he kept this up. Rivka could be the Devil and he could just be Lucifer. "I haven't got anything left in me. Or...it's there but I can't reach it. The things that make me *me*."

"We were sort of wondering about that hole in your chest."

Automatically, his fingers went to the wound, skirting around the edge. Several applications of Imogen's poultice had helped to take some of the tenderness away. He watched Imogen come in. "Good to have a witch for a butler."

"I'm not a witch," she said from the door, startling Georg so badly he almost lost his glass of wine. "My coven only let women be witches."

"You are a woman," Lucifer reminded.

"Ahh, if only you had been there in my youth, sire, you would have saved me so many years of confused yearning." Imogen graced him with a worrisome smile.

"I thought witches would be better about that kind of thing," Georg mused.

"It was seventeen seventy-one, nobody was good about that kind of thing," Imogen informed him. "They still aren't."

Georg wrinkled his nose.

For a small moment, Lucifer felt a little bit proud of the world he'd built up down here. Earth might have had a sun, it might have had all the attention and love God had seen fit to give, but at least none of his demons went to bed at night tortured by thoughts of bedding a member of the same gender or because the world saw them as something other than what they were. At least he'd given them that.

Humans hadn't started out so small-minded, but something had gone awry up there; Lucifer didn't know if it was part of His plan or not, but he really didn't think so. It had to be more negligence or miscalculation than intention.

"You were bound to come here eventually, better than you came on your own terms," Lucifer told her.

Imogen scowled at him. "If you could keep your infernal eyes *off* my soul, sire, it would be appreciated."

He nodded, unable to help himself from trying to categorize her sins. She'd likely have started out in the Fourth, dragged there by guilt instead of wrongdoing. She had a few accidental kills under her belt and a handful of other misdeeds, so she would have needed to finish off her stint in one of the other Precincts. Then up to Purgatory when her soul had been scrubbed clean.

"Stop," she warned like she knew what he was thinking.

He gave her a smile and she shuddered as if he had worms between his teeth.

He well might have, he didn't know. He hadn't seen himself in a mirror since before he'd died.

He took another sip of his wine.

Georg pulled his other leg up onto the chair. He looked cozy and Lucifer wanted to tuck a blanket around his shoulders.

"Is she a bad queen?" he asked, wondering if this question would get a better answer.

Georg sighed, rolled his eyes, and answered, "No, she's not a bad *queen*, but she's *not* the Devil. Hell doesn't need a queen...I mean, yes, the city needs a monarch, doesn't it? But that's not all you are."

"She could be the Devil."

"No."

"She could," he assured, "She needs...she needs time. She needs to go to Earth and she needs..."

He tried to think of what it was that had made him the Devil. It wasn't just the Fall or being barred from Heaven, it wasn't the rebellion or the pride or any one thing.

"I could do it to her, I could make her the Devil," he told no one in particular, overcome again by that odd urge to feed bits of himself to Rivka, to gorge her stomach with his flesh until her gut was swollen and hard.

"You're the Devil," Georg insisted.

"For now," he assured. He had named one of his grandsons as his heir, but he didn't know exactly when his abdication would come.

It wasn't that he could stop being Satan or that he could die, really die and never come back, but there would come a time when he would need respite. Maybe not forever and maybe not soon.

Or maybe it would be soon. He felt shaky, still, and tired. The world had become unsure and vast and frightening, and this was only Hell. He didn't know what would happen if he tried to set foot on Earth. He yearned for a bit of sunlight but didn't know what the hum and bustle of the human world would do to him.

Maybe it would do him good, even, to find some quiet Earthly oasis and lay in the sun. What he wouldn't give for a bit of sun. Maybe Rivka would have let him go someday if he had ever proved his worth to her.

He didn't know if he could even get there now. He could no longer feel the intangible strings that lurked beneath reality, the things that held the worlds together.

He dragged a finger around the cuff that still circled his wrist.

"I might be able to fix that," Georg offered.

Lucifer lifted his eyes and the younger man recoiled a little from his gaze.

"I'm a fair hand at magic."

"Not today."

Although, a small voice in the back of his mind suggested, if he went back without shackles perhaps Rivka wouldn't chain him again. Maybe she would give him the full space of his cell.

The door opened again, this time by the young half-human and the other demon. A common enough Hell-born thing with ash-gray skin and a comely face, though not much compared to Georg. Looking at him felt like looking into a black hole.

Lucifer stood and the gray demon's eyes followed him, somewhere between fearful and reverent.

He set aside his glass of wine and returned to the hammock so that no one could look at him anymore.

Georg's voice came right away, light and cheerful, asking Ira if they'd had any luck catching anything, saying he could go for a bit of fresh fish.

"We didn't catch anything," Ira said.

"Came close a few times," Hasbani added. "We've got to work on the bait."

After a week of brief, fireside chats and a handful of attempts at getting the cuffs from his wrists, Georg started to press Lucifer to come into the kitchen. After Lucifer capitulated to that, he tried to get him outside. That Lucifer staunchly resisted.

It was too bright out there, or too dark, depending on the time of day. It was always too big and he told Georg as much.

He didn't think he could have said it if anyone else had been around. Even now, he found himself retreating closer to the corner with each additional body in the room.

Imogen he didn't mind and Hasbani he could mostly ignore, but whenever Ira was around, Lucifer couldn't make it past the fireplace. He would tuck himself into an armchair and pretend to read, watching the shadows and only moving to stoke the fire.

He hated when Ira looked at him, hated it more when the little demon would try to talk to him.

There was no reason that someone he didn't know should look at him like that.

The closest he could come to placing Ira's face was a worker in the Third, Eodus, who could have been Ira's twin, with a few differences about the mouth and nose, but the same skin, the same eyes and jaw. Eodus didn't have curls though.

After dinner, Ira gathered up all their plates and washed them without being asked. Lucifer was loath to even hand his plate over to the demon; it wasn't his fault, there couldn't have been anything he'd done to warrant the level of nerves that Lucifer got from looking at him.

Unless he had betrayed him. Lucifer was inclined to think he had, but it didn't make sense for his butler to have brought along his betrayer during their midnight rescue.

Their fingers touched when Ira took his plate. Lucifer pulled back and the demon whispered, "Sorry," and brought all the dishes to the sink.

Once Ira had cleaned up, he lingered awkwardly in the kitchen, cast a baleful look towards Lucifer, and then announced, "I'm...I'm gonna go outside for a bit."

"You want company?" Georg asked.

"No."

He struck out into the night, his small figure silhouetted against the fading sky before he disappeared.

"Come outside with me," Georg said to Lucifer.

"No."

"Why not?" the young man pouted.

It was a disarming pout. "It's too bright."

"It's nearly dark."

"It's too dark."

"You can't have it both ways you know," Georg admonished.

"It isn't safe."

"I'll keep you safe," Georg offered and it felt like a promise, a vow that Lucifer could put his trust in.

He shook his head.

"Fine. You want me to work on that cuff?" Georg nodded toward his wrists. "I've been doing a bit of reading. I was looking through Manheim's *Theories of Unravelling Complex Magics* and I think—"

"Just a bit of reading." Lucifer grinned.

"Not my usual stuff, I've got to admit but Imogen didn't pack a single volume of *The Butcher's Wife* or *Lazlo Corbin*, so I guess I'll have to manage with getting your mess sorted," Georg told him.

Lucifer's smile widened. He pushed up his sleeve and offered his wrist to Georg.

The young man popped up out of his seat and crowed that he would be right back. He rushed off and came back with a thick tome with a lot of bookmarks. He set it down on the kitchen table and flipped through until he found the page he wanted.

He held out a hand and Lucifer was glad to place his hand in Georg's.

"I've really got it this time," Georg promised, taking a piece of loose leaf out of the book and smoothing it on the table. Across the paper he had crafted his own spell, penned neatly in handwriting that could have been used as a model for typesetting.

"You said that last time."

"Want to bet on it?" Georg challenged.

Lucifer did want to bet on it. More than he'd wanted anything in a while. "Yes," came to his lips unbidden.

"Fine. I get these things off of you, then you come outside with me. Deal."

"Deal," Lucifer agreed immediately, wrapping his fingers around Georg's wrist and pulling him close.

The young demon faltered, his eyes going wide, as Lucifer pressed a light kiss to his half-open mouth.

"It's done," Lucifer declared.

"Sire," Imogen scolded from the kitchen. "He didn't know—"

"But he made the deal," Lucifer reminded.

Georg stared at him for a moment longer, swiped his fingers across his mouth as if he could toss the kiss aside.

"I could have taken blood."

Color crawled up the young man's neck. He went to the kitchen, fished around in one drawer, and found a piece of chalk. He came back to the table and took up Lucifer's hand, drawing runes all over the cuff with the chalk.

Lucifer watched with some interest as the young man did what he couldn't.

When he'd finished with the runes, Georg started to chant, his enunciation careful and his intonation precise. It took about two minutes for him to finish the spell.

He released Lucifer's hand and the Devil raised an eyebrow, a smile spreading across his face until the cuff unsealed from around his wrist and clunked onto the table.

Georg let out a triumphant laugh, his whole face lighting up.

Nerves started to bubble in Lucifer's gut. "Three more," he murmured.

Still glowing, Georg reached for Lucifer's other hand, but Lucifer took his hand back. "No, come on, that's the deal!" Georg protested. "You have to let me at least try."

Not wanting to at all, but tied under the terms of the deal he'd struck, he let Georg take ahold of his other arm.

The other three cuffs went the same as the first, Lucifer's dread growing as each one clattered away.

Fear aside, he felt no different. The skin beneath the cuffs was raw and had an unpleasant, sweaty smell to it after so long without being able to breathe. But the cuffs, it turned out, were not what had been keeping him without his power.

Georg's smile faded when he fixed his eyes on Lucifer's face. "If...if you're not ready."

"No, that was the deal...just..." He rubbed his wrists, sickened by the feel of the skin there, wrinkled and moist and almost in danger of sloughing off altogether. "Could I have a moment to wash up a bit?"

"Go ahead."

Lucifer busied himself at the sink, getting a rag and some soap, carefully washing the newly exposed skin until he knew that he was just wasting time and was pulled to accompany Georg outside.

He could have fought it, put it off, renegotiated, but there was no point. He couldn't spend the rest of eternity inside. He'd never get back to the palace that way.

Georg opened the door for him and when Lucifer hesitated at the doorway, the younger man said, "You can hold my hand if you want."

Lucifer glanced down at him.

"Not cause I think you're sweet on me; Hansel always used to let me hold his hand when I was nervous about something."

Lucifer took his hand and they stepped outside together. He glanced up at the sky, filled up with an inexplicable terror at the sight of that vast emptiness.

Something winked up there where there should have only been darkness.

A star, except there were no stars in Hell.

They circled the house together. The thick blackness of the sky threatened to descend at any minute; the only light came from the small orb Georg had conjured. It wasn't enough. It would go and then it would be dark again, well and truly dark.

"Can I go back inside now?" Lucifer asked when they'd come back to the front door. He looked towards the door. It never got dark inside, not with the fire always going; it made the room overwarm and the others had complained, but he needed something in the fireplace, even if it was only embers.

"Was it as bad as you thought?"

"I want to go in."

"You can't stay in there forever. We need you out here in the real world."

There was something about the way he said it and how he trained those honey-colored eyes on Lucifer's face. "We're related, aren't we?" Lucifer asked.

"Technically. We're at least five generations apart, though."

Lucifer nodded, did some considering, and decided he could live with that. He leaned in and kissed Georg, for real this time; not something meant to do nothing but seal a bargain, but a kiss that made Georg mold his body against him.

He didn't remember the last time he'd wanted to kiss someone. It wasn't that it had been so long that he couldn't recall, it was that it had been excised from his memories. He tried not to think of the gaps in his memories, focusing on the warmth of Georg's mouth, the pressure of his body against his own, the way his arms slid around his waist.

Georg pulled back. "I can't, oh...fucking *shit*, you don't know how much I want to but I *can't*."

"Why not?" The world became desolate without the other man's body pressed against his.

"Because Ira's my friend."

"Oh."

"And you and him! It should be him, you miserable idiot, you should be kissing him!" Georg insisted.

"I don't know him," Lucifer said, incredibly impressed that Georg had called him an idiot. If anything, it made him even fonder of the lad.

Georg raked a hand through his coppery hair. "Fuck," he whispered to himself, "Fucking...you couldn't have just bought me when I was doing pleasure work?"

"I did think about it."

"Well, why didn't you?"

"I...I don't know." When he thought back, really thought about it, he couldn't put his finger on the reason why he hadn't bought an hour of Georg's time, why he hadn't bought a dozen hours with him. He had been in the brothel and Georg had offered him whatever he'd wanted, but he'd turned it down.

He remembered leaving the brothel without taking any of the workers to bed, but couldn't think of a reason why he'd gone to a brothel if he wasn't going to sleep with any of the pleasure workers.

"Go on, get back inside," Georg urged.

Lucifer went inside, retreating to the safety of his hammock to do some thinking. He kept an eye on the shadows and got up to stoke the fire if they crept over the room too much.

It was easier to cope with the fact that Lucifer didn't remember him if he kept the Devil out of sight. He was tired of being stared at like some kind of ghastly horror; he'd taken to spending most of his time outside, sitting by the lake. He had thrown the ring that Astrid had given him into it. He still hadn't managed to catch a fish and half the time, he didn't even cast a line, but that wasn't the point.

The point was to get away without having to say that he couldn't be in the same room with the man he loved any more.

Georg came down and sat beside him without a word. After a minute, he cleared his throat.

"What?" Ira asked.

"Managed to get those cuffs off."

Hope didn't even bother to show its face. "Any change?"

"No."

Ira nodded and stared off over the lake. He couldn't see more than a few inches in front of his face; he'd never been anywhere this dark in his whole life. The city always had lamps and lights going, but out here if the sky wasn't red then there wasn't any light.

Except that one pinprick.

He sighed and glanced up at the star.

"He, uh." Georg swallowed hard, loud enough for Ira to hear in the dark. "He kissed me."

"Did you kiss him back?"

"No!" A moment later, he added, "Not really."

"Why not?"

"What do you mean why not!"

Ira took some time to think about what he wanted to say so that he wouldn't mangle his words or his meaning. He felt around in the dark until he found Georg's hand. "I told you before, I trust you with him. And if he doesn't remember me, at least he's got you. Someone should be there for him. It's got to be awful for him right now."

"You mean that?"

"Sure."

Georg put an arm around Ira's shoulders and pulled him close. He kissed the top of Ira's head. "When I thought about this, it sounded a lot more fun. I sort of imagined we'd be taking turns or...all piled in together."

"Mmm."

"Maybe we'll get back to that."

"I hope so," Ira said, his voice cracking halfway through. He didn't know if things would ever go back to the way they should have been.

"Darling, are you holding up alright?"

"It's a lot to take in."

They sat together for a while.

Ira thought he would be alright, he thought he'd be able to ignore the hollow feeling in his chest but the more he thought about how things should have been, the worse it got. "I want to go to bed," he whispered.

"Then let's get you to bed." Georg pulled him to his feet, keeping an arm around him, and conjured up a small light to illuminate their path as they walked.

Ira discarded his clothes and crawled into the trundle bed. No one had yet claimed the main bed, but Ira couldn't help but imagine Georg and the Devil nestled in it together. It was an image that would have once filled him up with warmth and fondness for both men.

Georg tutted something about wrinkles and picked up the clothes Ira had tossed aside, folding up the things that could be worn again and hanging them. He tucked Ira in and kissed his cheek. "I was going to read a little bit, you don't mind, do you?"

"No," Ira lied.

It wasn't that he minded, really, just that he badly wanted someone next to him. Anyone. He would have settled for a cat.

"I'll be in soon, though," Georg promised.

"Goodnight."

Georg gave him a sad smile and headed over to the armchairs by the fire. He curled up with a book and even though the Devil was nowhere near him, a lick of envy wound through Ira's heart. He didn't want Georg to stay away from Lucifer, that wasn't it at all, he just couldn't understand what had gone wrong.

Lucifer should have remembered.

In the middle of the night, Georg came to bed and nestled right in beside Ira, brushing his lips across his neck and winding an arm around his waist.

By dinner the following night, Georg had coaxed the Devil into eating at the kitchen table with the rest of them. He'd done it with the most charming wheedling Ira had ever witnessed and thought that it wasn't fair, how good-looking he was. Even someone who didn't care for men would have been lured in by his smile and his pouts, especially if they were trapped together in a little house. No wonder Lucifer had kissed him.

The Devil sat at the far end of the table, hunched and twitchy. Twitchier than Ira had ever seen him. The fact that Lucifer hadn't gone through the house straightening everything out surprised him; maybe even that need to control his environment had been quashed during his time in the dungeon.

Georg jabbed Ira in the hand with his fork, not hard enough to do damage but definitely enough to irritate him.

"What?"

"You ought to tell him about your visit up to Earth."

Ira wrinkled his nose. He didn't think that anything that had happened up there would sit well with Lucifer, not the part about his son or the part about the contract.

"Maybe later," Imogen suggested, giving Hasbani an apologetic glance.

Hasbani shrugged. He hadn't said much to any of them, except to ask when Lucifer would follow through on his part of the deal. He spent the rest of his time either walking the land or out fishing; he had considerably better luck than Ira, but then again, he seemed to know what he was doing.

"Tell me what?" Lucifer asked Georg.

Georg flashed him a grin. "You'll have to ask Ira."

The Devil scowled and drew in on himself. He didn't so much as cast a glance Ira's way for the rest of dinner and when Ira started to gather the dishes, he wouldn't even hand over his plate.

Georg gave Lucifer a poke in the arm and took the plates over to the sink, telling Ira, "You go on, I'll do it."

"No, I—"

Georg quieted him with a kiss. "Go on. I need something to do."

Ira headed outside. He would have liked the excuse to linger a little longer. His suspicions of Georg having something up his sleeve were confirmed when about half an hour later, Lucifer edged out the door of the house.

Ira hadn't strayed far today. There was a pair of wood jays building a nest on the roof; Ira had been watching their progress for a while now and kept his eyes fixed on the male, green and crested, as he tucked in a few twigs. He wanted to look at Lucifer but didn't let himself, knowing it would send the other man right back inside.

"What happened on Earth?" Lucifer asked, sullen and not really looking at Ira.

He managed to gape only briefly before he closed his mouth. "Uh."

"He's won't tell me."

"He is sort of a brat," Ira admitted, not without a hint of pride. He didn't know what Georg had done to make his trip to Earth seem so interesting or how he'd gotten Lucifer so taken with him in such a short time.

"Well?"

"Oh, uh, I went up to visit Felix." He shrugged, hoping that it wouldn't sit the wrong way with Lucifer, who seemed to regard him as a potential enemy.

"Who?"

"Felix," Ira repeated.

Lucifer shook his head, brought his hand up halfway to his head, then stopped and shoved his hand in his pocket. "Who's Felix?"

"Your son."

"I...uh. I've got a few of those."

"Well, sure, but...well, Felix is just a baby."

The Devil's eyebrows shot up. "A *baby?*"

"He knows seven words."

Lucifer protested, "That's...I haven't...not in *years.* Centuries, I think."

"You really don't remember him?"

"No."

Ira raked a hand through his hair, not sure if he felt better that Felix was also among the things the Devil had forgotten. "Uh, anyway. He's doing well. I went up because I thought you'd be worried. Nearly got stuck up there, too..."

"Not such a bad place to be stuck."

Ira snorted. "You say that but...never mind."

"What?"

"There was this, it sounds stupid saying it out loud, there was this contract following me around."

For the second time, Lucifer's face shifted in surprise. "It was following you."

"Yes. Georg says usually you get them."

"Obviously."

"But, you know, incapacitated as you were—"

"And still am, apparently, I haven't seen one since we've been here. But why would they come to you? I have a wife and an heir and a trueborn daughter, they'd all be in line before...what? Some..." He glanced over Ira, his eyes cold and calculating. "What are you? A...clerk, or something? Some kind of librarian?"

"I'm a bookkeeper these days."

"Mmmm, knew it had to be something like that."

"And they came to me because of what *you* did to me."

His voice lost its sneering edge, softened and grew quieter. "What did I do to you?"

Ira considered his options and decided that showing was better than trying to explain something he still didn't really understand. He rolled up his left sleeve to expose his arm and show the five symbols there, running from elbow to wrist. They'd turned to dark pink scars, stark against the gray of his skin, and he took care to always cover his arm because of them.

The Devil reached for his arm, then stepped back. He shook his head. "I didn't..."

"You did. You didn't even ask first."

"I would remember." Lucifer stared at him with a kind of abject horror in his eyes. His fingers twitched towards Ira's arm again.

Ira looked at the star that barely showed against the darkening sky. He jutted his chin toward it. "You made me that, too."

Lucifer wrinkled his nose.

"I told Georg I didn't care if the two of you slept together. I mean...I know you don't care what I think, but he should be game now. He's had this awful crush on you for ages, ever since he first started working at Marius'."

"I remember."

A mean retort came to Ira's tongue right away, but he bit it back. "It was good I didn't know then, though, I would have been awful to him."

"Seems like a lot of effort."

"Hmm?"

"To go down to a brothel and yell at the workers for doing their jobs."

"Well, I mean, I worked there too," Ira told him.

"I thought you were a bookkeeper."

It was exhausting to have to rehash all the details of his life with Lucifer. "I am, but I used to take clients."

The Devil let out a derisive snort. "You? Who'd you take? Men who like to bugger little boys?"

"You."

Lucifer straightened up as if Ira had offended him. "Pardon?"

"You. You were one of my clients."

"I...how old are you, anyway?"

Ira rolled his eyes. "Old enough."

The set of his face changed, his lips pressing together and his eyes narrowing like he'd remembered that he didn't much care for Ira. His gaze flicked to the scars on Ira's arm again, then he turned and went inside, letting the door slam behind him.

It didn't feel like progress.

The sky had grown too dark to see anything, but Ira couldn't make himself follow Lucifer inside.

He picked his way carefully to the small paddock where they kept the horses. He didn't see why Georg got so worried around them, especially not when the roan one liked to come up to and have its nose pet.

He spent a long time out with the horses; by the time he heard anyone else coming, the sky had grown dark and he wondered if he should start carrying a lantern around with him. He turned towards the noise and squinted towards the bit of light bobbing his way, the flame of a candle.

If it had been Georg, it would have been a conjured light. "Imogen?"

"Yes." She approached the paddock and looked up at him, perched on the fence patting the neck of the bay horse.

"I fed them already."

"That's wonderful." She didn't go inside. "You can go."

"Oh, I don't really want..." He trailed off, wondering what she was doing out here anyway. "Have you been...?"

"I've got to drink something."

"Oh." Immediately, he pitied the horses. The two of them were large, hale creatures and judging by her appearance she hadn't been taking her fill from them either, but still, he didn't like the idea. "You could, uh."

"What?"

"If you wanted, I could, you know, I've never—"

She caught his meaning and gave a curt shake of her head. "No, thank you. Go inside, please."

He gave the horse one last pat and slipped off the fence, not wanting to leave them behind.

Imogen sighed. "I'm not taking more than they can give," she assured.

He turned and headed towards the house. Inside, he found Lucifer and Georg playing cards at the kitchen table.

A cursory glance led him to ask, "Where's Hasbani?"

Georg glanced up and, with a roll of his eyes, informed Ira, "In the toilet, probably struggling with those bindings. I offered to help but he just got all red and ducked in there."

Ira clucked.

"What! It's not like I *care*, I was just trying to help."

"It's not the same on Earth," Ira told him, "Poor lad's probably worried we're going to, I don't know, do whatever it is they *do* to people like him on Earth."

Lucifer cleared his throat and looked pointedly at the cards.

Georg shuffled through his hand, then set down a few.

Ira approached the toilet and rapped softly. "Uh, hey, everything alright in there?"

He could imagine Hasbani sitting awkwardly on the other side of the door, trying to actually relieve himself, but thought it would be better to offer and be wrong than to let him struggle on his own.

"Uhhh."

"I mean if you need help with anything."

The door opened a crack to reveal the young man, flustered with his shirt unbuttoned. Strips of fabric wound across his chest. In barely more than a whisper, he shared, "It's...I can't get the knot undone, it's twisted around and..."

"I can give it a shot."

Hasbani slipped his shirt off the rest of the way and turned his back to Ira, who set to work at the bandages in earnest. When he'd managed to loosen them, a wave of guilt passed through him at the sight of the red creases and bulges the binding had dug into his skin. He'd made a deal with Hasbani and was negligent in delivering his half.

"There you go."

"Thank you."

"Anytime."

Hasbani turned back around, clasping the shirt and loosened binding to his chest.

"It's dangerous to tie those too tight," Ira said.

Hasbani gave Ira a small, tense smile and then closed the door.

Ira sighed. He glanced towards Georg, who caught his melancholy look and beckoned for him to come over.

Ira shrugged and Georg insisted, "Yes, come on over."

He went.

Georg snagged him around the waist, pulling him onto his lap. "Don't tell me you're going to start sulking around because if we're going to be here much longer, I won't be able to stand it."

"I'm not sulking." He rested his head against Georg's chest, wishing he could be as content and cozy as he would be if Lucifer hadn't been watching them. Small as he was, Ira always managed to tuck into people's embraces and curl in their laps; it was worth all the jibes about his height to be able to do it.

Georg's fingers dragged through Ira's curls, sending a shiver down his spine. "Do you want to play cards?"

"If we had four we could play bridge."

"Ahh, there's got to be something for the three of us. Three can play I-doubt-it."

Lucifer set his cards down and swept up the rest of them, shuffling them back into a stack and setting them in front of Georg.

"Hey!"

Ira could hear the shout reverberate through Georg's chest.

"You were cheating."

Georg snorted. "Sure, and I stopped playing footsie with you."

Lucifer pushed back from the table and stood, drawing himself up to his full height. Ira thought he might do something drastic, but he only retreated to one of the armchairs.

"Maybe he'll play," Georg whispered to himself and called over to the other young man, who'd exited the toilet and gone to his hammock. "Come on, please."

Hasbani hesitated, then came over to the kitchen table.

"Besides, we've been holed up in here for ages and I don't think we've said two words to each other," Georg pointed out, shuffling the cards. "Ira, love, if we're going to play you're going to need your own seat. What is it, Hasbani, are you quiet or do you just not like me?"

Hasbani's hazel eyes widened, his vertical pupils making the effect unusually eerie. "Quiet, I guess," he mumbled.

Ira untangled himself from Georg's limbs and took his own seat, leaving Lucifer's vacated chair empty. "Four can play I-doubt-it, too."

The Devil pretended not to hear him.

"I really only did want to be helpful," Georg told Hasbani as he dealt the cards. "Sit down."

Hasbani sat, picking up the cards, his eyes on the table. "Hey."

He lifted his eyes to look at Georg.

"Tell me to fuck off if I'm being an ass. I don't know how you do things up there in that God-awful sun-roasted realm."

Ira chuckled.

"I just...I hate that you knew," Hasbani admitted, more to the cards than to Georg. He cast a sour glance in Ira's direction. "I thought it might be kept in confidence."

"Ira didn't say anything," Georg assured. "I've got other friends with the same kind of...uh..." He looked at Ira. "I don't know, what's the right word for this? Predicament seems so dire."

Ira shrugged. If any of them knew the right phrasing, it would be Lucifer. "Are you going to finish dealing?"

Georg resumed his task, chattering all the while, though he changed the topic to what, exactly, it meant to be the son of the angel of sleep, peppering Hasbani with all kinds of questions about what could he do and where he was from and what he had done before taking a job as a manservant in the Devil's palace.

The answers he gave were minimal at first, but after winning the first two rounds, Hasbani opened up a little more.

Imogen came in and accepted their offer to join them. She won four times in a row, that foxy smile of hers coming and going at unpredictable intervals, making it impossible to read her. Just when Ira thought he knew her tell and called a bluff, he was proven wrong.

The whole time they played, Ira kept sneaking looks at Lucifer, hoping no one else would notice. He thought that if Lucifer had played, Ira might have been able to catch all of his tells.

It was Georg who beat Imogen in the end. Once he had, he said, "I'd better quit while I'm ahead. And I'm beat. I've never been so tired from doing nothing all day. Do you want to come to bed?"

Ira nodded. His eyes had started to droop and he'd resorted to rubbing them viciously every so often to keep them open.

Georg gave him a nudge towards the bed they'd been sharing and, as Ira went, Georg headed over to speak with Lucifer. Ira couldn't catch what Georg said to him, his voice low, not furtive but intimate, nor did he hear the Devil's response.

He tried not to think about it too much. He failed in that endeavor, of course. Once Georg came to bed, Ira clasped onto him and wanted to cry.

The sight of mail had never sent such a shiver of dread up anyone's spine, Ira was sure of it. It didn't help that the envelope had crept up next to him as he'd been staring out over the water, his feet dangling off the dock.

He'd rolled up his trousers, he'd even thought about taking up Imogen's offer to teach him how to swim. Georg had offered to do so as well, but the idea of being in water that went over his head made his stomach quiver. He had leaned back on the dock, felt something crinkle under his hand, and looked down to see the envelope, addressed to Ira, proxy to the serpent's throne.

A groan found it's way out.

Hasbani looked over, setting down his fishing pole. "Are you feeling well?"

"I'm fine."

Hasbani raised an eyebrow, looking incredibly like his father. "I thought you were about to throw up."

"I might."

"Do you always give these kinds of mixed messages?"

Ira didn't answer. He searched around for his shoes, pulled them back on, and unrolled his trousers. He took the envelope and headed towards the house, past Imogen, who'd settled in beneath the tree that grew a dozen yards from the lake.

"I don't know if you want to head in there," she warned.

He didn't answer her either. He didn't want anything more to do with these contracts and didn't care what he interrupted to get rid of them.

He pushed open the door, assuming the clatter would interrupt whatever they were doing, but the sound had no effect on either of them. Not on Georg, writhing on his belly beneath the Devil, or on Lucifer. Ira watched, warmth seeping from his gut; in a detached way, he noted the disturbing lankiness of the Devil's limbs, something he'd never really seen in action from a distance before. Up close, being with him felt wrapped up and safe and warm.

From a distance, it sort of looked like Georg was being fucked by a skeleton, or maybe a scarecrow. Those months as Rivka's prisoner hadn't done his already thin frame any good.

The red marks on his wrists glowed against the pallor of his skin and Ira hoped that whatever Rivka was doing right now, it was horrible. He hoped she was miserable.

He cleared his throat and the two of them paused, looking over.

Georg pushed himself up onto his elbows and cocked an eyebrow. "What, love?"

He held up the envelope. "I've had about enough of these following me around."

Lucifer gave a small thrust.

A plaintive moan slipped through Georg's lips; he turned his head and bit his lower lip, sucking in a deep breath. "Do we need to do this now?" he asked when he'd regained his composure.

The Devil leaned in and Ira heard him rasp, "I don't mind if he watches," into Georg's ear.

Georg gave a visible shudder, rolling his hips back against Lucifer.

"Just...be quick about it." Ira threw down the envelope, sure that it would be back by his side in an instant.

He turned and left, not bothering to close the door for them. The sight of others going at it wasn't anything new for Ira; he didn't think there was anything that could be done between two consenting adults that would manage to shock him. It hadn't been what they were doing, it had been that they'd been doing it together and he'd been so excluded from everything that had to do with Lucifer.

He joined Imogen beneath the tree.

"I did warn you."

He snorted and tried to play things off. "Like I've never walked in on anyone fucking before? I work in a whorehouse."

"And how often are those people your best friend and your companion?"

"He's not my companion anymore." The words came out easy, unbidden and it took a moment for their meaning to sink in. Once they had, his face went hot while his stomach grew cold.

"Ira—"

"No, it's...he isn't!" Ira insisted. "How can he be? He has no idea who I am and whatever it was the first time that drew us together, whatever he saw in me then he doesn't now."

"Things take time."

Ira shook his head. "You weren't there. You...the very first time he saw me it was..." He licked his lips and wanted to cry, but pressed on, "It was different. No one had ever looked at me like that and people have looked at me *lots* of different ways." He picked at his nails and let out a sigh.

"I overestimated you."

He looked at her sharply.

"I didn't think you'd give up so easily." She slipped a hand around his left wrist and pushed up his sleeve. "He does this to you and you don't so much as mewl. He forgets a few things and suddenly you're not companions anymore?"

He tugged his hand back and fixed his sleeve. He scowled at her. "I don't remember asking for your opinion."

He thought he'd cowed her, but after a brief quiet interlude, she asked him, "Have you ever been alone?"

"Sorry?"

"I mean really alone. Like he was. In the dark. No food, no water, no people. Chained up."

"You know I haven't."

"I don't know that. Lilia Gotes isn't the most reputable madam. No need to keep up that sour look."

"How am I supposed to look when I'm being scolded?" he demanded. He knew how he was supposed to look: meek, acquiescent, apologetic. He'd had that molded into him at an early age.

She glanced him over. "I'm sorry. I didn't mean to scold. I've never been good with encouragement."

He pulled his knees to his chest and rested his forehead on his knees. Eventually, he turned his head to his side and asked, "You've been his butler for a while. Has this ever happened to him before?"

"He always comes back muddled after a death, but everything returns to him with time."

Her answer didn't provide any solace. When he'd slipped into the dungeon during the coronation, Lucifer had remembered him, said that he'd loved him. What could have transpired between then and his liberation to change things?

"Do you think that angel did something to him?"

"I think she did a lot of things to him."

He rolled his eyes. "What in the world would she gain from making him forget me? And Felix! Did I tell you that he doesn't remember Felix?"

The vampire straightened up. "You did not."

He shrugged.

"I thought you were all he'd forgotten."

"You think it matters?"

"It makes me worried that there might be more." She glanced towards the house, her back stiff. "And a ruler with gaps in his memory?"

She stood up, stretched, and brushed the dirt from her skirt. "I need to think." She headed off, striking out towards the woods on the other side of the house. There was a small patch included in the area she'd cordoned off. Not for the first time, Ira wondered what had become of the mage who'd worked the spell for her.

While she walked, Georg came out of the house and settled under the tree beside him.

"You smell," Ira told him right away. It was a musky, rich smell, more than just the smell of spilled seed and sweat, it was the smell of both of them, fantastically twined together.

Georg put both arms around him and pulled him into his lap. He nuzzled his face against Ira's neck and peppered his throat, jaw, and cheek with kisses. "Aren't you going to ask me how it was?"

"I don't have to, I know he's good."

Georg whined and butted his head gently against Ira's.

"How was it, kitten?" Ira twisted in his grasp and hooked an arm around his shoulder.

The younger man let out a luxurious sigh, melting against Ira. "It was all a bit of a whirlwind. Quick, but, you know, in that good way, somewhere between desperate and frenzied. Obviously, he hasn't been with anyone since before he died."

Ira remembered the last time he and Lucifer had slept together. It had been delightfully rough and quick, right before they'd gone to meet his wife; he'd begged Lucifer to come inside him. "Obviously," he agreed. "Was he as tender as an untouched lad on his first night?"

Georg chortled but sobered quickly. "You aren't jealous, are you?"

"No."

"Sad?" Georg asked.

Lying to Georg would be useless. "Sort of."

"Oh, darling, I...I shouldn't have."

"Of course you should have."

A shadow fell across them. "Funny how the two of you have decided it's up to you what I'm allowed to do."

Georg scowled up at the Devil. "Why do you think everything is about you?"

The Devil crouched beside them. "Am I not what you were talking about?" The question seemed cautious; his brows had knitted together, as though the answer genuinely concerned him.

"Yes, but not because it has anything to do with you," came Georg's reply.

"I don't understand."

Ira curled further into Georg's lap.

Georg's eyes remained on Lucifer's face. "Do you believe that you and Ira were together?"

Lucifer held up the envelope that Ira had brought into the house. To Ira, he said, "I believe that something has brought us to a place where contracts are coming addressed to you instead of to me."

"If you've got any ideas on how to get them to stop, I'm all ears," Ira said. "Because I've had enough of them."

"Tell me."

Ira scrapped his teeth over his tongue, not sure what to say.

"You were stuck on Earth," Lucifer prompted. "Yet you made it back. Tell me."

Ira sucked in a breath and related how he'd dealt with MacAfee, worried the whole time that he'd admit to some appalling mistake.

Lucifer crouched for the entirety of the story, his horrible red and gold eyes fixed on Ira's face. When he'd finished, he asked, "You gave him more time?"

"I didn't know what else to do."

"And the lad who likes to fish, what did you promise him?"

"Hasbani?" Ira looked towards the lake. "He was my man on the inside, to get you out."

"In return for what?"

"To make him the way he wants to be."

"Ah." Lucifer held out the envelope to Ira. "I can't open it."

"Georg could open it," Ira pointed out, hoping it would absolve him of some responsibility.

"Georg will be the Master of Records." Lucifer offered the envelope again.

Ira took it, broke the seal on the envelope, then handed it back, but Lucifer didn't take it.

"I can't."

"You're the Devil."

"I've got no power."

"You've got to have something," Georg insisted.

"I can't heal, I can't change shape, I can't feel the in-between place anymore. Those things I have been able to do as long as I have been the Devil."

A small wave of relief rolled over Ira. If Lucifer couldn't get through the place between worlds, then Ira didn't have to worry about the contracts. He didn't think all of them would be so easy to worm out of as MacAfee's; what if the time came for the Devil to pay his end of the bargain? Ira would have no idea how to do that.

He glanced down towards the lake.

If Lucifer didn't have his powers, then Hasbani would get nothing. He would have less than what he had started with. No job, a traitor to the queen.

That was less than ideal. And it was Ira's fault.

Ira said, "This is what you were afraid of. An angel could bind you, that's what you said."

"If I was a betting man, I'd say that's what she's done."

"If?" Georg asked.

Lucifer gave him a slippery smile.

"Oh!" Georg gave the Devil a small push. "But you made a deal with me, didn't you? About the cuffs."

"Mmm, making deals is different," Lucifer murmured. He reached out and took Ira by the hand. "I need your help."

The sensation of having Lucifer's hand around his again robbed Ira's tongue of words and his mind of thoughts. "I..."

"I can show you what to do."

"I don't want to," Ira whispered.

The Devil's long fingers tightened on his hand, sliding up to his wrist and over the runes on his arm. "Even if you are nothing else to me, you *are* my proxy."

He stood, drawing Ira up with him.

Ira gazed up at him, feeling small, unable to stop the tremble in his limbs. "I don't want to, please, Lu."

Gently and with that unyielding calmness that reminded Ira how old the Devil really was, the Devil said, "You don't even know what I'm asking for."

It took so little to undo him. A few soft words and Ira was falling for him all over again. "What?"

The Devil pulled him in close, still holding on to his left hand. "All you have to do is relax and let me guide you."

"That can't be all there is to it."

"Well, no, but you don't need to know the specifics. I'm not sure you could even comprehend them if I tried to explain. Now, relax. Take a deep breath."

Ira did his best, closing his eyes. If he'd had a pillow, he would have turned into it; he'd done it enough times. If he hadn't known how to relax when things had gotten rough, they would have hurt a lot worse.

This wasn't rough, it didn't hurt, but it did send a shivering, slippery feeling crawling all over his skin as he moved through the skin of reality. Starting with the tips of his fingers, the feeling consumed him. Lucifer pushed him further in, manipulating his hand to wrap around strings.

"Pull," came the soft voice in his ear.

He pulled.

Hell was left behind.

The strings pulled through and brought them to the other side. When Lucifer pressed his hand through into reality again, they had arrived on Earth.

Ira couldn't banish the feeling on his skin; it was like being covered in spiders. The sensation slipped inside his nose and ears, past his lips and filled him up. Inside and out, he was covered in horrible crawling things. The Devil released his hand, undoing his last tether to reality. His heart thundered in his chest and he couldn't hear past the muffled humming in his ears, nor see through the blur of tears.

He grabbed for Lucifer, needing something to hold, and when he couldn't find him, sank to the ground, pressing his hands over his ears and curling in on himself.

A pair of hands settled on his shoulders. "It will pass." Gone was that calmness from before; the Devil sounded just as unnerved as Ira felt.

He shook his head.

"It will. It always passes. Breathe."

He couldn't.

"Breathe, Ira." Lucifer's voice held a note of true panic, one that might not have been audible to anyone who didn't know him well.

It didn't matter how many times he was told to breathe, he couldn't, not evenly. All he could do was suck in small, gasping breaths.

Eventually, those hands left his shoulders and arms slid around his ribs, pulling him against a chest.

The sharp smell of astringent herbs filled up his nose. A heart thumped steadily and a hand moved up and down his back. The chest against his cheek moved with slow, deliberate breaths and after a while, his own breathing matched the pace.

"Are you calm?"

Ira nodded. As calm as he could be.

The Devil released him and when Ira dared to glance up at him, he thought he saw agitation. He dropped his gaze just as quickly.

"That's the worst I'll ask of you in this venture, so rest assured, it only gets better from here. Have you got the contract?"

Ira took the envelope from his pocket.

"Wonderful. Read it to me."

"All of it?" he whispered.

"The important parts."

Ira scanned over the contract but couldn't decipher any meaning. His nerves hadn't yet settled fully and he wanted to be back in Lucifer's arms. He rubbed his face and tried to read the contract again. This time the letters were more than shapes. "Uh. Patricia Young, she struck a deal to save her daughter from..." He glanced at the paper again. "Yellow fever. What's that?"

"It's a fever."

"Yeah, but why's it yellow?"

"Jaundice."

"Oh."

Ira looked around, took in the architecture of the buildings, and decided that it wasn't New York or Pickering. At least, as far as he could tell. It felt smaller, for one, and had a different smell as well as a balminess to the air that Ira didn't recognize.

It unnerved him to think that humans had so many cities when Hell had only one.

Well. Technically two, but that was a secret.

He didn't notice right away when Lucifer took off. Ira had to scan around to find him, but once he did he was an easy silhouette to pick out, heading down the street with his shoulders hunched and his hands shoved into his pockets. He didn't look right, not with his hair hacked so short.

Ira hurried to catch up with him, bumping into a small group of people huddled in front of a storefront. He mumbled a quick apology and by the time he'd done so, he'd lost sight of the Devil again. He stood on his toes to get a better look and when that failed him, grabbed onto a lamp post and hoisted himself up onto the base.

He saw nothing more than a few dozen humans bustling around.

And there, vanishing around a street corner, a bit of faded black silk. He hopped down and ran. He rounded the corner and spotted Lucifer right away. He grabbed onto the other man's arm.

Lucifer yanked out of his grasp, rounding on Ira with his teeth bared and his hand reaching for Ira's neck. He slammed Ira into the side of the nearest building, a brick wall that knocked hard against the back of Ira's head.

It happened faster that Ira could process and, when Lucifer withdrew his hand a second later, Ira almost didn't believe that anything had happened at all.

He touched his fingers to the tender spot on the back of his head.

Lucifer stared at him, his face twisted like he saw something disgusting where Ira stood. He looked slightly ill, even, and unsteady.

"Are you alright?" Ira asked.

"Fine. I'm...you. Are you alright?" Lucifer looked him over, reaching halfway for him, then drawing his hand back.

He'd picked his nails so badly that he had scabs instead of cuticles.

Ira nodded, even though he wanted to cry. "Fine."

"I didn't mean..."

"I know."

"How could you know?" the Devil demanded.

Ira didn't know what answer would satisfy that question. "You don't look right. You look sort of green. Do you need to sit?"

Instead of answering, the Devil braced himself against the brick wall, drawing in slow breaths.

"You haven't been fainting, have you?"

Lucifer's eyes flicked to his face. He shook his head.

"Do you think you might now?"

Instead of answering, Lucifer held out a hand, palm up. A scar across the meat of his hand, but it lacked the greenish-black discoloration that it had held prior to his death.

"Looks better than it did."

"One upside of dying," Lucifer said with a hint of a smile on his lips. "Bleed out and the body makes new blood."

"Good thing she didn't strangle you, then."

An odd giggle escaped the Devil. He pressed one bony finger into the scar. He looked over Ira for a while, searching over his face, his whole body down to the toes of his shoes. "I could believe it if you said we'd had some kind of...entanglement."

"But not that you asked for us to be official."

"*I* asked?"

Ira nodded and when Lucifer wrinkled his nose, he offered, "We don't have to talk about it. I know *I* don't want to talk about it."

"Why not?"

"Because you don't believe me anyway. I don't want to, to go through everything, dredge up all the things we've done just to have you look at me like I'm lying to you. Besides, if I started listing off all the things I'm not supposed to know, the things you told me anyway, it would just make you trust me less."

"What kinds of things?" Lucifer pressed, still leaning against the wall.

"I told you—"

"What kinds of things?" he asked through clenched teeth. Ira doubted he would bother to ask a third time.

"Things like...like the way you told me about the city on the other side of the mountains or that you miss Heaven."

After a moment of quiet consideration, Lucifer nodded. "You're right. I do trust you less."

Ira swept his sleeve under his nose, hating that this was making him tear up.

"Nobody knows about the other city."

"I do."

Lucifer straightened up and frowned down at Ira.

"What?" He shifted uneasily beneath his gaze. He'd seen the Devil turn such a look on others, but had never felt it himself.

"You shouldn't know things like that."

"It's not my fault you told me."

Lucifer mused, "And it's not your fault that I don't trust you now. But...Rivka said that it was you who betrayed me."

"Fuck what Rivka said! She's an *angel*, she took your throne. I...what I did, it was all an accident, I was just trying to find out more."

"Spying?"

He nodded.

"How do I know you aren't spying now?"

Ira hadn't expected this conversation to take such a turn and he didn't know how to turn it back. "If I was spying don't you think I'd be asking you questions?"

"I don't know." His eyes narrowed. "It...it could be a test. To see if she can trust me."

The mention of the angel again sent a flair of anger through Ira. How could he waste time thinking about that woman? "She *shouldn't* trust you! You're Lucifer, you're the Devil, you shouldn't be worrying what some stupid angel thinks."

"She was the only one who came."

"Because she was holding you captive! She didn't let anyone else see you. She *killed you* and you're worried about trusting *me?*"

Lucifer stared at him some more, in the wide-eyed, unblinking way that Ira had never seen before he'd died.

"Fucking...I said I didn't want to talk about this now stop *looking at me* and let's do whatever it is we came up here to do."

The Devil nodded and turned away from Ira, heading up the street again. This time, Ira stuck close to him.

He seemed to have some innate sense of where to go because he wound through the streets without hesitation and brought them to a small yellow house with green shutters and a screen door held shut with a small hook.

From inside the house came the voices of children and the smell of cooking, of long-simmering greens. Lucifer climbed the porch steps and rapped on the frame of the screen door. A girl of maybe ten came to the door, looked him over, and scampered right back inside the house, calling for her mother.

Ira couldn't help but snort. He covered his mouth with his hand and didn't meet the Devil's eyes when he cast a glare in his direction.

A brown-skinned woman appeared a moment later, a wooden spoon in her hand and a dirty apron about her waist. She was the touchstone for motherhood, at least as far as Ira could discern from his vague memories and what he'd gleaned from books.

She recognized the Devil right away, her mouth flying open in a silent gasp. She clutched the charm around her neck, her lips moving in some silent chant. She pushed open the screen door and closed the solid door behind her, her voice a hiss when she said, "Get out of here."

Lucifer raised an eyebrow. "You are Patricia Young."

"Nothing here for you, beast."

He held out a hand and Ira handed him the contract. He tried to present it to her. "We made a deal—"

"And Lisa is *dead*."

"Not of yellow fever."

The woman glared at him.

"You owe me—"

She snatched the contract from his hands and ripped it in two. "I don't owe you anything."

A moment later the contract was whole again and floating back to Ira on a breeze that wasn't blowing. It fluttered at his feet and he refused to pick it up.

"You owe me a favor. Specifically, your family owes me a favor. That is the correct wording, isn't it?" He glanced towards Ira.

With a huff, Ira picked up the contract, reread it, and nodded.

"I require the use of one of your children."

Ira didn't know what to make of that. Surely the man who'd made a law against laying with children wouldn't be out to harm them.

"Any one of them, it doesn't matter which," the Devil said. "But you know which one would be best."

The woman looked ready to argue until Lucifer placed a hand on her shoulder. With that touch, she shuddered and retreated back into the house. She came out with the girl who'd first answered the door.

"Ma, what—"

"Hush," the woman hissed.

Lucifer took the girl's hand from her mother's grip. "What's your name?"

"Mayella."

"Mayella, I'm not going to hurt you. I need a little bit of your time and then you'll never see me again."

The girl nodded, her narrow brown eyes fixed on the Devil's face.

"Lu, what—"

"I need you, too, come over here," the Devil requested.

"I...I don't know, Lu, what are we doing?"

Instead of answering, Lucifer led the girl over to Ira. He wrapped his hand around Ira's wrist and pulled him in close. "Take her by the hands."

Ira obeyed, not sure if he wanted to but afraid to argue.

Lucifer came behind him, his chest molded against Ira's back and his hands once again covering Ira's, making Ira feel like a puppet. He put his mouth next to Ira's ear and whispered, "Repeat what I say, exactly as I say it, or the spell will go all sorts of sideways."

"I don't want to."

"This isn't exactly how I like to do business either."

"I'd feel a lot better if you told me what we're doing."

The Devil let out a sigh, his breath whooshing against Ira's ear and making his stomach quiver. "I have need of eyes in this realm and there are few ways to get them."

"That's all?"

"That's all," Lucifer vowed. "Are you ready?"

Ira swallowed nodded.

The girl shifted anxiously.

Lucifer began to utter hushed words into Ira's ear, ones he couldn't understand. He did his best to repeat them exactly as Lucifer had. As he chanted what must have been the most stilted spell the world had ever witnessed, Lucifer moved his hands, drawing a bit of blood from Ira's thumb and swiping it over the girl's eyelids.

Mayella wrinkled her nose and pulled back slightly, but endured the rest of the ritual, staying perfectly still.

Finally, Lucifer released Ira and Ira released the girl. He put his hand in his pocket, let out a sigh of disgust and took Ira by the hand again, pushing both their hands into the pocket of his trousers. When he pulled their hands out, Ira had a coin clenched in his fist.

Lucifer wiggled his fingers into Ira's hand and snaked out the coin, then handed it over to Mayella. "People will come and ask you questions. They'll present you coins that look like this. That's how you'll know it's alright to answer them."

She nodded, staring down at the wooden coin. It had a single glyph carved on one side. "They won't hurt me?"

"Nothing will hurt you," he told her. "Not unless they plan to tangle with me."

"Oh." She frowned at him, then returned to her study of the coin.

He gave her a smile and a pat on the back then nodded towards her mother. He strode off the porch without another word to either of them.

Ira hurried after him, rubbing his arms to try to dissipate the feeling of Lucifer's body around his. No use in being reminded of something he couldn't have. "Why not do it to the woman?"

"Hmm? Oh. Children see things adults cannot. Now she'll see them forever." He looked up at the sun. "Are you in such a hurry to return to Hell?"

Ira shook his head, recalling the feeling of the place between worlds skittering over his skin. Bile rose in the back of his throat at the thought. It hadn't been like that when he'd traveled before, but he'd never been the one breaking the skin of reality or playing with the strings.

"Wonderful. There's...there should be a restaurant here called Dave's, it's on Pleasant Street. Popular, people should be able to point you right towards it. Let's meet there at nightfall."

"Oh."

"You object," Lucifer noted.

"No, I."

"What?"

"I thought you were saying we should get something to eat," Ira confessed.

"We could. Are you hungry?"

"No, but...never mind."

Lucifer shrugged and continued walking.

Ira hated him a little for not asking for clarification, hated him for not caring. He hated himself for mistaking anything the Devil did now for affection. He'd made his distaste clear enough; maybe it had been their closeness during the spellcasting, or how Lucifer had calmed him earlier, that had Ira seeing things that weren't there.

He kept pace with the Devil. "Doesn't it bother you?"

"Lots of things bother me. Your tie is crooked, that bothers me."

"That you don't remember things?"

"Of course it does."

Ira said, "You don't act like it. You just keep saying you've got to get back to that angel."

"You keep saying angel like it's a bad thing."

"Angels don't belong in Hell."

"I was an angel," Lucifer reminded as if that neatly summed up why Rivka had every right to be in Hell. "Are you going to keep following me?"

"What else am I supposed to do?" Ira demanded. "I've only ever been to Earth a few times and never by myself. I don't have any money or any idea where I'm going, I don't even know where I am."

Lucifer tilted his head. "Not very adventurous, are we?"

"It's another fucking realm!"

The Devil ruffled his curls in a way that felt more predatory than affectionate. "I'd like to see what they'd make of you in the Otherworld."

Ira ducked his head away. "I want to go home."

"I'd like to see you manage it on your own."

He had no idea where to begin and the idea of trying to breach the skin of the world on his own made his stomach turn. "Where did you want to meet?"

"Dave's."

Looking around, he tried to determine which way to go. None of it looked particularly appealing. He shoved his hands in his pockets, doublechecking for money. Not a penny. He walked a few feet, resigning himself to hours of aimless wandering and humanity demanding to know where he was from.

He glanced over at the Devil and found him staring up at the sky, his eyes fixed on the sun.

Part of Ira wanted to leave him there starting up at the burning ball in the sky, but a bigger part of him knew he couldn't. He went over and kicked his shoe. He repeated what June had told him when he'd first visited the realm, "First rule on Earth, don't stare at the sun."

Lucifer ignored him.

"Come on." Ira tugged his sleeve.

The Devil pulled out of his grasp. "You try spending..." He turned and looked at Ira.

"What?"

"How long? How long was I down there?"

"About five months."

"Five months," Lucifer echoed.

Ira nodded.

"That's it? Months?"

"Yes. How long did you think it'd been?"

"Years. I thought it had to be years." His fingers crept across his chest, slipping inside his shirt.

Ira pushed his hand away. "Imogen says if you keep doing that it's going to get really infected this time."

The Devil's eyes began to glitter and he wiped his eyes on the back of his wrist.

Ira glanced up and down the street, not sure what to do. A wave of unreality swept over him. "Do...Lu, do you want to talk?"

"What good will talking do?"

Ira shrugged. "I don't know, it always seemed to help."

"I don't think so."

Ira sighed. "Fine, stare at the sun some more. Have you got any money?"

"No."

Ira headed off, still not knowing where he was headed. Maybe he could find someone who liked his look; he wasn't above getting someone off to make a few coins. Or bills. He wasn't sure what they used for money here, or how much would be a fair price for his service.

He'd scout out restaurants, first, figure out the price of a meal and see if he could scrape that much together. He didn't think it was going to be dark anytime soon and he'd need to eat.

He ran a few different scenarios through his head, wondering how Earth's different customs regarding prostitution would trip him up. He could just as easily end up getting knifed or raped in some seedy alley or dingy backroom. Or in a nice room, it didn't have to be dingy, he imagined. Bad things happened in luxurious places just as much as they happened in dank ones.

The sound of footsteps behind him caught his ear and he glanced back to see Lucifer on his trail. He caught his eye and the Devil's cheeks turned pink; the sight of him blushing slowed Ira's step. "Need something?"

"I...I started thinking."

"Oh?"

"And now I can't stop. I...I'd managed to forget a little bit but now...now I know the sun is there, I know it's shining, I can *feel* it but I can feel the rest of it too," Lucifer said.

Ira had stopped walking and Lucifer had too.

"Creeping up." He rubbed his wrists. "I can feel those chains and I know it isn't dark, but it *feels* dark. It feels quiet. The shadows..." He gave the shadows cast by trees and streetlamps a furtive look.

"Are you hungry?"

"Yes."

"Ever been a pimp?"

"No," Lucifer answered.

"It's not hard. Come on, help me find someone to jerk off and we can get something to eat."

The corner of Lucifer's mouth turned up. "As charmed as I am by the offer, I think I've got a faster idea. Still involves sticky fingers, though. Come."

Ira followed a few steps behind until they reached a busier part of town. Lucifer gestured for him to fall back and he did, watching as Lucifer hunched his shoulders further and lowered his eyes. It didn't take more than half a minute for him to find a mark, a man in a sharp suit, who recoiled with a look of disgust when Lucifer bumped into him.

The Devil ducked into a small café and Ira followed. He found Lucifer tucked into a corner, a wallet resting on the table in front of him.

"You would be a pickpocket."

Lucifer shrugged; he remained quiet until coffee came. He stirred his drink for a solid three minutes before he sipped it.

"Feeling better?" Ira asked.

"No."

Ira gave him a bit of a smile. "I'm a good listener."

"I don't want to talk. I don't even want to think about it."

"Listen, I understand if you don't want to talk to me about it, but Georg is a good listener, too. You might not think so, he comes off as such a brat, but he really is sweet." Ira fiddled with his spoon and when he set it down, Lucifer reached over to straighten it. "You can't really mean to go back to Rivka."

"I don't know what to do."

"What about unbinding your power?"

"I need an angel for that."

"Are there any angels that would do it?"

The Devil shrugged. "I don't know, there aren't any that I've kept in touch with. With whom I've kept in touch."

"Not one?"

"No."

"And I don't imagine they're easy to coerce?"

The Devil shook his head and brought his coffee to his lips.

"You know there's souls from the Seventh out, don't you?"

Quietly, with a hint of guilt, Lucifer asked, "Is it a horrible mess?"

"They're killing people. Your people. And she can't take care of it. She's not even sure how many are actually *out*, you know. Spends all her time working on that stupid book and there's all sorts of foul things crawling around our Precincts. I don't think she's even laid hands on a soul."

"I'll think about it."

Ira rolled his eyes. He didn't think Lucifer would. A small part of him suspected that the Devil liked being their captive. They were better wardens that Rivka, surely, and taking the throne back wouldn't be an easy task. As long as Lucifer remained weak, he couldn't be expected to do anything more than get well again.

"Let me see your arm again."

Ira offered his left arm and Lucifer pushed up his sleeve. He resisted the urge to pull away as Lucifer traced over the scars, his mouth moving without a sound. He ran the edge of his nail over the scars, not hard enough to break skin but enough that Ira tried to tug his arm back.

He released Ira. "I should remember this. How can I not remember putting a piece of myself in you? Of all the things to forget! And even if I didn't remember it, I should feel it."

"You don't?"

"I feel...I feel more than nothing when I look at you. It's not blank, it's not like I've forgotten something. It makes me worry that if I look at you for too long I'll start forgetting other things. You are a void."

"I don't care for the sound of that."

The Devil sighed and rubbed his palm over his scruffy hair. "If I could just think straight maybe," he muttered to himself.

Ira didn't press the issue, worried that pushing him any further might undo the bit of equilibrium the Devil had regained.

They stayed in town until nightfall. Lucifer gave a brief glance up at the stars and wrinkled his nose as if they'd given him offense. Ira thought he heard him mutter than Hell didn't have any stars.

Without warning, he took Ira by the hand and pressed them through into the underneath. He wrapped his hand around a string and told him to pull.

Ira almost did, hesitating first because he hated the feel of it, but then because the string didn't feel right. It didn't bring to mind the house by the lake, it felt like the palace, the intangible mood of the place winding through his arm and settling in his mind.

He released the string and swallowed to keep down the bile that bubbled up from his stomach. "The right one."

"I need to see her."

Ira scoffed and felt around in the in-between place, his fingers finding strings wherever he went. He flinched from the touch of each one but pressed on. He thought of the house, thought of Georg and the scent of his skin right after Lucifer had taken him, of the horses and poor Hasbani, who might have gambled away his chance at getting what he wanted because Ira had thought the Devil would be whole when they found him.

The string floated over to him, curling around his hand unbidden. With his teeth digging deep into his tongue, he secured his grip on the string and Lucifer, then pulled, almost too irritated to be nervous.

When they arrived back in Hell, Georg yelped and scrambled away.

Maybe focusing on Georg so much had been the wrong way to travel, because they'd appeared practically on top of him as he sat at the kitchen table.

Shaking, he saw that Lucifer had been deposited unceremoniously onto the kitchen table, though luckily not in anyone's dinner.

Ira released the string and shook out his hand, then rubbed his arms, trying to banish that crawling feeling.

"Fuck! Oh, you scared the shit out of me!" Georg cried. "You awful thing, my heart almost came out of my chest!"

"Kitten," Ira managed.

Georg folded up into an embrace right away, his fingers raking through his curls. "You were gone for so long, I got worried."

The crawling of his skin subsided where Georg touched him. Eventually, it dissipated altogether, leaving Ira exhausted. He leaned against Georg and pleaded, "Come to bed, love, please. I'm so tired."

"Of course."

Ira couldn't get to sleep until Georg had nestled in close to him again and buried them both beneath the covers.

The nothing person that Ira was picked at the edges of Lucifer's mind. He couldn't shake the emptiness from his head and the sight of those deep pink scars against the gray skin disturbed him in a way they shouldn't have. No other hand could have made those marks except his and not remembering it tore at him in ways he didn't like.

He didn't trust him, he hated looking at him, and spending a day on Earth with him hadn't done anything to change that.

Ira hadn't done anything to him and, under any other circumstance, Lucifer likely would have found him inoffensive. He'd even felt bad watching him cry after his first time touching the strings between the worlds. It wasn't an easy thing to endure and he wouldn't have wished it on someone he despised. Too many trips would likely drive a Hell-born thing like him mad; he wasn't made of the right stuff to go traipsing around the place between realms.

The poor creature had gotten himself messed up in things in which he had no right to be involved.

Pity aside, Lucifer hated seeing him. The neatest solution would be to do away with him altogether. It would be easy, he was so small, and his slender body looked soft instead of lean. He wouldn't be able to put up much of a fight.

The idea wiggled into his head and settled into his stomach. He'd be tender as a milk-fed lamb.

That wasn't an option. It couldn't be. Slitting the throat of an unsettling but harmless whore-turned-bookkeeper wouldn't be an auspicious addition to his reign or to his personal accomplishments.

And, without Ira, he'd have no way to traverse the realms.

Not to mention how upset the others would be, especially Georg. He tried to put aside thoughts of Ira in any capacity.

When he set upon the dishes that had been left to soak last night, the first thing he came up on was a knife. He abandoned the dishes entirely and went to stoke the fire.

It did little to calm his nerves because it only made him wonder if he would like the taste of his flesh better roasted or raw.

Raw, he decided.

Imogen found him like that, crouched in front of the fire with the poker in his hand, thinking of different ways to kill the demon.

"Sire?"

He glanced over.

"How are we today?"

"Fine, Imogen, thank you."

"You don't look fine," she told him, "And Earth has a way of wearing you out."

He shook his head. "Not this time. I almost enjoyed myself. Or, I think, I could have enjoyed myself if things had been a little different."

"Oh?"

"If I could have gotten there on my own, for example, and if that little wretch hadn't been following me around," he growled under his breath.

The vampire came over to stand beside him, her arms folded across her chest as she looked down at him. "You know that woman was feeding you nothing but lies."

"Meat."

"Sorry?" Imogen asked.

"She was feeding me meat."

"And probably hunks of bread and a bit of water, she wanted you alive for some reason," the butler conceded. "But she didn't do your head any favors."

He rocked a little; he didn't like to think about this. "She was kind to me."

"Have you seen yourself yet?"

His hand brushed over his hair. "No." He fixed his eyes on the fire; he had no desire to see himself. The toilet was thankfully free of reflective surfaces, though he'd seen Georg set out a shaving mirror some mornings, usually after Ira teased him for giving scratchy kisses.

Lucifer's fingers spread over his own cheeks. Not a hint of stubble. He'd never seen an angel grow a beard. Maybe some of the new ones could do it, he didn't know any of them. Except Rivka.

Imogen left his side and went to rifle around somewhere else. He could hear the tinkling and he imagined he should have expected it when she returned and held out the small, round mirror to him.

He pushed her hand away before he'd even had a chance to consider looking at himself.

"Sire."

"Imogen, I don't—"

"Look at yourself, sire, and tell me again that the angel was kind to you," she insisted, pressing the mirror into his hand.

He glanced down and caught a glimpse of his hair, unkempt and lank. There was nothing he could do about it, not at this length, anyway.

"It's not what I'm supposed to look like."

She gave him a small smile. "You know you always say that after you come back."

"I do, don't I?"

When her hand closed over his and angled the mirror towards his face, he allowed it.

She asked, "But what are you expecting to see?"

"I don't know," he lied as he turned his eyes towards the mirror.

Structurally, his face had remained the same, the same slope to the cheekbones, the same narrowness to the nose, and proud set to his jaw. The mouth had changed, he supposed, but only if he smiled. The lips went from reasonably and, he thought, handsomely plump to stretched and thin when he smiled a certain type of smile. He poked at the corners of his mouth, giving his best swallow-you-whole grin and found the effect unsettling, especially when his teeth, black like bits of obsidian, showed. Ugly.

The coloring was wrong. The eyes had that uncommon red tint to them, the skin had no color at all, and that resolute blackness of his hair, teeth, and nails.

He knew that his bones would be the same and brushed aside the urge to slit open his arm to check.

He sighed, poking at the circles beneath his eyes and the blue-green veins that showed through his skin. The skin had taken on a slightly more translucent quality since his death. There was a new thinness to the face, too, hollows where there hadn't been before.

"How often did she feed you?" came Imogen's voice, gentler than she had any right to be when speaking to him.

"I don't know."

"And how much?"

"Enough so I wasn't hungry." He didn't like that note of kindness in Imogen's voice; she was his butler, not his friend. She was meant to run his house and make him do the things he needed to do, not to hold his hand while he waffled between wanting his throne and wanting Rivka to bestow another kind touch.

He handed back the mirror.

"You were hungry when we found you," came the reminder.

"I was..." he trailed off. *I was bad.* Even his rebellion in Heaven had not provoked such a response from the Almighty. Barred from Paradise, yes, but not...not held as he had been in that cell.

Even with the full heat of the fire baking his face so dry he thought it might start to crack, even though he was already too close to the flames, he wanted to edge closer, especially when he recalled the darkness of that cell. Especially in the last stretch. He didn't know how long Rivka had left him well and truly alone. He didn't want to know.

If five months had felt like years, then he didn't want to know if he'd been broken by mere weeks in the dark.

He reached his hand towards the flame and the tips of his fingers started to hurt, first only a smarting ache, but then real pain.

Imogen pushed his hand back before the skin could start to bubble. "Hasbani caught some fish."

He didn't know what she wanted him to do with that information.

"Come help me cook."

The corner of his mouth twitched. Imogen didn't eat, which left her cooking skills with something to be desired. He'd been scarfing down more than his fair share, of course, but now that he had a few meals under his belt he could tell that becoming better acquainted with things like salt wouldn't do her any harm.

He followed her to the kitchen. The fish had already been gutted and scaled. He poked at them, trying to recall what kind of fish they were and how best to cook them. Bits of information like that were slippery, but that had nothing to do with dying and more to do with living too long.

"Eyeshines," he whispered.

"Hmm?"

"That's what Elisa used to call them when she was little. Good fried." He tilted the fish and the eyes, still clear, flashed in the firelight.

Imogen made a gesture that suggested he should do as he saw fit.

In almost no time at all, he rediscovered the easy rhythm he usually had in the kitchen. Cooking had a set of rules and, as long as he paid attention to what he was doing, things couldn't go disastrously awry. Ingredients and utensils had no will of their own and he found comfort in that.

Still, he watched the shadows out of the corner of his eye as he worked.

Imogen remained nearby to help him locate anything he might need or to tell him that they didn't have any.

"Are you sure we haven't got any more garlic?"

"I looked twice, sire."

He clucked his tongue and eyed the two cloves she'd been able to scrounge up. "People are going to get the wrong idea about you. Vampires and all that."

"About me? We'd have garlic if *you'd* leave that hole in your chest alone. I brought a dozen heads at least. Or did you want it to get infected?" she asked.

"Ah."

She raised her eyebrows. "That's what I thought."

He turned back to the pan, resigning himself to not having enough garlic.

"And I didn't think we'd be out here for so long," Imogen admitted.

"How long did you think we'd be out here?"

"A week or two. But I didn't anticipate finding you in such a state."

Embarrassment bubbled in his gut. He poked at the fish, wanting to flip it so he had something to do, but knew it wasn't ready to be flipped. He rubbed his nose and cleared his throat.

Imogen didn't say anything, but Lucifer could feel her eyes boring into his back. He tried to ignore it. He had little luck and finally glanced back at her once the fish had been flipped.

"Just say it," he demanded.

She gave him a wide-eyed look of misunderstanding. "What do you mean, sire?"

"Whatever it is you want from me."

"I want to see you well."

With a roll of his eyes, he gave a grunt and gave the fish a poke, shredding the delicate flesh. He grunted again and crossed his arms. "Then you won't mind staying out here a while longer, then."

"I want you to stop feeling sorry for yourself and figure out how to get rid of that binding. The city is going to shit, you know that, don't you? There's all kinds of nasty souls running amok. The people, *your* people are frightened."

The bubbling in his stomach doubled and he feared he wouldn't hold anything down for much longer.

She said, "You told me once that it was my job to look after the city, too."

"I recall."

It had been the first day she'd worked for him, when he'd been giving her a tour of the palace and grounds, before she'd gone by Imogen and long before she'd worked up the nerve to grow her hair and don a dress anywhere but in secret. He'd taken her up to the highest tower in the library and shown her the view of the city from such a height. He'd pointed out the lazy wind of the River Elbe and the mountains in the distance, the Empty Plains where the souls fell.

He had told her, "You aren't just working for me, you know, you're working for all of them."

"I don't follow."

"Sometimes I need a push. Sometimes I need reminding."

"What kind of reminding?" she'd asked. Her voice had been different back then, not in pitch but in the amount of bitterness it had held. Everything in those first years had been a growl or a snarl; now her words came out delightfully husky.

"That I care for all the things I've created. You're to help me care for this city. It's more than just a household I've asked you to watch over. I hope you're up to it."

"I'll do my job," she'd grumbled with an irritated tug at her suit jacket.

He came back to the present and took the fish from the pan before it burned.

"I don't want to push you too far, sire, God knows you've had enough of that," Imogen said, "But you cannot stay out here forever. Your city needs you."

"I know." And he did. "I have to go back."

She let out a groan. "I thought you were made of stronger stuff, I really did. What did that angel do to you?"

He glanced over. "No. I have to go back. But not yet." His fingers brushed over the wound in his chest. "I'll try to think of the angels that might help me. Get that little gray wretch to bring me up."

"It's good to hear you say that."

As he put another fish in the pan, he felt the need to remind, "Saying and doing are entirely different. I don't know if there's an angel that would do more than spit on me."

When dinner had been cooked and the other three had come inside, Lucifer felt older and uncommonly maternal. Sometimes these types of feelings bloomed in his chest, but normally only when confronted with an actual child. They were so young, the three of them; Imogen had some years under her belt, but these other three weren't much more than children.

He brushed aside those thoughts, especially when he considered that he'd definitely had sex with Georg and the others seemed to think that he'd done the same with Ira.

He forgot about feeling maternal altogether when Georg hooked his foot around Lucifer's ankle and told him, "Better cooking than we've had since we got out here."

The compliment sent a wave of heat through him and he could feel his cheeks burning so hot that he knew his face had to be pink all over.

Georg gave him a broad grin and he had to look away.

He spent the rest of dinner with his eyes fixed on his plate, methodically picking out and stacking all the little bones from his meal. When his plate had been cleared and he had nothing with which to occupy his hands, he realized how dry his lips had become from his time so close to the fire.

It started with chewing and then moved to picking. He picked at the rough bits of skin, peeling them off but even that didn't satisfy him. Before he knew it, the taste of blood permeated his mouth and his fingers were scrabbling towards a knife that hadn't been cleared yet. His other hand grasped one lip and tugged it down.

He'd gotten the knife halfway to his mouth before a hand grabbed his wrist and yanked it down.

"Lu, that's not a great idea," Ira told him, thoroughly startling him, not in the way that made him jump, but that made him freeze up for a moment.

He pulled his wrist back and left the knife on the table. "Nobody calls me that."

"I do."

"The sentiment stands," Lucifer replied, a little unnerved at how close he'd come to slicing his lips right off his face without even realizing it.

He'd hoped to see hurt or disappointment flash across Ira's face, but all he got was a resigned sigh and a tired look.

Georg, on the other hand, absolutely glowered at him and slid his arms around Ira's shoulders, drawing the smaller man into a hug. He nuzzled his face against Ira's and told him, "Don't worry, dear, he's going to feel like an absolute ass when he remembers who you are."

The thought of killing Ira reared up again in Satan's mind. It would be easy, even weakened as he was, and it would make it so that nobody kept telling him that someday he'd remember taking this little nothing of a demon as not just a casual fuck or a lover but his public companion.

"Angels," Imogen reminded as he took his leave from the table and curled up in his hammock.

He couldn't comfortably stretch out in the hammock and his spindly body demanded the luxury of stretching out in the as yet unslept-in bed. He couldn't, though, the bed was too far from the fireplace and too close to the trundle bed that Georg and Ira shared.

He curled up in the hammock, drawing his blankets in all around himself while he tried to think of an angel who would come to his aid and not of sinking his teeth into the little demon's throat.

A day did not bring to mind any of his former brethren who would lend him a helping hand. It also didn't do much to banish his thoughts of killing Ira.

He needed a distraction.

A few hours spent organizing the kitchen cabinets and avoiding the shadows did nothing to improve his disposition. Even alphabetizing the bookshelf had no effect. When there was nothing left to do inside, he spent a full hour lingering near the door, thinking about going out. When he finally managed to brave the outdoors, he found Georg sitting on the shore of the lake and nudged his thigh with the side of his foot. "Come inside."

The young man looked up at him. "I'm reading."

Lucifer squinted out over the water. It should have been a beautiful sight, he should have appreciated it more after so long held in that cell. "You can read later. Come inside."

This time Georg didn't so much as glance his way. "Maybe I don't want to. Maybe I already got everything I wanted from you."

The thought had not crossed Lucifer's mind. It rested firmly within the realm of possibility that he'd only been a notch in the lad's belt. Not everyone could say they'd fucked the Devil. "Please."

"You really know how to sweep me off my feet."

Ira, who had been lying on his stomach beside the younger man, piped, "He wants you to—"

Georg smacked Ira with his book. "Shut up. He can figure it out on his own."

Lucifer caught the gilded letters that glimmered on the cover, *Compendium of Those Who Remained Vol.1* by Sinayah Wu, who was not one of the Fallen, but the daughter of one. It was dry reading, but he recalled when the half-human had come to Hell seeking knowledge about the angels who hadn't joined him in his fall. At first, he'd turned her away, but she'd persisted and he'd always had a soft spot for people who didn't take no for an answer. She'd given him a copy as thanks.

Ira let out a little chuckle and grinned at Georg, his finger sliding between the pages to mark his spot.

Georg swooped in to press a kiss to his lips. It started as a small kiss but turned to one that Lucifer couldn't take his eyes from, watching Georg's tongue slip past Ira's lips. He forgot about the book and filled up with a familiar but always unsettling mixture of lust, hunger, and murderous intent. A small whine escaped his lips and he nudged Georg again. "Come inside."

Georg pulled away from Ira, grinning. "Do you mind?"

"Have fun, kitten."

Georg kissed him once more.

Lucifer took the young man by the arm, pulling him to his feet.

Inside or out, it didn't matter to him anymore and Lucifer would have taken him in full view of all the others, but Georg grasped his hand and lead him inside before he could make any suggestions to that end.

"You could ask a little nicer," Georg reminded as they passed through the doorway.

"I could ask a lot less nicely, too."

Georg dropped his hand. "You'll get nothing out of being mean to me. I don't go for that, not even if you're paying me."

Lucifer hadn't expected such a reaction and mumbled an apology. This venture felt foolish, now, and he had half a mind to tell Georg to go back outside.

"What's got you in a mood?" the young man demanded.

"I need to think about something else."

Georg looked him over, the expression his face somewhere between pity and affection, gave an understanding nod, and twined his fingers with Lucifer's again. "I know what to do for that."

He maneuvered Lucifer onto the edge of the bed, then climbed onto his lap, straddling him, making Lucifer forget that an instant ago he'd thought about asking him to go. The pressure of his mouth banished his hesitance altogether and in moments, he found his fingers scrabbling over Georg's skin, his teeth nipping here and there.

Georg rolled his hips, closing the last bit of a gap between them, then slipped his hand between the Devil's legs. His fingers barely slid over his length but that was enough to have Lucifer crying out.

The body wasn't new, but it had died, and he remained more sensitive to some sensations than he would have been normally. It wasn't bad, but it made things go quickly. Georg hadn't seemed to mind last time, he'd even giggled and give him a kiss when Lucifer had mumbled that it had been a while.

Georg moved from the bed to his knees, his fingers undoing Lucifer's trousers as he went. He didn't waste time teasing or removing the rest of Lucifer's trousers, either, but slid his tongue over the head of Lucifer's cock right away.

It elicited a moan and a shiver.

"Lay back," Georg advised, resting his hand on Lucifer's chest and giving him a gentle push. "I'll make it last, too, keep your mind busy for a while."

Heeding his advice, Lucifer lay back, his eyes squeezing closed when Georg's lips encircled him.

This was the distraction he'd needed, something easy and calm, that filled him his head with thoughts of nothing but the wet heat of Georg's mouth. He wouldn't have to worry about a single thing, he could pretend that he wasn't shirking his duty and half-mad to boot.

He thought about nothing, especially not Ira.

He focused on the small sounds that Georg made and barely recognized the sounds coming from his own mouth.

Something niggled at the back of his mind, something he hadn't noticed when he'd been eyeing the shadows and waiting for them to fill up the room, or when he'd been gnawing all the skin from around his fingernails.

There was a wall there, something built to keep things in.

Better to leave things as they were, who knew what was so bad that he would lock it away.

Except.

Except it would be easy to push past that wall right now, his body filled up with peace, with heat and a lazy euphoria. What could be so bad, really? What could be worse than where he'd been?

He pushed.

Then he remembered.

"Stop," he said, starting to sit up. "Stop, stop."

"What?" Georg pulled back. "What's wrong?"

"Ira."

"What about him?"

"I remember."

"Oh." Georg wiped his mouth on his wrist. "Oh!"

Lucifer stared at him for a moment, then started to rush, things coming together all at once as he tucked himself back into his clothes. All of a sudden there was nothing more he needed in the world than to see Ira. He needed it more than he'd ever needed Georg's mouth around his cock.

He found the demon still lying on the shore of the lake, but on his back now. He'd put his book aside and had his eyes closed. Lucifer rushed over to him, almost breaking into a run, and dropped to his knees beside him, skittering his hands over the demon's chest.

With a small shout, Ira sat up and scrambled away, his face twisted with worry, as though he thought the Devil would have some malicious intent.

"Raspberries," Lucifer said.

"What?"

"You were reading. I thought you were your brother at first."

"Oh."

"*Ira.*" Even the name felt good to say. "Oh, fuck. Shit. I'm…" He didn't have the words for what he felt.

Ira stared at him, concerned still scrawled across his face, and Lucifer knew that he'd ruined everything. What had taken more than a year to build had all been undone in less than a month. Sorry wasn't the right word, an apology couldn't suffice. This, more than anything, would be his undoing. To remember him and to have lost him anyway.

His fingers reached for the hole in his chest; maybe he could push through to his heart and take it out, make it stop twisting and aching like that.

Ira pushed his hand down. "You need to stop doing that, you're making it worse."

He held on to Ira's hand, staring down at the fingers, dark gray stark and lovely against the white of his own. The individual fingers became hard to make out through the blur of tears.

Ira took his hand back and Lucifer heard the rustle of clothes.

What he thought would be Ira's flight turned out to be an embrace.

Ira put his arms around his neck and pulled him in close, pressing a kiss to the side of his head.

Lucifer crumpled against him, ruined. He shouldn't have been weeping, he should have been making things right. He should have been finding a way to fix forgetting about him, to get them back to where they should have been.

"You haven't got to apologize," Ira assured, making Lucifer realize that the inane words he'd been mumbling had been variations on 'I'm sorry.' "You had a rough go, love."

"Tell me I'm yours."

"Of course you are, Lu, of course, you are." Ira's voice had a shake to it. He placed a hand on the back of Lucifer's head, drawing him in tighter, and kissed the top of it. "There you go, love, go on. You're alright."

Lucifer continued to blubber into the smaller man's chest. Ira made small shushing noises until the Devil went still, the wound over his heart aching from the exertion of crying like that. He sank lower in Ira's grip, nestling his face into the demon's lap.

"What'd you do to him?" Imogen demanded, her voice coming from somewhere above them.

"He's remembered," Georg said.

Lucifer had not noticed him come down from the house or that he'd seated himself a foot or so away from them, legs crisscrossed and his elbows resting on his knees. He had his chin propped on one fist like he was watching some entertaining display.

"All of it?" she asked.

"All of it," the Devil confirmed. Later, he would have to sort through all these memories and put away the ones he didn't like to keep floating around in his head.

"And how does that sit with us, sire?" Imogen inquired.

"Poorly."

"Mmm, I thought it might. I'd hoped you'd do your remembering with a little more finesse."

"What have I ever done with finesse?"

Ira's fingers traced circles along his scalp and it sent prickles all over his skin.

"I was thinking about killing you." Lucifer ran a finger over the fabric of Ira's trousers until the texture made the pad of his finger go numb.

"I accidentally helped usurp your throne."

He pushed himself up and scrubbed his hands over his face, hoping to restore some sense of clarity. It didn't work. Thoughts tumbled over each other in his mind. "I've got to talk with him. The rest of you should go away."

Georg and Imogen glanced at each other, then at Ira, who gave them a nod.

Once the other two had gone, he picked at the worn silk of his shirt. "Things were an awful mess last time we really saw each other."

"You had a knife in your chest, yes, I recall that."

It mustn't have been easy to witness, but that hadn't been what Lucifer had meant. "About Tabby. That night. Shit, it was...not ideal. We didn't get a chance for anything to settle."

"What do you want to talk about?"

"I don't know. It feels like something we should talk about."

"I don't want to talk about her. I don't want to talk about any of it," Ira said.

"What do you want? Not in a general sense, of course."

Ira picked bits of grass off his trousers. "I wanted you back. I didn't think much past that."

"I see."

"I know that before all of this you'd made mention of wanting more—"

"I want as much as you're willing to give, nothing else."

"You haven't got to lie, Lu, or try to cover things up because you think I'll rebuff you," Ira assured him.

"You won't rebuff me?"

"I'll do my best to be nice about it if I do. Please, don't make me parse this all out now. I haven't been able to even talk to you in ages."

Lucifer nodded.

"I missed you."

He nodded again and made himself ask the question he'd been dreading since he sat up. He didn't have any interest in hearing Ira say something that would shred him apart, but he needed to know. "Have things changed between us?"

"I'd say so, darling, I watched you die."

"Oh." The word came out as no more than a hoarse whisper.

"It made things clear. More clear than they had been. You haven't got to look so nervous, love, and I told you to *stop* trying to pick at your chest." Ira took his hand and pushed it away from his chest again. "I'm going to have Imogen bind it up again. Look at me."

Lucifer raised his eyes to Ira's face.

"Things are going to be strange for a while, I think. Until we've got you unbound and back on the throne, until you've had time to readjust to being out of that cell. But, uh, I guess what I'm getting at is that if you'd still like for us to be an official pair, then I'd like that too. I'd like to go on as what we were before the mess with your wife and the throne."

"Oh." Lucifer swallowed. "Yes."

"Yes, you'd like that?'

"Yes, I'd like that," Lucifer confirmed. "Do you think that maybe we ought to make it, well, you know, official on paper?"

"Is that more or less official than carving it into my skin?" the demon asked, his mouth tipped into a smile.

Lucifer's stomach clenched.

Ira tightened his grip on his hand. "Forget I said anything. We can talk about all this some other time. You look terrible. Have you eaten yet?"

"No. All the shadows started to come out and I had to fix the fire."

Ira let out a sigh and gathered Lucifer into his arms again. "Then let's get you something to eat. Do the shadows do that a lot?"

"Yes."

This time the demon huffed. He pushed himself to his feet, brushing off his trousers, then tugged on Lucifer's shirt. "Come on, get up."

He stood and it felt wrong, suddenly, to be taller than him. if he could have changed his shape he would have wanted to shrink down into something small enough to curl in his arms. "Ira."

"Hmm?"

"I love you."

"I love you, too."

"More than I should."

"I swear if you start telling me that you're going to hold me captive," he warned but didn't finish the thought.

Lucifer felt the need to probe, "You'll do what?"

Ira rubbed his face and kept it cradled in his palms for a moment, then he murmured, "I might just fucking let you," without looking at the Devil. He rubbed his eyes then gave Lucifer a push towards the house.

Even though he wasn't hungry, Lucifer let Ira goad him into eating with sighs and huffy stares when he didn't finish everything on his plate.

"Tell me..." he began but trailed off. It didn't feel right to ask about this so soon, he didn't want Ira to think he'd already moved on. He played with his fork.

"Tell you what?"

"You went to see Felix."

Ira's face softened. "I did."

Checking the urge to wrap his arms around Ira, he asked, "How is he?"

Ira's eyes followed the movement of his hand towards his waist and its retreat. He moved into his arms and recounted his visit to see the child. While he spoke, his fingers constantly found their way to Lucifer's hair, sliding through the shaggy locks.

"I can't believe what she did to your hair."

"I did it."

Ira pulled back, his nose wrinkled. "Why?"

"I couldn't get it clean."

With a small sigh, Ira touched his forehead to Lucifer's. His hands cradled the Devil's cheeks. "So you don't know *any* angels?"

The question struck him as out of place juxtaposed with the tenderness of their posture. He had felt treasured a moment ago, a far cry from the crawling feeling of worthlessness that had settled over him recently. The question brought back that sense of being useless.

"I know a lot of angels. The problem is that they don't like me."

Ira said, "You don't seem to like them much either. Wu has an addendum for every entry, you know, just for what you had to say."

Lucifer didn't know what he meant; he'd never bothered to read the volumes Wu had given to him.

"Samael takes himself too serious, Uriel never shuts up, Jophiel is a snitch," he recited, "Thus spoke Lucifer."

"Jophiel *is* a snitch."

Ira sniggered and put his arms around Lucifer's neck, kissing his cheek. "You look *awful.*"

"I'm sorry." He wanted suddenly to hide his face.

"And not your usual sort of awful," Ira continued.

"My usual sort?" He didn't like to think that he usually looked awful.

"You know, the...the eat-you-up smile and the slinky prowling around, the good kind of awful."

"Oh."

Ira seemed to realize he'd hurt Lucifer's feelings and caught his mouth in a kiss. "It's a really delicious kind of awful."

"But it's still awful."

"Would you like it better if I was calling you beautiful?"

"I never thought that lies were part of our relationship."

"They aren't, darling." Ira moved in again, his kiss feather soft.

As much as Lucifer wanted to pull back and accuse Ira of trying to soothe his ego, he wanted the kiss more. He reached up to rake his fingers through the demon's curls, an uncommon surge of envy rumbling through his chest. It had never happened before, and it took him a while to place the source of the feeling.

It was the hair.

It was more than that. It was the healthy smoothness of his skin, the softness of his lips, the suppleness of his flesh. He wasn't some scrapped together thing, a feeble jumble of bones and skin with a permanent hole in his chest.

Suddenly, Lucifer was hungry, despite the bits of food that Ira had made him consume. He didn't want bits of bread and cheese or a few apple slices, he wanted flesh, raw and dripping and *hot*, torn from the bone.

He wanted the little demon trembling, absolutely quaking. His fingers dug into the meat on Ira's ribs.

"Ow."

He put his mouth to Ira's throat, his teeth digging in, aching for the snap of sinew and the easy chew of raw meat.

"*Ow*." Ira pulled back, his hands firmly planted on the Devil's shoulders.

"I'm sorry." He was, he hadn't meant to hurt him, he hadn't even realized what he was doing.

Rubbing the set of teeth marks on his neck, Ira removed himself from the Devil's lap. "I think you broke the skin." He sounded incredulous more than angry.

Lucifer shook his head. He hadn't tasted anything but skin, though he could see a blood blister on his neck. "I'm sorry. I..." He rubbed his face. "I don't know what came over me."

He hadn't tried anything like that with Georg, but then again, Georg didn't inspire the same kind of feelings in his chest. He didn't feel the need to make Georg part of himself or to put bits of himself into Georg.

He wanted Ira back in his arms and ran his fingertips over Ira's arm, taking a loose hold of his wrist. "Ira."

The younger man rubbed at the bite mark. "I know, I know. It...it just *hurt*."

"I'm sorry."

"Don't get dramatic about it," Ira warned. He put a hand on Lucifer's shoulder and kissed the top of his head. "How've you been sleeping?"

"Well enough."

Ira snorted.

"Terribly."

"Maybe the hammock has something to do with it."

He ducked his head and bit his lip. "I can't sleep anywhere else."

"You're not sleeping in there," Ira pointed out. "What harm can it do?"

"I'm not tired," he lied. Exhaustion had seeped into his very bones, but he didn't think sleeping would do much to improve that kind of tiredness.

Ira rolled his eyes and didn't say anything more about sleeping. "You've got that look on your face."

"What look?"

"The one where you're thinking about things I can't understand."

"Ah."

"You want me to leave you to it?" Ira asked.

If Ira never left his side again it would be too soon. He shook his head.

"Then come outside. It's about a thousand degrees in here, I'm sweating like...well, I was going to say like a pig, but—"

"Pigs don't sweat that much."

Ira moved in close and gave him a quick kiss. "Exactly." He tangled his fingers with Lucifer's and gave the barest hint of a tug.

It was enough to get Lucifer on his feet, following Ira out the door all the way down to the lake without a single thought. With his hand in Ira's, he didn't feel so much like the sky would fall down at any minute.

Georg still had a pencil tucked behind his ear and his head bent over the first volume of Wu's book and he saw that Ira had been reading the second.

"What's got you two reading about angels?" he asked as Ira drew him down to sit. He sprawled out on the grass and then curled on his side. His back felt exposed like that so he rolled onto his stomach, giving himself a better view of who might be approaching.

"Because you need angel magic," Georg reminded.

"And you're sure we can't just ask one of the Fallen, right?" Ira asked. "I'm sure June would—"

"I wouldn't advise it," Georg interrupted. "Angels get, uh, sort of queer when it comes to the Fallen. Corruption and all that so a lot of their spells are safeguarded against unholy things."

"Listen to you, when did you become an expert on angels?" Lucifer teased.

Georg didn't seem to recognize his teasing and waved a hand. "There was a whole section in my Principles of Magics course. About which kinds of magic not to mess with. Angels and fairies." He ticked them off on his fingers.

Lucifer considered that maybe seeing Georg as a flighty slut had been an oversight. He was that, for sure, and it was a delightful thing to be, but Lucifer took comfort knowing that the Record Office would be in good hands when Georg inherited it.

He peered at the book in Georg's lap and saw pencil marks on the page. "You wrote in my book."

"You never read it. The binding wasn't even cracked."

"You're a monster."

"Don't be dramatic," Georg scoffed.

Not feeling dramatic but absolutely justified, he continued, "Absolutely abhorrent. I'm disgusted. It's beyond words."

"If it's beyond words then you should shut up," Georg murmured, his eyes still on the book. He flipped the page.

Ira advised, "Don't try to talk to him while he's reading. It makes him grumpy." He took up his own book and rested his head on Lucifer's back. The book remained closed, though, sitting on his chest.

Lucifer rested his head on his arms, his face turned towards Ira.

Eventually, the book did open and the other two remained absorbed in their reading until dinner time.

Ira had paused in his reading to rest his eyes a little and get a drink of water. He'd brought one to Georg, too, because although they'd convinced the Devil not to let the fire burn so high, it was still warm in the house.

Hasbani had a sheen of sweat across his brow and wet patches on his shirt.

Ira went over and banked the fire a little more, earning looks of approval from the others but one of distaste from the Devil.

Imogen had already thrown open the windows.

"Listen to this one," Georg said. "The Devil notes here that Demiel is an utter piece of shit. Do you have anything nice to say about anyone? And that's the information you have to give to this poor woman? Making her write something like that in what was *clearly* an academic endeavor."

"Are you still reading that?" Lucifer asked.

"Yes."

"*Why?*"

"I was under the impression that we needed an angel. Ira pointed out that the new ones probably wouldn't have any cause to help you."

Ira went over to Georg and looped an arm across his chest, resting his chin on the younger man's head. "And Georg wondered if some of the older angels might have some lingering fondness for you."

"Which I'm starting to doubt," Georg admitted, "If they feel about you how you feel about them. Haniel is something to look at, that's for sure but doesn't have much in the way of brains. Perhaps the Almighty was feeling particularly shallow when He created that one. You're *mean*, you know that?"

Lucifer couldn't help but smile.

Every so often Georg read another line out loud, but other than that, the only sound was the clink of Hasbani doing the dishes.

The sky had darkened and Ira's eyes started to droop, no doubt aided by the emotional exertion of the day. Things between him and Lucifer still had an uneasy feel, but it was better than the emptiness of before.

He stretched up on his toes and yawned, feeling the Devil's eyes on him.

"Tired?" Lucifer asked.

Ira nodded. They'd agreed to continue on as official but agreeing was different than doing. He didn't know what Lucifer intended anymore and that bite on his neck had worried him a little. He didn't think the Devil had ill intentions, but he did have instincts that Ira didn't fully understand.

"I might turn in." His hand went to Georg's back on instinct.

Georg took up his hand and pressed a kiss to Ira's knuckles. "You go ahead. I want to do a little more reading."

The Devil's eyes had been fixed on the two of them the whole time and when Ira glanced over at him, he had that hungry look in his eyes again.

It made him hesitate to ask, but he asked anyway, "What about you, love? Are you tired?"

Lucifer's gaze darted to the hammock.

That Ira couldn't abide. Sleeping scrunched up in a hammock wouldn't do him any good and, more than that, Ira didn't want him there. He offered his hand and long enough passed that Ira thought he wouldn't take it.

When he did, Ira's knees went a little weak with relief.

Neither of them spoke on the short journey between the kitchen and the bed, nor as they disrobed. It turned an act that took no more than ten minutes into a lengthy process, full of aborted glances and awkward smiles.

Ira had imagined their reunion differently; he hadn't considered it possible that so much time would pass between seeing the Devil and being recognized by him.

Lucifer scooted into the bed, ungainly enough that a fond grin spread across Ira's face.

"What?" the Devil whispered.

Ira shook his head and crawled into bed beside him, only pulling up one of the thin sheets. "Trying to roast us alive, aren't you?"

"It's too dark." Lucifer hadn't relaxed into the mattress but huddled up in the corner, his knees drawn to his chest.

"Come here."

"I..."

"Come here," Ira insisted, "Let me hold you, love, and if it's still too dark for you then we'll find a tealight."

Slowly the Devil unfolded from the corner. He lay on his side and Ira slid right up behind him, putting one arm beneath his head and the other over his chest. Skinny as Lucifer was, it wasn't a feat to wrap him up entirely. His arm would go numb before the night was out, but it was a small price to pay to do this again.

He brushed his lips over Lucifer's shoulder; the other man vibrated, about ready to crawl out of his skin. "Shh, darling. Try to breathe." He made the conscious effort to slow his own breathing, hoping Lucifer would match his pace.

"I can't."

"A little longer."

The Devil acquiesced but after another minute, he whimpered, "Please, I can't."

"Alright." It wouldn't do any good to torture him like this. "Alright, I'll be back in a second."

He slipped out of bed and went over to Georg, whispering his request for a small light. He hadn't meant to whisper but the words had stuck in his throat. Georg conjured him a dim, red light and said, "Hansel used to make these for me."

"Thank you."

Before he could head back, Georg put a hand on his arm. "If the two of you want space..."

"Kitten..." Ira felt guilty even broaching the idea.

"I understand."

"Just for a little while, until we've settled in more."

"I don't have to sleep in the other bed, either," Georg offered.

"Now you're just being silly." Ira squeezed his hand. "You're still my dearest friend. You know that, don't you?"

"Yes."

Ira didn't quite trust the melancholy note in Georg's voice. "We promised."

The younger man gave him a small smile. "Of course."

Ira brought the light back to Lucifer, who had curled into a ball. He hung the conjured light in the air beside the headboard. "Better?"

Lucifer gave a nod.

When Ira had lain back down and put his arms around Lucifer again, the Devil uncoiled somewhat. By the time his breathing evened out and his body went slack, he'd tangled his legs with Ira's and given Ira's fingers a gentle nibble.

The next morning, Lucifer kept one hand firmly on Ira at all times and would, at least once an hour, bring some part of Ira to his mouth and give it a tentative bite. Never as hard as he'd done the first time, but always catching a bit of Ira's flesh between his teeth.

"Izidkiel is a drunk," Georg pronounced over their midday meal.

Lucifer paused with Ira's hand brought halfway to his mouth. "Poor sod really is."

"That almost sounded like affection." Georg looked up from the book and looked at Ira. "Love, are you really going to let him keep chewing on you like that?"

Ira shrugged. It didn't hurt that much. It felt almost reassuring and more than a little possessive, which sat fine with him considering that a day ago Lucifer hadn't cared for him at all. He tightened his grip on the Devil's hand. "It doesn't bother me."

Georg sighed at him. "Anyway. You're meant to be reading, too."

"I finished my half."

"You did not! You don't read faster than me!"

Ira reached over and tucked a lock of hair behind his ear. "No, but I also didn't spend all morning in bed."

Color crept becomingly across Georg's face. "So you didn't find anyone?"

"Tzadkiel is the angel of mercy," Ira said with a shrug. "And a soft-touch, apparently."

"You didn't think that was worth mentioning?" Imogen demanded.

Ira shook his head. "Not really." He glanced towards Lucifer, feeling guilty. "His idea of a soft-touch probably isn't the same as ours."

Imogen sighed and eyed the mark the Devil had left on his neck. "Maybe you're right. Sire?"

"Tzadkiel...well, she isn't exactly my idea of a soft-touch, to be honest. Wu had some difficulty detecting sarcasm," Lucifer admitted. "But she does take her job seriously. She...well, she could show mercy, but it's just as likely to be the kind of mercy that has you slitting your daughter's throat before she can sin."

"Oof." Georg marked his page and set it down. "Are you willing to risk that?"

The Devil's face contorted, then he shrugged. "I don't have a lot of other options, do I? I've got to ask someone for help. Might as well start with her."

"Or we could start with the drunk," Ira suggested. "Sounds like more your type."

Lucifer gave him a smile and drew Ira's hand to his mouth; he pressed a kiss to the knuckles.

Ira tightened his hand reflexively, ready for the bite that was sure to come. It did, but gentler than normal, not even as hard as a pinch, leaving the barest impression on his skin. The look in his eyes was hungry, but it was the most affectionate type of hungry that Ira had ever seen.

"We'll start with Tzadkiel," the Devil told them, the most decisive he'd sounded in ages.

"When?" Ira asked.

The strength in his voice faded when he suggested, "Now, probably, would be best."

Ira nodded, his stomach quivering at the idea of having to touch on the strings that bound the worlds again. He swallowed and hoped he would be able to keep down his lunch.

Lucifer stood, straightened his clothes, and nodded towards Georg. "We'll need you, too, Master Schreiber."

"What for?"

"I can't summon her if I'm still bound. We'll need to pay a visit to that awful Reinhart man."

Georg huffed. "No way around that?"

"What did Hiram do to you anyway?" Ira asked, recalling the coldness between the two of them.

Georg rubbed his nose and didn't look at either of them. "Some of the things he had to say about our illustrious Prince weren't particularly flattering."

Lucifer grinned. "Just think how glad dear Hiram will be to see me in person."

"You should go armed," Imogen advised.

"I don't think so. Doesn't exactly scream 'trust me,' does it?" Lucifer's eyes danced over Georg, over his smooth shoulders and the easy muscle of his arms and chest. "But Georg might consider putting on a touch more in the way of clothing."

"Is it going to be boiling hot up there?" the younger man demanded with a scowl.

"No."

Georg grumbled as he dressed and once he had, the Devil asked, "Shall we?" His hand crept across Ira's shoulder and then skimmed down his arm, molding over Ira's hand the same way he had last time they'd traversed realms. He offered his other hand to Georg.

Georg twined his fingers with Lucifer's.

Ira sucked in a deep breath and dug his teeth into his lip as soon as he felt the slither of reality over his fingertips. When Lucifer guided his hand to one of the strings, he jerked back as soon as he touched it. Knowing what it would feel like made it that much worse.

Lucifer tightened his grip on Ira's hand and kissed the top of his head. It was a small comfort, but it abated the roiling in his stomach somewhat.

Of course, the roiling doubled when Lucifer closed his hand over one of the strings. "Pull."

Ira pulled and a moment later, they were standing not just in Pickering but in the living room of Hiram and Phaedrus. He stumbled and expected his knees to hit the floor, but Lucifer gathered him up and held him close.

"I've got you," Lucifer murmured.

"I'm going to throw up."

"Keep breathing."

He swallowed, his mouth filled up with saliva. Being sick remained a real possibility.

The Devil's hand moved slowly over his arm. "You're alright, you are, keep breathing," he soothed.

Ira nodded and scrubbed his sleeve over his cheeks to get rid of the tears. He pulled in a breath through his nose, which made an unattractive noise as he'd sucked in a lot of snot. He blinked back the tears and looked up when there came a lot of clattering from the stairs.

Hiram, mostly undressed, came running down the stairs with his fingers crooked and a nasty looking orb glimmering between them. "You!" the mage barked. The spell in his hand didn't fade once he recognized them.

"Peace, Reinhart," Lucifer warned, his arms still around Ira.

"You know decent people give notice, they don't just show up."

"Darling?" Phaedrus appeared on the balcony that overlooked the living room, a robe half-pulled on.

The Devil gave a gleeful chuckle.

"I heard you were missing," Phaedrus said.

"No way to greet your Prince," Lucifer scolded.

Phaedrus pulled on their robe the rest of the way and descended the stairs, passing their husband on the way down. They knelt before the Devil, though Ira noted that they didn't lower their head and touch it to the floor.

Lucifer raised an eyebrow.

Phaedrus narrowed their eyes.

"Just a little, for old time's sake," Lucifer said, a pout on his lips.

Phaedrus dipped their head forward enough to expose the back of their neck but didn't touch their forehead to the floor.

Once Phaedrus had completed their bow, Lucifer said, "Rise."

Phaedrus stood and gave the Devil a long look. "What can I do for you, my Prince?"

"I need his books."

Hiram, on the stairs still, tucked himself into his trousers more securely. "I don't owe you anymore. I've done the favor you asked of me."

Lucifer turned his eyes to Hiram, widening them to a beguiling size. "Is that all Felix is to you?" he whispered.

Hiram made a sound of disgust.

"Speaking of the boy."

"He's asleep," Hiram informed him.

Lucifer nodded and Ira thought he saw disappointment flit across his face. "Just the book, then."

"Don't be stupid, Hiram; he's sleeping, you can still look at him when he's sleeping." Phaedrus put their hand on Lucifer's elbow.

They pulled Lucifer away, leading him towards the stairs, leaving Ira standing there, still uneasy, the feeling of that place still worming through his mind.

Georg put a hand on his shoulder and drew him in.

"Phaedrus!" Hiram protested. "I don't—"

Upstairs, a baby started to squall.

Phaedrus gave Hiram a push. "Nice job, you woke him up."

The human flushed all over.

Phaedrus slipped in close to the man and nipped his earlobe. "You probably would have done that anyway by the time I was done with you."

The pinkness across his skin deepened to red.

"Bring him down to see me!" Georg called to Lucifer as the Devil continued up the stairs.

"Right in my ear," Ira grumbled, stepping out of Georg's grip and rubbing his ear as if would do anything to help.

"I'm sorry."

Hiram watched them from the stairs, distrust scrawled all over his face.

Georg rolled his eyes and urged, "Go on, get dressed, we're not going to do anything."

The mage shook his head.

"You know, for someone married to a demon—" Georg began.

"Phaedrus *isn't* like you."

"And how do you know what I'm like? What we're like?" Georg demanded.

Ira shook his head and pulled Georg closer to him, nestling his face against his shirt. "I wouldn't bother, kitten. He's clearly made up his mind." He sniffled, wishing he could get that feeling out of his head.

Lucifer returned with Felix on his hip, his gaze captured by his son; the room could have been burning and Ira didn't think he would look away. Across his face was the sorriest expression Ira had ever seen, love and loss all muddled together.

Hiram glared daggers at him the whole time and Phaedrus scolded him for it, pulling him into the kitchen and hissing so softly that Ira couldn't catch what they were saying.

The Devil spoke to his son the whole time, telling him how much he'd missed him, that he was sorry he hadn't visited in such a long time. "You're so big, darling, look how much you've grown."

Ira didn't think the child understood much of it, but then again, he didn't know much about children.

"And how long before he takes him back!" Hiram shouted, his voice carrying out to the living room.

Felix started to fuss.

"Oh, shh, little one, don't worry, just a bit of squawking," Lucifer soothed. He rubbed the child's back. Louder and firmly, he called, "Hiram, come out here."

"And now he thinks he can come into *my house*—"

"Hiram Montgomery Reinhart, come into this room and speak with me. We have business together," Lucifer repeated, his voice not growing in volume, but something about the pitch felt wrong. It was a hair deeper and almost layered.

Phaedrus pushed their husband into the living room. "I'm sorry, my king—"

"No need for apologies." Lucifer turned his gaze to the human. "Hiram, if you have a grievance with your end of our bargain, speak."

The fire seemed to have gone out of the mage when facing Lucifer directly. That sort of thing happened a lot; Ira had seen at least a dozen demons claim they didn't fear their Prince and pale at the very sight of him when he arrived. "No, I, I..."

"You clearly have complaints. What are they? That I visit the child I could not keep?"

"It's...you visit *a lot.*"

"And yet it feels like I never see him." Lucifer brushed the back of his fingers over Felix's cheek with a melancholy tenderness that Ira hadn't seen in him before. Watching the Devil with his son set an odd feeling stirring in Ira's belly, one that almost felt like regret. "It feels like a thousand years between each visit. Do you know what it's like, Hiram, to be away from your child?"

"No, I don't but..." The human looked at the floor, then brought his hand up to rub at his eyes. "I'm afraid I will. I'm afraid you'll take him back."

"I can't," Lucifer said. "I am not a fit parent and Hell would never be safe for him. Those who seek him would find him easily there and...and it seems that I cannot even keep myself safe. He remains with you."

Felix squirmed, kicking his legs and reaching for the floor. Lucifer tightened his arm around him and brushed a kiss across his cheek, then set him on the ground. He watched him carefully make his way over to Phaedrus.

Felix raised his arms and demanded, "Bibi up."

Phaedrus lifted the child and gave Lucifer an apologetic look.

"Besides." Lucifer tightened his hands into fists and Ira would have bet that if someone checked his palms, there would be deep marks cut into the flesh. "I came because I need your books. I need to summon someone."

"Someone?" Hiram asked.

"An angel."

"The books don't work on angels."

"That's what they want you to think. Go on. Volume two, isn't it?" When Hiram didn't move, Lucifer repeated, "Go," with enough force to make Ira recoil.

Hiram hurried up the stairs after that.

"Honestly, you'd think I was coming by every weekend," Lucifer huffed when Hiram had gone.

"He's had a hard time holding on to the ones he loves," Phaedrus reasoned, "Can you blame him for worrying?"

"I'd be a hypocrite if I did."

The Fallen turned a critical eye to the Devil. "You look—"

"Phaedrus, if you tell me I look terrible...!"

"You look tired, my king. Very tired."

"I am bound."

"Grave indeed."

Georg leaned in close and whispered into Ira's ear, "Do you think everyone from Heaven talks like that or just the two of them?"

Ira giggled and tried to stifle it in his hands when Lucifer looked his way. He couldn't stop, though, not even with those awful eyes trained on him. It made things worse, being stared at like that and it lent his giggling a hysterical edge, until he had tears streaming down his face and stitches in his sides.

By the time Hiram came back downstairs with more clothes on and the book tucked under his arm, Ira had stopped laughing, his face aching and his chest echoing with a strange hollowness.

Lucifer took the book. "Thank you. I'll bring it back as soon as we're done."

"Back?" Hiram hissed. "You never said—"

"Or did you think I should summon an angel to your house? I'm sure Tzadkiel would be interested to see where I've been hiding the most recent antichrist."

The mage crossed his arms but didn't argue. "You'll need the dictionary."

Georg raised his eyebrow. "For what?" He held out an expectant hand and Lucifer handed him the tome. He flipped through a few pages. "Long-form script?"

"Germanic," Hiram informed him. "It can be difficult to translate."

Georg chortled and closed the book. "You want difficult I'll send you something out of the Fellborne codices. Purely logographic, written in concentric circles to indicate importance and in alternating direction within the circles to indicate order, left-right and up-down, I swear the fucking translations end up looking like word searches."

"Oh."

"Mmm, people write their entire thesis just translating one page."

"That sounds fascinating," Hiram admitted.

"I really can send you a copy," Georg offered, forgetting his enmity with Hiram, as he always did in the face of being able to have a real discussion with someone.

"*Don't,*" Phaedrus warned, "You've got enough on your plate running a school, you haven't got time to go deciphering the writings of some Hell-born war clan."

Lucifer cleared his throat. "Ira, do you think you could manage to bring us somewhere a little more suited to our task?"

The thought turned his insides to jelly, but he nodded his head. It would be better to do this away from prying eyes and he had made the trip three times already, a fourth wouldn't be his undoing. This was like all unpleasant things; if he endured it enough times, eventually it wouldn't bother him.

Lucifer held out his hand and Ira took it, doing his best the calm his trembling in his own. The Devil tightened those spidery-long fingers around his hand but didn't move them past the skin of reality. His lips tightened and the angle of his head changed slightly, his awful eyes fixed on Ira's face.

"Just do it," Ira insisted, his voice low and, to his shame, shaking.

"No." Lucifer's fingers brushed over his face the same way they'd brushed over Felix's. "I shouldn't be asking this of you." He spoke the words as if he'd realized something terrible about himself.

"I can do it."

"You can do a great many things, love, but I don't want to see you broken because of it."

The way Lucifer looked down at him, Ira almost forgot the others in the room. They hadn't had a moment like this yet, one where Lucifer felt like their Prince instead of a thing that needed to be protected. Ira realized he'd been staring up at him with his lips parted like some untouched schoolboy waiting for his first kiss. He closed his mouth and looked away.

Lucifer cleared his throat again, harder than he had last time. He pulled in a slow, deep breath. "There's...somewhere around here that's empty, there's has to be. We'll find somewhere else."

He led Ira out the door and Georg hurried to keep up, the book tucked under his arm. "You know, I've never summoned anything before, let alone an angel."

"I didn't imagine you had." Lucifer glanced his way.

Georg said, "I'm only pointing this out because it could go wrong."

"Angels are hard to kill."

"That doesn't make me feel like you have faith in my abilities."

"I have a lot of faith in you, Master Schreiber. I wouldn't have brought you along otherwise."

Georg absolutely glowed at that and a petty spark of envy stirred in Ira, envy that Lucifer had faith in Georg but none in him.

A few minutes with a bundle of thin, gray paper left the Devil with ink smudged on his fingertips and, apparently, all the information he needed. Ira trailed behind him and Georg as they walked together and fell to discussing what kinds of changes Georg would need to make to have the spell work properly.

"It's a few simple substitutions, really, I think you'll be able to manage."

"I think so." Georg had the book peeled open already, his finger trailing over the pages briefly before he tucked it back under his arm.

He pulled it back out every so often as they walked and whispered something to himself. Ira knew he itched to sit down and read through the whole thing. Any other day Ira would have found it endearing.

Now, though, he only wondered if unbinding the Devil would also mean putting an end to Ira's usefulness.

"It would be faster if I brought us somewhere," Ira said, still behind the other two, and when neither of them said anything, he repeated the statement more loudly.

Lucifer glanced back at him. "No, you haven't got to worry about it. We can hire a cab."

"Have you got money?"

"What need have I for money?" he asked, then gave a small smile. "I begged a few dollars off Phaedrus before we left. It should suffice."

"Mm."

"No need to worry."

"Mm."

Lucifer's face twisted a little, but he didn't say anything else. He hailed them a cab and asked to be brought to a farm a few miles outside the city limits.

The driver frowned and the expression doubled when Lucifer produced the bundle of notices to show him the exact location. "What business do you have there?"

"Is my business not my own?"

"Three people got hacked up there, I figure it's best to let the dead rest. And I *don't* figure the police would want any rubberneckers," the driver said.

A lie came to the Devil's lips so easily and confidently it made Ira doubt everything the other man had ever said to him. "Of course they don't, but it's my business to help the dead rest. When such evils have been done, it's best to do a cleansing. Master Schreiber?" Georg handed over the book when Lucifer put out his hand. Lucifer flashed the cover and continued. "It's a delicate matter and the remaining family members would like to have it done as soon as possible. They can't sell the farm in good confidence as it is."

"You work with the university?" the man gave the three of them a long look.

In a dark three-piece suit, Ira knew he looked respectable. Georg wore slim trousers with a plain shirt and a cozy cardigan; if he'd had spectacles perched on his nose he would have been the picture of a serious university student. The kohl around his eyes and rouge on his lips skewed the look a little, but Ira figured the real obstacle to the deceit lay with the Devil himself. He looked ill, as well as shabby in his thin, oversized silk clothing.

The Devil gave a solemn nod of his head. The seriousness of his face lent a quality of asceticism to his appearance.

The driver grunted and nodded for them to get into the cab.

The ride to the farm passed in silence, with Lucifer's face turned towards the window and Georg's head bent over the book.

Ira fidgeted, picking lint off his trousers, and wondering what things would actually be like when the Devil had regained his throne. Georg had left behind a life in shambles and Ira wasn't sure how quickly or easily that could be repaired, or if Georg even wanted to repair it. He thought that he should tell him he could continue to share the apartment for as long as he wanted.

"You look bored."

He glanced up to find that Lucifer had fixed his gaze on him.

"You always look like you've got so many better places to be," Lucifer said.

"I know. Mistress used to tell me I should try to look less like I think I'm better than everyone."

The smile that tipped up the corner of Lucifer's mouth wasn't one of his terrible grins, but a small, fond one that inspired almost no horror. "It always felt like interrupting you when I came to trade."

"I...I'm sorry. Mistress didn't like me reading but Nial said that..." A bit of a chuckle escaped. "Nial said it let people know that I was at least old enough to know how to read past chapter books."

Lucifer snorted.

"You don't look *that* young," Georg told him.

"Kitten, haven't they got jokes in that hoity-toity part of the Ninth where you live?" Ira asked.

Georg pursed his lips and returned to his reading.

"I'm not bored," Ira confessed softly.

"No?" Lucifer asked.

"I'm worried."

"About what, love?"

"That things won't go back to how they're supposed to be."

Instead of asking what he meant, Lucifer nodded. "Time will tell. It always does."

"I liked what we had."

Georg stole a guilty glance towards the Devil. Worrying that Lucifer would prefer Georg over him was not high on Ira's list of worries, but it would have been a lie to deny it altogether. That hadn't been what he'd meant, though.

Lucifer didn't ask him to elaborate and the ride's silence returned.

Once the cab brought them to the farm, Lucifer brought them into the farmhouse to procure the pencil Georg requested.

"Don't write in this book," Lucifer warned as he handed over the pencil.

"Then you'd better get me some paper because I'm not about to ad-lib this spell."

With a huff and a fond smile, Lucifer fetched him a pad of paper.

Georg settled in at the kitchen table, the lead scratching pleasantly over the paper as he worked, humming to himself.

Lucifer took Ira by the hand and led him outside to sit on the steps of the porch. The sun hung low in the sky. Ira hadn't witnessed many sunsets but the way that Lucifer stared at the horizon, Ira would have guessed that he'd never even seen one.

Somewhere off to the left of the house, Ira could hear some kind of bird. Chickens, maybe.

"I liked what we had, too," came the quiet confession. "I loved what we had. I don't think we got nearly enough of it."

"You wanted more," Ira reminded.

"I did but it hadn't been much more than a year. I would have waited. I still would."

Ira had to ask, "What if I never wanted the same things as you?"

"I would have tried my best to give you the choice."

A long sigh pushed past his lips and he leaned against Lucifer, resting his head against his arm. "And what if I do want it?"

"I would tell you not to rush."

"Because I don't know..." Ira hesitated. "I don't know if I want it because I'm afraid or because I missed you or because I was going to want it anyway. But I do."

"Do what?"

"Want more. More than a few days at a time."

Nervous fingers slid through the Devil's hair and he licked his lips, his tongue darting out between his obsidian chip teeth. Ira thought he even saw his jaw tremble. "I..." He moved forward, then shook his head and pulled back. "I want to eat you."

It took a moment for Ira to process. The answer wasn't what he'd expected.

"More than just swallowing you whole, I want...I want to make you scared and I want to bite you. Hard. I want meat between my teeth."

Ira scrambled for anything to say. "Uh. Just me?"

Lucifer nodded.

"Why?"

"I..." The slow rise and fall of his thin chest was the only movement between them, the bones showing starkly against his skin. He had his eyes fixed on Ira's face, on his mouth. His hand started to inch up his chest, oozing towards the gaping wound that Imogen had threatened to stitch shut.

Ira put his hand over Lucifer's and pushed it away. He hated watching him push his fingers inside his chest like that, hated it more seeing them come out covered in blood. Making contact seemed to break the spell that had held the Devil still because once their skin touched, he unwound, rushing forward to catch Ira's mouth with his. He kissed with enough fervor to make Ira think that maybe this was just another way to eat him alive.

The bites came when he caught Ira's lip between his teeth and tugged, releasing before the point of real pain, and they came when he nipped Ira's throat, sucking hard enough that Ira would have bruises.

Still, Ira arched against him and when he clambered on top of Ira, pressing him on to his back, against the hard wood of the porch, Ira wrapped his legs around the other man's hips.

His hands roamed everywhere, not gentle or exploratory but possessive, as though he were checking to make sure everything was as he'd left it. He pulled at clothing, pushing up Ira's shirt and ripping at the fly of his trousers, not bothering to do more than undo the fastenings.

No one had ever fixed their mouth so eagerly around his cock nor engulfed him so fully so soon. It was a greedy, desperate sliding of tongue and lips, the Devil's hands pressing his hips onto the floor so he couldn't buck or roll in time with the other man's mouth.

He could feel the Devil's throat open up to allow his shaft to slide in deeper, swallowed up by the slick muscles, and though he'd performed the act himself, he'd never had anyone do it for him. His hands searched desperately for something to hold but found nothing, his heart hammering, the groans and grunts escaping Lucifer pushing him closer to spilling.

His fingers found purchase on his own clothing and he cried out, louder and harsher than he'd ever done, a wordless shout as he spilled, his hips finally breaking free of Lucifer's hold as he thrust up.

Lucifer let out a long, low moan as he swallowed. When he pulled back, he was flush and panting. He rested his cheek against Ira's belly, his fingers idly traveling up and down his side, white stark against gray.

They lay together, breathing ragged, and Ira filled up with some sense of unease. Something more than melancholy or regret brought tears to his eyes and he hurried to scrub them away. He didn't want to cry, he had no business crying after something that had felt so whole and good.

His breathing hitched and Lucifer lifted his head. As soon as he took in Ira's face, he sat up all the way. "What is it?"

Ira shook his head. He pushed himself up and set to arranging his clothes. It was the only tangible thing he had at the moment, the only task he could set for himself to keep the sharp sense of loss at bay.

"Love, what is it? Was...Did I..."

Ira shook his head.

"Should I have stopped?"

"No!"

"Then what?" the Devil asked.

"Just...just *hold me*, please."

Lucifer scooped him up, pulling him onto his lap and wrapping his arms around him. He cradled him close to his chest. His heart still clattered erratically against his ribs and Ira swore that he could hear a faint squelching sound escaping from the wound in his chest. "Ira, please, what's wrong?"

"I love you, Lu, I love you so fucking *much*." The words came out as a growl but only so they didn't come out as a sob. "Don't ever go away from me like that again."

"Oh." Lucifer's long fingers tangled in Ira's curls as he tightened his embrace even further.

Nothing could be done to stop the tears after that and when they came, they wracked his whole body until he thought his ribs would break and he would never be able to breathe normally again. It was more than crying, it was a desperate, keening wail, the way he'd never been able to cry when he'd watched Lucifer die.

The Devil sniffled and kissed the top of his head, holding him even after he had exhausted his store of tears.

Georg came out of the house with a few pieces of paper grasped in one hand and cleared his throat. "If, well, if you two are ready, I've got this all figured out."

"That quick?" Ira asked.

The younger man looked at the floor and tapped the toe of his shoe against one of the boards. "You were crying for a long time."

An embarrassed sigh passed Ira's lips and Lucifer kissed his temple.

"Let's get this done," the Devil sighed. He gave Ira's thigh a pat.

Ira clambered to his feet and brushed himself off.

Georg smoothed down part of his shirt for him. He clasped Ira's hand and searched his face.

"I'm alright."

George kept ahold of his hand for a little longer.

Lucifer stood and stretched, twisting his shoulders so his back popped. He let out a small groan.

George hesitated, his eyes moving between the two of them, then turned to head inside.

They followed Georg into the house, hovering near the edge of the circle he had chalked onto the floor.

"You're ready?" Georg asked.

"Yes," Lucifer said.

The young man hesitated, cleared his throat, then asked, "You sure?"

"Yes."

Georg nodded decisively, cleared his throat once more and, after a nervous giggle, began the chant. He read carefully, his voice rolling over the words and sending shivers down Ira's spine.

He rubbed his arms and fidgeted, shuffling from foot to foot until Lucifer gave him a small push and widened his eyes with a nod towards Georg. Ira stilled himself and tried to be content with playing with his fingers.

Several minutes after Georg had stopped reading and, as Georg and Lucifer stared into the empty circle, Ira had to mention, "Nothing's happened."

"It takes time," the two of them said together.

In time, a form began to appear, the form of a short woman with bobbed chestnut hair and amber skin. She had broad hips and full thighs and wore a sleeveless tunic that showed well-muscled arms. A sword hung on her hip. When she turned to survey the room, her stance low and solid, he glimpsed a long dagger at her back.

Ira hadn't expected the angel of mercy to look so prepared for a fight.

By the look on Lucifer's face, neither had he. The Devil half-looked at Georg, an eyebrow arched. "Are you sure you got me the right one?"

Georg scowled at him. "It's *your* fucking book, if the spell doesn't work—"

"It's not *my* book."

"And *you're the one who's been to Heaven*," the young demon continued.

The Devil drew himself up taller and huffed, "She didn't look like that—"

"Bringer of Light." The angel had her hand rested on the hilt of her sword. Gray eyes flicked over the Devil's form. "Tzadkiel?"

She nodded.

"I remember you being...smaller." He appraised her again.

"Small didn't do me any good."

"And you've been, what, training with those pretty golden soldiers of His?" the Devil scoffed.

Her mouth twisted into a snarl. "Why have you brought me here?"

"No offense meant, darling, muscles look good on you. Fantastic arms, really. I'd love to see your back, actually, that's always—"

"Why am I here?" the angel growled, her fingers tightening around the hilt.

He pressed his fingers into the bones of his chest. "I'm in need of a favor."

Immediately, her eyes narrowed. "I owe you nothing, beast."

"Uh. I worded that wrong, I think. I need help."

Ira watched her hand go slack around the hilt and her eyes widen, but the expression only lasted for a moment before she redoubled her grip in the sword, drawing it halfway out of the scabbard. "What are you playing at?"

"Nothing. I need help."

"With what?"

Lucifer rubbed the back of his neck. "I'm...well, I don't suppose you know what's been going on in Hell?"

Tzadkiel rolled her eyes. "You mean with the notary? They're saying she killed you."

"That's not incorrect," the Devil admitted.

"You?"

He nodded, tugging on his clothes.

"*You* were killed by a notary."

"I'm afraid so."

"He Himself, Prince of Darkness and Lord of Creepy-crawlies brought down by a notary," she marveled. "We thought this had to be one of your little schemes. Like the one you pulled with that boy's soul."

"Lu was sick," Ira piped, hating to for anyone to think that Rivka could have beaten him if he was at his best. He regretted his intrusion, however, when color crept across the Devil's cheeks.

"I wasn't—" began Lucifer's protest.

"You look sick," the angel noted, finally removing her hand from the sword altogether.

"I'm not *sick*."

Tzadkiel raised an eyebrow. "So you must come crawling back to Heaven to regain your throne?"

"Uhhh, it wasn't quite what I had in mind. Rivka has me, well, she's bound me somehow," Lucifer admitted quietly. "And angel magic, well…" He shrugged. He didn't look directly at the angel.

"Has been beyond your grasp for millennia?" Tzadkiel guessed, a sneer stretching her lips.

"Something like that. Can you unbind me?"

"I'm sure I could."

No one moved.

Georg cleared his throat and Ira demanded, "Well?"

Tzadkiel glanced towards the circle on the floor and Lucifer scuffed away the chalk with his shoe.

The angel stepped out of the circle. "You really do look awful."

Lucifer said, "Yes, well, if you could be quick about it."

She raised an eyebrow and walked past him, angling for the door. "Good luck to you, Light Bringer."

The Devil slumped somewhat but made no protest.

"Aren't you going to help?" Ira demanded.

Tzadkiel didn't spare him a glance, continuing towards the door.

He hurried to catch up with her, putting a hand on her arm and regretting it immediately when she caught him and twisted his wrist back hard enough to drive him to his knees.

"A demon should think twice before laying its hands on an angel."

He tried to ignore the sharp pain shooting through his arm. He reminded, "You said you'd help."

"I said I could."

"I thought you were an angel of mercy, not syntax."

She twisted his arm harder.

He yelped.

"Let him go, Tzadkiel," Lucifer requested, sounding tired and not at all forceful.

When she didn't, the Devil strode over.

She released Ira before Lucifer moved more than three steps. He fell back, and she drew her sword, swinging it in Lucifer's direction. "No closer," she warned.

He put his hands up. "Peace."

"I haven't got time to waste, not with Heaven it the state it is. Stay back unless you want to die again," the angel warned.

"What state?" Lucifer helped Ira to his feet, his fingers probing Ira's wrist. "Does this hurt?"

"No."

The Devil gave his cheek an affectionate stroke and looked back to the angel. "Tzadkiel, what state?"

"Think, beast, how would one of our notaries be running unchecked?" the angel asked.

"Surely the Almighty—"

"Has many things with which to concern Himself."

"He doesn't know?" Lucifer asked.

"He knows all."

With a sigh, Lucifer scrubbed a hand over his face. "If you won't help, can you at least point me towards someone who will?"

"Help you? No angel would stoop so low."

"Is it me, or does mercy mean something else in Heaven?" Georg wondered.

"It means something different in Heaven," Lucifer informed him. "There are fourteen acts of mercy."

"None of them include unbinding the Devil," Tzadkiel confirmed. "I can, however, admonish the sinners among us."

"I didn't figure angels would be so...intentionally obtuse," Georg said, shuffling through his paper and taking the pencil from behind his ear. "Who was next to try? The drunk one?"

"Oh, no, not poor Izidkiel. I don't think I would trust him with anything more than opening a bottle of sherry," Lucifer said, turning away from Tzadkiel. "I think it might become necessary to force a few hands."

"Meaning what, exactly?" Ira asked.

"Meaning that there are a handful of angels who have weaknesses. Soft spots, easy to pierce."

The three of them oriented themselves towards each other; Tzadkiel remained at their backs. Ira heard her take a few steps towards the door, but not the sound of the door opening.

"Who's the softest?" Georg asked.

"Hamay was smitten with Rania for the longest time. I think that would be easily exploited. If we summoned Rania—"

"You won't lay a hand on her," Tzadkiel announced.

Lucifer glanced back towards the angel, who had made it all the way to the exit but hadn't done more than put a hand on the knob. "I thought you were leaving."

"You're not going to—"

The Devil said, "I'll do what I must and if that means snatching a couple of the lesser angels and putting one of them to the knife, then so be it."

Ira didn't know if that was Lucifer's true intent, but his fingers found the scars on his forearm. He had no delusions about what Lucifer could do to people who crossed him, or how many people he could hurt to accomplish something he saw as necessary. Ira had seen him swallow traitors whole.

Lucifer turned his back on Tzadkiel and went over to stand beside Georg. "Summon Rania first, she's a slip of a thing, she won't be hard to control. We might be able to force her hand without getting Hamay involved. The fewer angels, the better."

Tzadkiel drew her sword again and put the point to Lucifer's back. "If you even try, they'll be waiting for you to come back from the dead again."

Without thinking, Ira moved in towards the angel. She didn't have her eyes on him, her gaze darting between the Devil and the spell Georg had started to call up.

"Don't! Another word and I'll sever his spine," she warned Georg.

She never even glanced Ira's way. People tended not to in confrontations, not unless he was what they'd been fighting over.

He slipped the knife from her belt and tangled his fingers in her hair before she had time to balk and by the time she had, he'd brought the blade up to her throat. It had the unnatural green-silver sheen that angel's blades were supposed to have. It made him think the knife would be coated in poison, too.

His voice wavered as he instructed, "Drop your sword."

"The poison doesn't work on angels," she warned.

Lucifer slowly turned to face him, a look of pleased but cautious bewilderment on his face.

"Knives do, though, I bet." He tightened his fingers in her hair, not with any intent to be cruel, but because he didn't want her to slip out of his grip. She stood a hair shorter than he did; pressing so close to her felt almost obscene and made his stomach hurt. "Drop your sword."

It clattered to the floor. Lucifer bent to lift it. The right size for her, it looked like a child's toy against his lanky frame. He tested the weight and balance.

"You're going to unbind him. That's it, it's all we want." Ira swallowed hard and shifted his grip on the knife hilt. "Please."

"Please, he asks as he holds a knife to my throat," she sneered.

Ira looked to Lucifer, hoping the other man could tell him what to do. He hadn't moved with the intention to do any of this, but he'd had Lucifer back for hardly any time at all.

With a glance down at the blade, Lucifer nodded. "Let her go, love."

Ira stepped back, lowering the knife. He didn't like the feel of it in his hand but kept his grip no matter how badly he wanted to toss it away.

"Take your leave, Tzadkiel. I have work to do," the Devil advised.

"Don't summon anyone else."

"I cannot leave an angel on my throne and I cannot wait three centuries for this binding to weaken on its own."

The angel balled her hands into fists, then let out a sigh of disgust. "You're foul."

Satan raised an eyebrow. "It's your choice, Tzadkiel. You can help or someone else will."

She thrust out her hand, palm up but her fingers curled slightly as though she had no interest in touching whatever was about to be handed to her.

Ira, for a moment, thought she expected Lucifer to hand her sword back, but he placed his hand in hers.

She recoiled, then gripped his hand and yanked him closer, securing both hands around his. "It's going to hurt."

"And I feel so wonderful now."

She chanted, the words hushed.

Ira watched as tendrils of light started to emanate from the angel's hands and wind up Lucifer's arm. Lucifer's nose wrinkled and he took half a step back. His tongue poked out from between his lips, plainly caught between his teeth. Blood oozed past his lips as the tendrils wound around his whole body until they all came to rest in a central location, over the hole in his chest.

The lights sank past his clothes and into his skin. The angel released him and wiped her hands on her tunic.

"Is it done?" Ira asked.

Tzadkiel sniggered. "That? That was only to find where she anchored the spell."

Looking clammier than usual, Lucifer drew in a deep breath. His tongue flicked out to wet his lips and left a smear of blood over his mouth.

"Can...if I hold his hand, will it ruin the spell?" Ira asked, heat crawling up his neck and over his cheeks. It had to be a stupid question, but he didn't know much about magic and less about angel magic.

She glanced his way. "Are you joking?"

"You said it was going to hurt," he insisted.

"Darling, I'm touched, but you haven't got to worry about me," Lucifer said, his casual tone betrayed somewhat by the shake in his voice.

"She's got to remove the anchor, it shouldn't matter what he's touching," Georg offered, more helpful than the sneer on the angel's face.

He handed over the knife to Georg and put his hand in Lucifer's. The other man took it right away.

"Are you ready now?" Tzadkiel asked, "Or did you need a teat to suckle, too?"

Georg wound an arm around Lucifer's waist and asked, "Are you offering to let him suck your tit? That's sort of inappropriate given the circumstances."

The woman hissed something unkind under her breath, then plunged into the spell without out asking if they were ready.

Lucifer stiffened, his back arching and his hand tightening on Ira's hard enough to hurt.

With both hands, she tore open the front of Lucifer's shirt and pushed one of them into the wound, her voice still rising and falling steadily with the cadence of her spell. At that, the Devil's legs went limp and he struggled to brace himself against the other two.

Georg tightened his arm around the Devil's waist and pressed closer.

He fainted altogether when Tzadkiel drew her hand back, covered in gore but also clutching something.

Georg took the majority of the Devil's weight, almost as if he had known this would happen.

Ira thought at first the mess in her hand had to be his heart, but she opened her grip to reveal a hunk of something dull and dark. She dropped it to the floor and it shattered into nothing, leaving behind only a smear of blood.

Together he and Georg lowered Lucifer to the floor. Ira touched his face. "Love, come on, now."

"He'll be alright," Georg assured but Ira didn't know if it was spoken from a place of knowledge or hope.

The angel reached for her sword.

Georg swatted her hand away with the flat of the knife.

She yanked her hand back. "If I was going to kill him I would have done it already."

"Back up."

She stepped back several yards, almost to the other side of the room and Georg slid the sword her way. She had it sheathed in a heartbeat. "And my knife?"

Ira had no qualms with tossing the knife in her direction.

She grabbed it and was out the door just as fast, likely off to find someone friendlier who would send her home.

"Lu." Ira gave him a bit of a shake.

"Let him rest a bit." Georg extracted himself from the tangle of limbs. He pushed aside the torn silk of Lucifer's shirt and leaned in to examine the wound.

As far as Ira could tell, it was unchanged.

Georg stood up and stretched, then scrubbed his hands over his face. "I need a drink. I need several."

Ira nodded, not taking his eyes from Lucifer. He adjusted himself so he sat on the floor and arranged Lucifer on his lap.

"Poor thing." Georg looked down at them, then asked, "Would it be bad of me to go through their cabinets?"

"Yes. I'll have some of whatever you find."

With a snicker, Georg headed off into the kitchen. He returned several minutes later with an unlabeled bottle of something clear. He sniffed it, took a swig, then passed the bottle to Ira.

It burned going down and made his eyes water. His stomach threatened to throw it back up almost as soon as he had swallowed. He pressed the back of his wrist to his mouth and drew in a few deep breaths. "That's *vile*."

Georg took another sip.

"How can you drink that!"

"Not as bad as half the shit Rogg brings to parties." Georg set the bottle on a side table. He came to sit on the floor beside Ira, resting a hand on Ira's thigh. "What do you think he'll do about Rivka?"

"I hope he kills her."

"You do not."

"I absolutely fucking do, Georg. I hope he rips her into little pieces." He traced his fingers over the planes of Lucifer's face, something he hadn't been able to do for half a year. He certainly wanted Rivka dead for that offense alone. "How long do you think before he wakes up?"

"I don't know." Georg took another swig and went over to the window, pushing aside the curtain. "Dark out," he mentioned.

Ira barely registered his words.

"There's a bedroom down the hall. I could wake him up, probably, but don't you think we should let him rest?"

"Mhm."

Together they lifted him and settled him into the second bedroom. The mattress in the first had bloodstains all over and when they'd opened the door, the air had been thick with the smell of old gore.

The second bedroom was relatively free of stenches and blood. They pulled back the covers and Ira pulled off his shoes as Georg tugged off the remains of his shirt.

"Looks a little better, I think," the younger demon said with a glance towards the wound.

"Maybe."

They pulled up the covers and tucked him in.

His chest moved shallowly and every few minutes he would twitch or grunt, which Ira took as a good sign. People who were dying surely moaned or groaned, surely they tossed and turned or lay perfectly still. That's what happened in all the books.

Georg put an arm around his shoulder and pulled him close. "Come on, darling, we can't just stare at him until he wakes up."

"I should be here."

The younger man gave him a bit of a tug. "We'll scrounge up some dinner and check in on him in a bit."

"I'm not hungry."

Georg pulled him closer, wrapping him up in a tight hug, lifting him off his toes slightly. Ira melted against him, pressing himself even harder against Georg. "I'll make dinner, alright, and you can wait with him."

Ira nodded.

Before Georg let him go, he kissed him, a warm, searching kiss that made Ira want to cry again.

He sniffled and scrubbed at his eyes. He didn't think he had any more tears in him.

"What's wrong?" Georg asked.

He shook his head. "I don't know."

Georg settled him into the armchair in the corner of the room and wrapped a blanket around his shoulders. "I'll bring you something to eat."

"Thanks."

He nestled deeper into the armchair and tried to fix his eyes on Lucifer. Sleep claimed him all at once, at first just a few slow blinks of heavy eyelids, and then he was gone.

The smell of frying eggs woke Lucifer, sending an ache through his stomach all the way up to his mouth. The bedroom smelled, too, a faint stench that marked anywhere that had seen a violent death.

He pushed himself up and he realized that it hadn't been the smell of eggs that had woken him. He felt stiff and sore and more than that, he felt raw, like he'd been scrubbed with sandpaper inside and out.

Very coarse sandpaper, he decided as the bedsheets slid down his bare chest and sent shivers through him, set his skin to throbbing.

Pins and needles tingled all through his legs when he set his feet on the floor.

Pork. He smelled some kind of pork. Bacon or maybe ham. Not sausage. Who would be cooking in a house that had seen a triple homicide not a week past?

In the kitchen, he found Georg in front of the stove and Ira wrapped around the other man, his cheek against Georg's shoulder.

He spent a long time watching the two of them, knowing that the moral and sensible thing to do would be to leave them alone. He could go now, make the break clean and quick. He'd leave a note, of course, and even started to draft it in his head.

Ira would take it hard, but he'd shown a resilience Lucifer couldn't wrap his head around. If he could survive a childhood and more than a decade of whoring at the Trade House, he could survive a break-up. He'd be better off for it, too.

Georg would bounce back in no time at all and he would comfort Ira through the sting of being set aside. Georg was a better match for Ira than the Devil would ever be. They were good men, both of them, and they'd be happy.

And they were adorable together.

Lucifer stopped drafting a break-up letter and started imagining what it would look like to watch the two of them go at it. Or, on a more tender note, to see them cuddled together and tucked into bed.

It would be good for Ira to have someone to keep him company when the Devil couldn't; Lucifer anticipated that a lot of his time would be spoken for once he returned to the city.

"People died here, you know," Lucifer told them.

The two of them pulled apart.

Ira scurried over to him, throwing his arms around him and squeezing hard.

A whine passed the Devil's lips and that gave him an idea as to how poor his state really was because Ira didn't have the strength to best a ten-year-old.

Ira released him and danced back, his hands flying to his mouth. "I'm sorry."

"No, I'm...a little sore, is all," Lucifer said.

"Hungry?" Georg asked.

He nodded.

"Even though people died here?" Georg asked, a bit of a smile playing on his lips.

He nodded again and sat when Georg put a plate on the table.

"Someone ought to eat it, it was just going bad," Georg reasoned. "And I fed the chickens, so, you know, that's got to count for something."

Ira hovered off to the side and when Lucifer met his eyes, he asked, "How are you feeling? I mean, overall. Do you feel, well, have you been unbound?"

Jabbing the corner of a piece of toast into an egg, he watched the yolk swell then break, oozing everywhere. As he chewed, he thought, reaching into himself and evaluating his state. Unbound. What a funny way to think of himself. How could he be unbound when he was tied so thoroughly to Hell?

His fingers danced around the scabby edge of the hole in his chest. He sucked in his breath through his teeth when he strayed too deep and sent a sharp twist of agony through him. "I think so."

"You think?" Ira asked.

He scooped a bit of egg and ham onto the toast and chewed some more. Raw as he was, he didn't want to put anything to the test, but it had to happen at some point. He flexed his hand then stretched it out, pushing so the fingers changed, longer and thinner, sharp at the ends, talons now instead of fingers.

He pulled back in on himself before he lost control of it. His head had started to throb and he thought it would be best not to push his luck with shape changing for a while.

"Oh!" Georg cried and turned back to the stove, snatching a few more pieces of toast out of the oven.

The young man tossed the slightly burnt toast onto a plate and flushed.

Lucifer took a few more bites of food, barely able to stand the rough crumb of the bread or the gooeyness of the yolk. He bit into a piece of bacon, encountered a particularly chewy bit of fat, and almost threw up.

He pushed the plate away, wiped his fingers on his trousers and realized the other two had been staring at him instead of eating their own food. "What?"

"You're not hungry?" Ira asked.

"Starving, just..." He looked over the plate again. "Not for that. Not for...not for food in the traditional sense, I don't think."

"Oh."

"I'm not still thinking about eating you," Lucifer assured him. "Not any more than I usually do."

Ira and Georg exchanged a nervous look.

"Eat," Lucifer insisted.

He wanted something to eat but it wasn't flesh and it wasn't breakfast. He wanted something soft and easy to chew, something that wouldn't slide down his throat or stick to his teeth. He felt reasonably certain that it was either mushrooms or bean curd. Imogen would be able to scare some up for him once they got back to Hell, either way.

When they had finished, the two of them whisked away the plates, washing up, and putting everything away. Aside from the lingering smell of breakfast and the chalk circle on the floor, no one would be the wiser that the house had seen guests.

Lucifer pushed himself up. He wrapped one arm around Ira and kissed his hair. "Hold on to Georg for me, darling."

Ira wrapped his hand around Georg's and pulled him closer. "Are you up to it?"

"Love, don't go asking silly questions, of course, I'm not. Now, hold on tight, I don't want to end up losing one of you in the nowhere place," Lucifer warned.

Ira's grip on him redoubled.

"Of course, if you were together, that wouldn't be so bad, it's really Master Schreiber who needs to be careful," he mused.

He considered what would happen if Georg were to get lost there, then pulled them all through into the in-between place. He wrapped his hand around the correct thread and tugged. In no more than a moment, they were all safely in the cabin, although a little too close to the kitchen table.

He didn't usually travel through with so many people and he'd need to be more careful in the future, otherwise, someone would end up as part of the furniture.

"Shit," he said upon seeing the book cradled against Georg's chest.

"What?" one of them said, he couldn't quite tell which through the buzzing in his ears. That awful feeling slithered over his skin and under it; he'd had no right to ask Ira to touch those threads. He could hardly believe the demon had weathered three trips without cracking altogether.

"Forgot to bring back Hiram's book, now he's really not going to like me," Lucifer said. He blinked several times, hoping to clear away the speckles dancing in front of his eyes.

He had no luck.

Maybe jumping right into interdimensional travel so soon after regaining his powers hadn't been the smartest idea.

"Imogen," he began, looking around but not seeing the vampire.

"She's outside, do you want me to get her?" Georg asked.

"Tell her I want mushrooms."

He teetered and felt himself start to fall, but he'd lost consciousness before he hit the floor.

When he did wake, he had the feeling that a lot of time had passed. Some of that feeling came from the change in lighting and the slick, sweaty feeling that clung to his skin. He wondered how long he could pretend to be unconscious before the others caught on.

Probably not long. Imogen caught on to everything.

There he was shirking his duty again. He had deals to keep and an angel to dethrone. And Hiram's book to return.

He pushed himself up, noting that the raw-nerve tenderness had faded, replaced with a lingering soreness that he preferred.

Almost as soon as he sat up, Ira appeared by his side, putting a hand on his cheek and asking if he was alright.

"I'm fine."

"You were out for days," the demon informed him.

That gave him some pause. "How many days?"

"Eight."

He winced and reached up to touch the hole in his chest. He found a bumpy seam of scar tissue and didn't know how to reconcile the feeling of disappointment.

"You shouldn't get out of bed," Ira insisted, his hands pushing Lucifer back as he tried to get up.

"Don't be silly. I'd like to have a bath and something to eat, then I think...I think there's something pressing to which I must attend," Lucifer said, scanning the room for Marius' son. He could have delayed his half of the bargain but didn't see the point.

The young creature had waited too long for what he was owed and he needed it desperately.

He swung his legs out of bed and Ira planted himself in front of the Devil as he protested, "Lu, please."

He tried to stand but Ira didn't move back. Lucifer wrapped an arm around his waist and lifted him easily as he stood.

Ira squawked, securing his legs around Lucifer hips and his arms around his neck as though he thought the Devil might drop him.

Holding Ira felt like holding a child.

Something lighter than a child, Lucifer decided, it almost felt like holding nothing at all. Although he ached a bit, more than that, he felt strong and whole. He felt like he could make another star, like he could grow to the size of the mountain and swallow his city whole. He could throw himself open and go on forever and swallow the world.

Maybe eight solid days of sleep had been all he'd needed.

Maybe it had been all he'd needed for years. He couldn't think of the last time he had slept for so long.

"Take a bath with me."

"Alright, fine, put me down so I can get it ready," Ira said.

Lucifer didn't put him down. He carried the smaller man over to the copper tub propped up against the wall by the fireplace.

With a curl of his fingers, it floated into place on the rug before the hearth and with a wave of his arm, the tub filled up, sloshing and bubbling to the brim with steaming water.

"Now you're showing off," Ira scolded.

Lucifer set him down. "You like me better weak and useless?"

"I think I like you no matter what," Ira admitted and didn't necessarily sound pleased about it. Ira looked him over and crossed his arms.

"What?"

"No, nothing, I just...I don't think I've ever seen you this filled out."

Lucifer glanced down at himself. Still thin, yes, but not as scrawny as he'd been these past years.

"You look good."

"The body does what it wants," Lucifer told him, hoping that Ira couldn't see him blushing from the compliment.

Lucifer climbed into the too-hot bath as Ira shed his jacket and rolled up his sleeves. The smaller man didn't join him but did wash his back for him.

"So, once I've made my glorious return to the city and restored the throne to its usual state of insipid self-indulgence..." Lucifer began.

"And you round up the souls from the Seventh?"

Lucifer sunk a little lower in the water; that had almost slipped his mind and he didn't like the idea of going back to a city with so much disorder. The souls should have been where they belonged and the fact that they weren't made his stomach bubble unpleasantly. "Yes. After that. What are your plans?"

"I'm sure I've got a ton of bookkeeping to catch up on. I told Marius just to leave it all until I got back and I'd bet ten serpents he hasn't touched a single page."

"Yes, well, that..." Lucifer said.

"But what?"

"But, uh...you know, I carved my indelible essence into your flesh and contaminated you with my soul."

Ira dumped a bit of water over Lucifer's head and sudded up his hair. "It sounds so charming when you say it like that."

Lucifer momentarily forgot what he'd been meaning to say, too consumed with the feeling of Ira's fingers kneading his scalp. He tilted his head and squirmed beneath Ira's attentions, his eyes fluttering closed.

Then Ira doused his head again.

He sputtered and wiped the water out of his eyes. He raked back his hair from his forehead and turned to face Ira. "Maybe..."

"Maybe what, love?" Ira asked.

It should not have been so hard to ask this. He had fought for the Almighty and fought against Him. He had wrestled beasts twice his size and he'd been married to Tabitha for centuries. Still, his tongue stuck to the roof of his mouth and he had to clear his throat before he could make himself ask, "Maybe you could move in with me."

"Maybe," Ira agreed. He leaned in to give Lucifer a kiss then pulled back with his nose wrinkled. "You taste like soap."

Maybe.

It was a lot better than no, which was what he'd expected.

Lucifer stood and toweled off.

Ira nudged him towards the kitchen table.

Lucifer opened his mouth to protest and Ira told him, "Imogen had us out combing through the woods for mushrooms so you'd better come eat them. Georg got bit by this awful-looking spider thing."

He sat at the table.

"It had about a dozen legs. Do you want bacon or butter?"

"Butter, please."

"We haven't got any garlic," Ira warned.

"That's fine, darling."

They sat together quietly for a few minutes, cleaning and slicing mushrooms. Ira took the mushrooms to the stove, threw a pat of butter into the pan, and mentioned, "If I did move in, I might still keep my apartment at the Inverness."

"Whatever you want."

"Just, you know, since it's already paid for," Ira explained.

"That would be fine."

"And Georg has been living there."

"Ira, darling, whatever you want. It was just an idea." It was so much more than an idea; it was a desperate need, one that he had no right to ask Ira to bear. The thought of sleeping alone in the palace made him wish he could avoid going back.

If Ira didn't want to move in, he wouldn't force him, he'd gnaw off his fingers before he forced Ira to do a single thing.

The demon turned back to the stove and told the mushrooms more than he told Lucifer, "It wasn't a bad idea, I'm not trying to say that."

Lucifer said nothing.

"And the other thing," Ira began but didn't continue.

"What other thing?" Lucifer asked eventually.

"Georg and I, we're friends, you know."

"I know."

Ira turned around and brandished the wooden spoon he'd been using to stir the mushrooms. "So if you're going to go on sleeping with him, you'd better not mess anything up. I won't have it."

"I'll handle him with the utmost care," Lucifer promised, having never intended to do anything otherwise. "And what about the two of you? Do you plan to keep sleeping with him?"

Ira shrugged. "I don't know. Maybe. He is handsome." He gave the mushrooms a stir. "Probably. Only sometimes, though, you know. Just...as friends. But not anybody else."

The smell of mushrooms made its way to the Devil and he stopped thinking about Georg and Ira together and started to think about stuffing his face.

"And you either," Ira said when he set a plate of food in front of Lucifer.

"Me either what?" Lucifer asked.

"We talked about Georg, we didn't talk about sleeping with anyone else," Ira reminded him.

The thought of taking anyone else to bed hadn't crossed Lucifer's mind. Of course, his options had been limited lately, but even before that, thoughts of anyone but Ira had hardly crossed his mind. "Of course not, darling."

"Good." Ira put his arms around Lucifer. "You are mine, aren't you?"

"Just for you," Lucifer agreed, nestling into his embrace. It had been so long since anyone had wanted him like this, wanted him to be just for them in the way that Ira did. The right blend of possession, care, and flexibility. "I love you."

"I love you, too." Ira stepped back and gave him a kiss. "Go on, eat, you need to keep your strength up."

Lucifer ate his way through all the mushrooms that they'd gathered and thought he could do with some more. He didn't voice it, though, not wanting to seem greedy or ungrateful. He helped Ira wash the handful of dishes they'd dirtied, then asked, "Where's Hasbani?"

"Fishing."

The Devil made his way towards the door and Ira threw a pair of trousers at him. He stepped into them and found them tighter than they should have been, the silk clinging to his legs instead of hanging off of him.

"Oh, so that's what you look like in clothes that fit," Ira called after him.

Lucifer felt his face warming again.

He headed towards the lake and found Hasbani at his usual spot on the pier. "I'm told my companion struck a deal with you."

The half-Fallen squinted up at him. "Yes."

"You might want to reel in your line."

"Right now?"

"Are you anticipating a particularly good catch?" Lucifer asked.

Hasbani didn't reel in his line, but he did stand, wiping his hands on his shirt. "No, but, I just...isn't there anything that needs to be done first? Or...I don't know, it's so..."

"You only need to tell me how you want to be."

"I want to be how I am inside on the outside," Hasbani said quietly.

"Alright, but I don't think being covered in blood and loose organs is going to be a very good look for you," Lucifer warned.

"I want to be a man. Properly."

Lucifer sighed and pressed a hand to his own chest. He dug his fingers in, almost missing the wound, and told Hasbani, "As someone who lived millennia without a body and whose current body sometimes changes shape of its own free will, I have to tell you, that word is mostly meaningless to me."

The young man stared up at him.

"I need anatomical specifics is what I'm trying to tell you. You can write it down if you don't want to say it out loud."

Hasbani whispered something.

Lucifer leaned down. "A little louder, dear. I'm old and my hearing isn't what it used to be."

Hasbani raised his voice a hair and it was enough for Lucifer to catch his requests. Lucifer asked a few questions, just to make confirmations and pull out a little more detail, before he felt that he had a good grasp on what Hasbani wanted out of this exchange.

He set his hands on to Hasbani's shoulders and began to work, rearranging things here and there. Once or twice he thought about pausing to clarify something, but thought better of it and made a few executive decisions on his own. It was better to muddle the minor details than it was to lose the lad's shape altogether overthinking things.

When Lucifer had finished and removed his hands, Hasbani collapsed and threw up all over the Devil's feet.

Lucifer stepped back and recalled that he usually had people fast for a day or two before he went rearranging their shapes like this.

"I'm so sorry," the young man groaned.

"Perfectly alright." Lucifer helped him to his feet and gave him a pat on the back. "I have business to attend to in the city. I imagine you might want to stay here for a few days and...adjust, yes?"

Hasbani nodded, running his hands over his chest, over the slightly altered planes of his face. His fingers lingered on the new lump on his throat and skated over the hint of stubble on his cheeks.

"After that, you're welcome to return to your job at the palace."

"I..."

"Don't answer me now," Lucifer told him. "Think. Adjust." He looked over the young man, pleased with his own work. "I know it can be overwhelming to be...different all of a sudden."

Hasbani nodded, then started to weep.

The Devil looped an arm around him, trying to ignore the cooling vomit splashed over his feet. He rubbed the lad's back and cradled him close.

"Thank you," the young man gurgled, his voice full of phlegm.

"We made a deal, there are no thanks to exchange."

Hasbani quieted for a moment, then heaved another sob and cried for several more minutes. Once he had calmed, Lucifer washed off in the lake and walked Hasbani to the house.

The poor thing stumbled here and there, not used to the adjusted center of gravity or length of his new stride. Lucifer stopped at the door, knowing if he went in he might lack the resolve to leave again for days.

"I'll be back," Lucifer told Hasbani, "If they ask where I've gone."

Hasbani nodded and Lucifer wasn't sure he'd been paying attention.

He reached into the underneath and stepped through.

The throne room, which had been doubling as a great foyer for several centuries, looked nothing as it had when Lucifer had left.

First of all, it had a throne. She'd dragged the thing out of storage and set it up on a dais beneath the balcony. It was a spindly thing made of ghostwood that had long since darkened to black with scales carved into the wood, made to accommodate his long frame and tendency to sprawl when he had to sit for too long.

Second, the whole place had been decorated with banners depicting several types of ravens.

Third, there were no cats. There should have been at least four or five black cats sprawled out on the floor, rolling over to expose their bellies or watching passers-by with lazy, jewel-toned eyes.

When he appeared, the movement in the room stopped.

Several of the guards dropped their spears. Several more lowered them in his direction.

One fool pointed her spear at his chest and lunged.

He plucked the spear out of her hands and used the butt to knock her onto her back. He twirled the spear in his hand and rested the tip beneath her chin.

She stared up at him with purple eyes the size of saucers.

Young. Probably the same age as Georg. Definitely nowhere near as smart, if she'd thrown in with the angel, but young people did tend to be stupid.

"You really should pick just one of these," Lucifer announced to the room and used the spear to gesture to the half-dozen raven banners. "Too many and people will get confused. Poor branding."

No one moved.

"Fetch her, wherever she is." He gave the young guard he'd disarmed a bit of a kick and she scrambled away from him, bolting for the exit, to fetch the queen or to throw up in the bushes, he didn't know.

Lucifer moved towards the throne, letting the spear fall to the floor. He stepped onto the dais, settled into the throne, and waited.

As he waited, he recalled why he'd stopped using this throne.

His ass went numb after just a few minutes.

Marlow appeared from the woodwork and leaped up onto his lap, kneading him viciously and scraping her tongue along his jaw. She began to purr and he ran his hand down her spine. She rubbed her face against his and licked his nose.

"I missed you too, beautiful," he cooed.

A woman moved forward and told him, "I can take that, sire, if you want me to put it out."

The idea of putting any of the cats out had never crossed his mind.

"Who are you?" Lucifer asked.

"Thraxis, sire, one of the cat keepers."

"Cat keepers don't put cats out, Thraxis," he told her, taking in the scratches all over her arms and hands. "Where are the rest of them?"

"They've mostly been hanging around the garden."

"Let them in."

"Sire?" she asked.

"You heard me, go let them back in."

She hesitated and looked towards the front door as it opened. She shrank away into the crowd as Rivka entered, trailed by the purple-eyed guard. She no longer looked so tall as she had before; her dappled silver skin didn't glimmer as beautifully now that he'd been reminded of the sun.

She walked in, smooth and calm, climbed the dais, and leveled her sword at his chest. "Up, back to the dungeon before I have to kill you again."

He smacked the blade away. "Rivka, last time we tussled you found me terribly weakened. You won't find me that way this time."

She raised her chin, tightened her grip, and pointed the sword at him again.

Marlow hissed and Lucifer placed the cat on the dais.

He stood, taller than the angel. Taller than he had been a moment ago.

He would settle back to his usual height, he hoped, or all his trousers would be too short on him.

"The Almighty has been slack to allow you to romp around down here for so long," he told her. "And I was slack, too. I have to thank you for opening my eyes, at least."

He stepped forward and she didn't move her blade.

He slid one finger along the edge, pushing it aside and opening his skin and dripping blood onto the floor.

Three quick steps and he had her face in his hand, dribbling blood down her cheeks and throat.

"The rest, though, I can't thank you for at all."

She writhed in his grasp and he lowered his grip, closing his hand around her throat. After a moment longer, she ceased her wiggling, her hands clawing at his.

"But I'm going to find a way for you to make amends," he promised her.

He brought up his free hand and with one nail began to carve runes across her face. She gurgled and grunted, her eyes bulging wildly as he worked.

When he finally released her, her skin had gone from dappled and beautiful to mottled with blood. Her silver eyes glowed like moons and he thought about adding a moon to the sky to accompany the star he'd made.

He released her and she collapsed at his feet, choking and coughing. She scrambled to her knees and started to scream when she touched her face.

He went to wipe his hands on his shirt and realized he'd never put one on.

"Take her to the dungeon. In my old cell. And someone get me a shirt." At first, no one moved and he glanced out over the people in the throne room.

He put a foot on Rivka and pushed her off the dais, sending her tumbling off to land with a thud. "Now."

Two guards came forward and scooped Rivka up under the arms, hauling her away as she continued her wails.

Someone else brought him a shirt.

He walked the palace with a gaggle of servants, pointed out all the things that had to go, and demanding to know where all his old things were.

"Some things were burned, my Prince," a one-winged woman told him.

He rounded on her. "Burned?"

She cowered. "I'm sorry, my Prince."

"All of it?" he demanded.

"Everything that didn't fit in the other cells."

He sighed and rubbed his eyes. "Well, have all that brought out. God, Imogen will know where to start. Burned! Really?"

The one-winged woman nodded, still cowering.

He rolled his eyes and walked away from her. He checked all the rooms and stood in the middle of one of the spare bedrooms for a while.

He'd meant to have such a different life from the one he'd had. The thought of having to redecorate everything almost set him to weeping. Everything had been as it should have been for so long and now he had no cats and too many hideous banners.

Once he'd walked his palace and had them restore as much of it as could be restored, he brought Ira, Georg, and Imogen from the cabin.

Imogen scolded him for it and he gathered from the flush in her cheeks and the smear of blood down her front, that he'd interrupted her feeding.

He ignored her and gestured for Georg and Ira to follow him.

Ira grew noticeably cautious when they headed up to the second floor, higher than Lucifer had brought a guest in centuries.

"I know the two of you have taken up sharing the apartment at the Inverness together," he began, "And you're obviously free to do as you want but..."

He nodded towards the door, not sure how to say what he wanted.

Ira tried the door and found that it opened not into a spare room but into his apartment on the fourth floor.

"It's still technically *in* the Inverness, I just...you know, bent space-time a little bit," Lucifer explained. "I thought it might make things a little easier. I know you like having your own space."

Ira stared into the apartment.

"If you don't like it, it's just as easily undone," Lucifer hurried to say.

"The things you do in half-measures," Ira muttered.

"Half-measures?" Lucifer asked. "I manipulated the laws of the universe for you."

Ira raised an eyebrow.

"Again!"

"Kitten, go ahead, give us a bit of time," Ira said, giving Georg a push towards the apartment. "Start spreading the word for us, yeah? Especially make sure you tell Astrid. And then can you bring me one of my suits? You know which one."

"I can't wait to see the look on her face," the younger man said with a nasty grin. He kissed Ira on the cheek and pulled closed the door of the apartment behind him as he left.

Ira took Lucifer by the hand and brought him back downstairs. "Is Rivka dead?"

"No. She is useful now, though. Or will be, soon. Tzadkiel mentioned something about Heaven being all out of sorts and I'd really like to know more about that."

"And when do you plan to start with that nonsense?"

"I imagined after I had the Seventh back under control," Lucifer told him.

"Reasonable."

"I thought so."

Ira opened the door to Lucifer's bedroom but didn't bring him towards the bed. Instead, he scowled at the severe new furnishings and went over to one of the boxes that had been brought up from the dungeon and rifled through it.

Ira sorted through the clothes for a while then handed Lucifer a change of clothes and asked, "I don't imagine you know what Imogen did with your tiara?"

"It's not a tiara." Lucifer stared down at the pile of silks in his hands, not sure why Ira had decided he needed something else to wear. Finer things than what he wore now, trousers and a vest and a beautifully embroidered shirt. What need had he of these?

"Well, you'll need it."

"For what?" Lucifer asked.

"The Revel." Ira headed to another box and dug out a pair of boots. He tossed those Lucifer's way as well.

"What Revel?"

"This one, love," Ira told him. "I'm declaring one, right now."

"I don't know if you can do that."

"If I can make deals and travel through the underneath, I certainly think I can declare a Revel." Ira stood on his toes to kiss him, sweet and chaste. "I was really hoping you were going to eat her."

"I will, later, when I've gotten what I need from her."

Ira nodded. "Good. We'll have to find that crown. Did you plan on leaving the throne down there?"

"You don't like it?" Lucifer asked.

"Oh, no, I'd just like to see you kneeling in front of it," Ira told him. "With my cock between your lips," he added for good measure.

"I can do that."

Ira grinned. "Later, though, get dressed, everyone's going to want to see you. I'll be right back, I'm going to get changed, too."

By the time Ira had come back, dressed in the teal suit that Lucifer loved, the Devil had not just found his own circlet but had one for Ira as well.

"You might as well have it now," Lucifer told him.

"Was it Tabby's?" Ira asked warily.

"No. It's yours." He set the circlet on Ira's head, nestling it safely among his curls. "I was going to wait and try to make it sort of special, but then you said that bit about half-measures."

"When did you make it?"

"Before Tabby left." Lucifer slipped his fingers under Ira's chin and tilted his head to get a better look at the crown. "It suits you."

Ira smiled up at him, then took him by the hand. "Come, dear, your people await. Georg says they're already burning things in the Eighth—in a good way! Don't worry. We missed our Prince something awful."

"And those who supported Rivka?"

Ira rolled his eyes. "Worry about them when you're worrying about the souls," he advised. "Right now we're celebrating."

He made it sound so simple.

Lucifer tightened his grip on Ira's hand and together they headed out to join the Revel. A proxy could declare one, after all, it seemed because, by the time they made it to the Ninth, they'd started burning slap-dash effigies of the angel.

What Everyone Deserves
2017 Rainbow Awards Honorable Mention
"Although the story deals with some real 1950s issues – discrimination, homophobia, interracial couples and hate crimes – it did it in a way that perfectly suited the characters and the story." - Divine Magazine

In this 1950s period drama, Junius is a New York City fertility demon with a crush. Ever since falling from heaven he's been alone. Except for the mothers and children he watches over.

James Kelly Rosenburg, a black soldier with snowflakes in his hair, walks right into his life with a big problem. James Kelly, turned vampire during the war, is new to New York and its prohibition against vampire killing in city limits.

Junius offers to teach him to overcome his bloodthirsty instincts and live a proper Manhattan life. Their growing friendship leaves them both conflicted as they explore a city both welcoming and alienated by their kind.

That Doesn't Belong Here
2018-2019 Rainbow Awards Honorable Mention
"I liked the ... atmosphere that he created, alongside the paranormal creatures that roam the street. I liked that he wrote characters I could emotionally care for. If Ackerman writes another LGBT fiction, I will give it a try for sure." - Ami, The Blogger Girls

That Doesn't Belong Here begins when Levi and his friend Emily discover an impossible creature in an abandoned pick up. The thing is wounded, frightened and the two friends cannot leave him to the mercy of rubberneckers and tourists. This novel explores what it means to be a person, as the creature, Kato, begins to display not mere intelligence or friendliness but what can only be explained as humanity. The question of who we are allowed to love arises for Levi and Kato, as they are not just crossing the boundaries of gender or sexuality, but of species.

www.ingramcontent.com/pod-product-compliance
Lightning Source LLC
Chambersburg PA
CBHW071747190726
48292CB00003B/899